I have had the opportunity to review this amazing book and it is a knock out! Scott Taylor shows you a side of life not often talked about in polite circles. It's not only a life adventure, but also a courageous journey of spirit. From darkness into the light and then... As a novelist myself, I am impressed with the depth of being in this first novel. Cheers to Scott Taylor, for a most dynamic first novel. This is a MUST READ!!!

Andreah,
Author of: But I Still Love Him and Acceptance

In Scott Taylor's first novel (Passing Through Oblivion) guilt, self-destruction, and redemption are harsh and rollicking steps in John O'Rourke's riveting dance into oblivion (which is) peopled by top hats, gowns, and jewels. On the outside, his new journey has just begun. Fasten your seatbelts for a great ride!

Sheila Kindellan-Sheehan,
Author of: Cutting Corners and The Wrong Move.

PASSING THROUGH OBLIVION

By Scott Taylor

Amethyst House Book Publishers
Scarborough, Ontario Canada
www.amethysthouse.com

PASSING THROUGH OBLIVION
By Scott Tayor

Copyright © 2008

All rights reserved, including all reproduction rights of any portion, in any form whatsoever.

ISBN 978-0-9735663-7-6

"To Ally"

"The Author wishes to acknowledge the following people:
My late mom, Sonia, and dad Bruce, for everything, my brother, Brett, along with Lorri and Sundance for their open-door policy so often in the past, Mother Goose for being my second mom and making sure what damage I could inflict upon myself was limited during the craziest time of my life, N.D. for being my friend and always absolving me, my other close friends, past and present, who I love and appreciate for all they've given me over the years, Peter, my publisher, for his endless encouragement, advice and friendship, and to Mitchell."

Prologue:

You could say I knew John O'Rourke. I still do, truth be told. I see him now and again, coming here or going there, always on the run and trying his best to be helpful. And although we don't spend as much time together as we used to, I can call him my best friend without a shadow of a doubt in my mind that he feels that way about me too. John was once what some of us here call a troubled soul, and he did little at the time to disprove that notion. That's about when I came into his life - and he came into mine. This story, however, is not about our friendship, though that's certainly part of it. No, this story is about love, loss, guilt and redemption. It is a story about life and about death.

I asked John once if I could tell when the feeling struck or when I thought it might do someone else some good. He thought about it for a while and his eyes drifted off as they do when he's thinking deeply about something. When they came back and focused on me again, he smiled warmly and told me he'd be honored if I told it. I believe he meant it, too, because he had that way about him. When he really meant something, anyone who knew him could see it. So, my friends, this is his story, at least as much of his story as I know, and I'm pretty sure I know all of it by now. It began on a perfect summer morning. It began with a loss.

Chapter One

John O'Rourke, 39 years old, the surviving member of his immediate family, stood rigidly as the last casket was lowered into the frozen earth. This was the small casket; the one John requested to be lowered last so that its occupant wouldn't be alone in the darkness. It was the one that contained his only child, a boy he and his now-deceased wife Wendy had named Henry, after John's favourite writer, Henry Miller.

"Ashes to ashes, dust to dust . . ."

Three fresh holes in the ground, one beside the other in perfect unison. Three stars falling from the sky in a brilliant ball of fire. As I said, it began with a loss.

*****

"We don't have any answers yet," the girl stammered, clearly uncomfortable with her job for the day. She shuffled quickly from foot to foot and mindlessly pulled and twisted her hair with her left hand. She might have pulled it out entirely if not for her right hand, which held the red pen she was using to check off the names of the deceased as their surviving relatives appeared before her. One after the other, ashen, uncomprehending faces streaked with new and old tears arrived. She had been on scene that Saturday; a junior public relations representative for Trans-American Airlines, which before that day, had a spotless record. Like they say, there's a first for everything. The elderly, the young, mothers, fathers, and confused children stumbled to the desk softly bumping into each other to ask if she was sure that their mom or dad or grandpa or niece had been on that plane. Was she absolutely certain? Maybe they missed it or took another one. But every time, the young girl pulling on her hair with her free left hand was certain. When it became John's turn to talk to her, he noticed the number of names under his own.

Liam O'Rourke
Wendy O'Rourke
Henry O'Rourke

Why did the airline choose *her* to speak to the families? She couldn't have been more than twenty-five, and even at that she looked still younger. Must have drawn the short straw, John thought. After all, the PR department existed solely to sell the public on the benefits of flying this airline, not to console widows and orphans. He suspected a senior executive was at that moment speeding to the airport to begin damage control. In PR lingo, they called it "damage control." The accident had happened so unexpectedly - when doesn't it? - that the only person immediately on the scene to deal with shocked family members was this young woman with increasingly unkempt hair. Dead bodies were littering the earth and John O'Rourke was feeling sympathy for a terrified employee of an airline whose name he would never forget. He most certainly didn't know how to feel about that. "I'm so very sorry, sir," she mumbled. "I don¹t know exactly what they want me to tell you, except that I am so sorry for your loss."

*****

He watched the small box slip into its place. It was covered in white linen, as his mother's coffin had been minutes earlier when it was lowered. Three days later, the airline still hadn't told him what had happened, but he didn't really care. The engine blew up, the hydraulics shut down. Would any reason in the world bring his wife, child and father back? Would there be gratification, closure, a sense of unavoidable destiny if he knew why the safest mode of transportation in the world had failed those he loved? How about giving him comfort for why he had rescheduled his own flight so he could finish up a little business, as he had told Wendy, before joining them for their first family vacation since Henry's birth. He'd finish up that one last column for the paper so they'd have it for the weekend edition. He would only be a day behind them, he promised, when Wendy resisted. What was a single day, he kept asking. What could it hurt? Wendy was in the first trimester of her second pregnancy when it happened. In the paralyzing fear of that endless moment, at least one of them didn't know to be afraid.

*****

At the wake, John scurried from wall to wall across his kitchen floor like a cornered animal. He studied the table and counter, both covered in food, from every angle as if it was a living thing. Why do people bring food to things like this, he wondered, as he again surveyed the mountain of casseroles and cakes and salads piled throughout the room. Why do people bring fucking salad to things like this? Do they think I'm concerned with my fucking cholesterol?

"You? You brought food, too?"

Will swung around from his duty at the table, unsure of what he had done wrong at such a delicate moment. "What do you mean?" he asked quietly.

"What I mean is, who's fucking hungry right now? Should we have served hot dogs and beer at the funerals? Did I commit a social faux pas by not having munchies at the cemetery? I mean, this is all great, but where's the pizza? That's what everyone wants!"

Will stood rigid, trying to control a small anxiety attack
"There are a couple warming in the oven, I think."

John clapped his hands. "Fucking well done! Now everybody will be happy. And why not? Now there's more for us to eat!"

"Don't do this, Johnny. I can't begin to imagine how you feel, but there are a lot of people who are hurting right now, too, and they're just trying to do what's best for you."

John picked up a kaiser roll from Will's platter, bit into it and threw a perfect strike into the kitchen sink. "I need a drink, Will. You gonna have one with me or am I drinking alone today?"

Will grabbed a couple of plastic cups from the table and hurriedly filled them with scotch, as if he'd been salivating to do so already. "To better days," he whispered.

"I don't think they can get much worse," John snorted. "Finish yours and fill them up again. I've got to dull my senses if I'm ever going to get through this day."

Will filled the cups again. "But only for today, okay?"

"You're the doctor."

*****

The beaming red numbers of the digital clock read 4:15 a.m. As had been the pattern for the previous three nights, John O'Rourke was fighting sleep, drifting off only to be jolted back to reality twenty or thirty minutes later. When he did sleep, there were always the dreams. Some were short, like the coming attractions of a movie he didn't want to see. Others were the movie itself. Most of the bed sheets were scattered on the floor from his constant tossing. He moaned softly, an unconscious reaction to the familiar, unwelcome movie now playing in his head.

Chapter Two

Another Monday morning, another week of work. John sighed deeply and grabbed his notes as he reached for the doorknob. Light headed from lack of sleep, he made a mental note to pick up some sort of sleeping aid on the way home from work. He was still having trouble focusing his eyes as he closed and locked the door behind himself. He couldn't shake the feeling that something wasn't right, as if he was in an unfamiliar place. Resting his head against the door, he summoned the will to get on with his day, but before he could move the door opened and he nearly fell through onto the foyer floor.

"John? What are you doing?"

He swiveled his head around, at once embarrassed that someone had seen him in such a position and wondering who it may have been. It was a woman, a little younger that he was, with a look of concern spreading across her face. She seemed familiar, but John couldn't place her. He guessed he must have seen her in the building once or twice.

"John," she repeated with a hint of impatience in her voice, "are you all right?"

He looked at the woman, squinting his eyes to see her through the fog of his insomnia, but it was no use. He knew her, but he didn't know her at the same time. "Um, yeah, I'm fine, thank you," he mumbled with slight embarrassment. "I'm just on my way to work." He was the type who could rarely recall faces or names, and he felt awkward whenever someone he didn't know spoke to him as if he was more than a passing acquaintance. This was especially troubling now because he had the feeling this woman was more than just a friendly stranger - perhaps much more. They must have bumped into each other one evening as John was coming home from a bar. He never remembered to whom he spoke on those nights, which were now increasing in number. He rubbed his burning eyes again.

"What do you mean you're on your way to work? I think you've put in a long enough day for anybody. Come on inside, honey. Dinner's almost ready and the little guy has missed you." She went back into the house leaving the door open.

John gave his head a good shake, trying to get his bearings. Now he knew he'd seen that woman before, but the memory of her was murky, like looking at someone through the ocean water. And what did she mean by coming home from work? And who was the little guy. "Of course," he cried, slapping himself on his forehead. It was another one of those dreams, but having deduced what he thought was the obvious, he expected to wake from it like people always do when conscious overpowers fantasy. He was surprised, though not unhappy to find his scenario continuing. John laughed softly to himself, resigned to his fate. "Okay, Alice, you've just passed through the looking glass. Let's go see tonight's Mad Hatter."

He heard the woman's muffled voice from inside the opened door just as a little boy bolted out towards him.

"Daddy! Daddy!" the boy squealed with delight. "Daddy's home from work!" he hollered, as he wrapped himself around John's left leg.

John's first inclination was to shake the boy, who appeared to be about five, loose. He'd never been entirely comfortable around children, a trait he had always disliked, but instead he found himself placing his hand on the boy's head.

"I missed you today, Daddy. Guess what?"

"What?"

"Chicken butt," laughed the boy. "Knock-knock!"

"Uh, who's there?"

"Boo!"

"Boo, who?"

"Why are you crying, Daddy?" asked the boy, laughing harder than before.

"Henry," called the woman. "Bring your father in for dinner."

John went along with Henry. After all, this dream was a hell of a lot better than the other ones had been. He looked into the boy's (his son's?) bright, blue eyes. "What do you suppose Mommy made for us tonight?" he asked.

"I hope pasghetti. I love pasghetti."

"I know you do," said John O'Rourke. And, not surprisingly, he did.

They strode through the door holding hands. "Here's Daddy, Mommy," beamed the boy.

The pretty woman with the long dark hair turned from the stove where she had been busy ladling out the spaghetti sauce onto three plates and walked over to where John was standing. She kissed him warmly and deeply on his mouth, stroking his cheek with her hand. "How was your day, my love?" she asked.

John giggled. "Well, it's been different, but it seems to be turning out pretty well."

She looked at him with endlessly deep eyes. John noticed she had the same dimples in her smile as Henry did.

"Well, you just started your practice a week ago, so I bet everything is going to be different for a while until you get into a routine. We'll talk about it after dinner, if you like, my brilliant man." She turned her attention to her son. "Henry? Do you remember what Daddy does at work?"

Henry looked up from his Spiderman action figure with a beaming smile, obviously proud of himself. "Daddy's a writer. He makes stories that go in the newspaper."

"Right, honey, good for you," she said, kissing him on the top of his head.

I like the way he says it, John thought. In real life, I'm a columnist, and a burned-out columnist, at that.

"Would you like some garlic bread tonight, sweetie?"

"Sure," John replied. "That sounds great."

"Good. I'll toast some and-" The phone rang, stopping the woman short and scaring the hell out of John, who dropped a fork onto the tile floor. "Hello? Oh, hi Tracy. Just a second, okay?" The woman covered the mouthpiece with her hand and turned to John. "Honey," she whispered, "can you make the garlic bread without setting the place on fire? It's Tracy and I want to see how things are going with her husband. I'll just be a second."

John nodded and got up from the chair to find a knife. Curiously, he knew which drawer to open. He began to slice the crusty French loaf taking in its warm, fresh aroma. "Henry, want to help Dad with dinner tonight?"

The boy jumped up and scampered to the counter. Okay. Can I cut the bread?"

John smiled and shook his head. Maybe when you're a little older, pardner. Tonight, I thought we could play a game while I slice the bread. That sound okay with you?"

"Sure, I love playing games with you, Daddy."

"Attaboy. Since you were so smart to remember what I do at work, I thought we could see how smart you really are, okay?" The boy smiled and nodded. "Good, let's start with an easy one. What's Mommy's name?" What is Mommy's name?

Henry's eyes twinkled. "I know that one. You call her Angie, or angel," he said, giggling over the "angel" part of his response.

Okay, John thought, her name is Angie. He rolled it around in his head. I think I like Angel better, he decided.

Angie hung up the phone. "Look at you two," she scolded. "One slice of bread so far." She smiled slyly at John. "It's a good thing for you you're so talented at some other things otherwise what use would I have for you?"

"Yeah. Daddy knows how to fix my bicycle," added Henry.

"That's just what I was talking about, sweetie," she said with a wink.

They ate dinner, the three of them, discussing the events of each other's day. John enjoyed listening to Angie's stories, watching her eyes twinkle as she spoke. She possessed an obvious joie de vivre that was infectious. After the dishes had been placed in the dishwasher, they played a game of Memory, in which the goal was to find pairs of cartoon animals among the cards placed face down at random on the table. To John's delight, Henry played competitively and well, finding a purple giraffe near the right-hand corner of the cards and its mate near the centre. It took little effort to let him win.

"Way to go, sport," John said as Henry showed each parent his large stack of cards. "I didn't know you were so good."

"I always win, don't I, Daddy?"

"Every time," John confirmed.

"Okay, young man, time for bed," Angie said. "Give your dad a goodbye kiss."

Henry jumped into John's arms, the warmth of his small body a beautiful comfort, and he placed a soft kiss on his dad's cheek. "Goodbye, Daddy," he whispered.

"You mean goodnight, don't you, buddy?"

"I love you, Daddy. Goodbye."

John physically felt his son leaving him as a pain in his stomach grew. "I'll see you tomorrow, right buddy? I love you."

Henry only smiled and waved.

"I'll be right down, honey," Angie smiled, though John thought he noticed sadness in her eyes. "Maybe you could light a fire?"

John found some old newspapers lying beside the fireplace and carefully stacked the dry kindling on top of the pages he'd torn for the fire's base. He added a couple of small logs and lit the paper with a pack of matches he took from his shirt pocket. The wood was dry and the fire started quickly, burning brightly within a couple of minutes. Looking around the dimly lit living room, he spied a stack of CDs and placed one into the player. He smiled as the room was enveloped with the soft brilliance of Beethoven and sat back on the sofa waiting for his angel to reappear. When she did a few minutes later, she was wearing one of his flannel shirts that fell just above her knees. Her dark hair cascaded below her shoulders and John wondered if she was wearing anything underneath the shirt. He hoped she wasn't and looked forward to finding out for sure. She sat beside him, melting into his form.

"Nice dream, huh?" He asked.

"What do you mean?"

He was quickly afraid that talking about the dream would end it, and he didn't want that to happen - at least not yet. "I just mean that everything is so good that it feels like a dream. Like nothing this good could ever happen to me in real life."

She craned her neck to softly kiss him. One of her hands made it way slowly up his thigh. "I wonder if we can find a way to make it even better."

John held her and was delighted to find that she was indeed naked beneath his shirt. He slid his hands over her breasts and felt himself grow with excitement.

"Ummm, I love when you do that," she purred.

He unbuttoned the shirt from top to bottom and kissed each breast longingly. "I love you," he softly growled.

Angie moaned and pulled him on top of her. "Let's see how much, big fellah."

"What about Henry?" he whispered.

"Who?" she smiled.

They made love in front of the glowing fire, softly and teasingly at first, then with a passion and urgency that John had never before experienced. "Not bad for an old married couple," she said breathlessly after they both came in torrents of spasms, moans and tangled limbs. Her face was crimson and her hair exploded in every direction.

"I don't know what I did to deserve this," John said, his voice shaking partly from the power of his orgasm and partly from raw emotion. "But I'm glad I have it."

"You just had to truly want it," Angel answered. "You had to do no more than look at your life and decide what was most important to you. John, you gave up too easily." She gently pushed herself away from him and began to dress.

John caught his breath. He knew it was coming to an end, as he was certain it eventually would. "I'm sorry," he gasped through the rising lump in his throat. "I never knew how happy I could be like this."

"I know, John. You've always been the type to harbor good intentions and poor execution. I believe that you sincerely want what's best for everyone, but you've also lacked the courage to do what's necessary. Sometimes you have to face down your demons if you ever hope to move past them. Running from them only allows them to grow stronger until they really are too big to overcome."

John could feel tears running down his face. "You left me, you left me here alone," he sobbed.

Angel smiled sadly. "You're the one who has gone, John. Before anything happened to us, you left our world to find one of your own."

Cold, deep guilt crushed him. He cried with more fury, his back hurting with each sob. "It's too late, isn't it? What if I did something to join you?"

"You have to stop running, John. You have to stop running to the next big thing."

He closed his eyes to kiss her one last time, but felt nothing. It didn't surprise him. He awoke hopeless, alone and empty. There was only one thing he could think of doing.

Chapter Three

"Are you sure about this, John? Once the papers are signed, it'll be too late to change your mind."

John O'Rourke stopped for another long look at the house and nodded. For six months it had stood as a hollow reminder of the laughter and love - and life - that used to bounce off its walls. For six months he had felt like a soulless spirit, neither alive nor dead as he wandered the hallways, recalling the painting and wallpapering of each room, hearing the voices, like ghosts, come to him everywhere he looked. The flooded toilet where Henry decided to see if his G.I. Joe could survive the deadly whirlpool; the blinds he had spent an hour installing backwards before Wendy came in to save the day; the bedroom; the bed. John wearily gazed at the real estate agent and smiled wanly. "I hope they enjoy it," he said as he signed the papers.

"But the furniture? The blinds, the pillows on the beds even? I'm in this to make money, John, but I hate to see someone throw their life's possessions away. You're only thirty- five. Keep your things. They'll take the house, no matter what. It's only a happy coincidence for them that it came entirely furnished."

"All this is from a different time," he whispered. "It doesn't belong to me anymore."

"Won't you at least sell it? I can set up an estate auction for you."

"I don't want money from this. Just tell them to keep what they want and to give the rest to charity."

The papers at last signed, the two men shook hands and John walked one last time through the entrance of the home he and Wendy had found just as their lives together were beginning. Before leaving, he paused to listen. The voices were quiet. He ran his fingers softly along the wall and found a flaw in its smoothness. A small hair from a paintbrush was entombed in the light khaki paint. He rubbed his fingers over it again and again. "Nothing's ever perfect," he sighed, as he left the house for the last time.

Chapter Four

John had been advised against making the epic drive across the country in January. Everyone had told him to wait the winter out and leave - if he felt he must - deep into the spring or summer when conditions would be safer. But John knew what horror a lazy, breezy summer day could bring just as easily as any in the winter. Besides, he wanted to escape right away. The guilt was crushing, the stares from those who meant well suffocating. If he couldn't move to a foreign country - or a foreign planet, which would be even better - Quebec would have to do. It was the polar opposite of Vancouver, he figured, and a new year called for a new start. A job with a sister newspaper under the Trans-Can umbrella was waiting for him where he again would be a city columnist. What's a couple of days in a hotel room if it snows, he reasoned? He would just order pizza and watch TV if it came to that. Snow squalls, though, especially in Northern Ontario, can blast from out of nowhere, turning a sunny day into a true life-or-death experience, they'd argued. But John had to go. Only one other person knew his true reason, and she had promised on her mother's name not to tell anybody.

But there was still one mission to complete before he could turn the page and begin all over again. There was still the matter of Wendy's parents, who had treated him like a son and who had offered him their home and love after the accident. John had to drive one last time to Eugene, Oregon to say goodbye - at least for a little while. He parked outside their small house, the one with the immaculate lawn free of leaves and cut evenly at an inch and a half. Tom Weston was a stickler for detail and his lawn fell into the category of one of his details. He mowed it every week without fail, and as far as John knew, he had never missed it for anything other than driving rain or the odd snowfall. True to his character, Tom owned a barely used snow blower for just such an emergency. In fact, he even started it up from time to time just to allow the oil to run through it and "get the bugs out." John knew of only three times the machine had been used, but his (former) father-in-law made certain it was in good working condition just in case. The garage that stored the snow blower was also pristine - not just for a garage, but for any room inside the house. A green, spotless carpet covered the entire floor, a workbench in the far corner was always free of dust and tools hung in unison both from smallest to largest and in families from a pegboard. Screwdrivers were with screwdrivers, hammers with hammers, small to large, left to right.

Even after six months, John had no idea how the loss of his daughter had affected his father-in-law, who had always been as stoic as the garage was neat and orderly. To open up and spill feelings was not Tom Weston's way. He had been a major in the U.S. Navy during Vietnam and although he preferred to talk about almost anything but that time, the training he received was never far from the surface. John made himself smile once thinking about old Tom Weston sitting in his reclining chair barking marching orders to his wife.

"Come on, Elizabeth, dinner time, step to it! Left, left, left-right-left!" John surmised that the massive pain Wendy's parents felt was something that would always live inside of each of them, rarely acknowledged, but slowly poisoning them over the years until they woke up, ate, spoke, and worked as if on auto-pilot, much like zombies. John imagined them ten years in the future sitting at the breakfast table with little to say to each other and even less desire to say it. They would never be able to reclaim their lives, John was quite sure about that. Wendy had been their only child and they had doted on her from birth.

Tom Weston answered the door with a smile and predictably firm handshake. "John," he smiled, "it's good to see you, son." But the pain in his eyes betrayed his hollow words. In fact, he was not happy to see John because the sight of him involuntarily opened the box he had been trying so hard to lock. John standing on his front porch hurt him, and that was something he didn't like at all.

"Tom, it's good to see you again," John replied. "I'm sorry I haven't been in touch as often as I should've been the past few months, but . . ."

"It's been a difficult time for all of us, John, no need for apologies. We all deal with it in our own ways. Come on in, Elizabeth has been looking forward to seeing you. Can I get you a splash?"

John placed his left hand on his father-in-law's left shoulder as he removed his right hand from Tom's grip, which caused him to absent-mindedly flex his red fingers. "It's a little early for me, Tom, and I'm heading north straight from here. I'd love a coffee, if you have any."

Tom craned his neck towards the kitchen and called for his wife. "Beth, come on over and say hello. John's here."

Wendy's mom, who had always looked more like her older sister, padded to the foyer, where the men were now standing. John stifled a gasp as she came into sight. She had aged 20 years in the six months since the accident. She had allowed her store-bought auburn hair to gray, new lines of despair creased her face, she was slightly stooped and the usual dancing eyes lay deep in their sockets. "Hello, John," she said through a false smile. "It's nice to see you again." But John could tell it wasn't nice to see him at all. Much like in Poe's Telltale Heart, John believed Beth knew his secret and so standing in front of her was terrifying. He had no reason to believe this, but it was a feeling he hadn't been able to shake.

"It's good to see you, too, Beth. I hope you've been keeping well."

"Pshhh," she replied between pursed lips. "As well as can be expected, John." Then she abruptly turned and headed for the kitchen. "I'm afraid we don't have any real coffee," she called. "Will instant do?"

John replied that it would as he and Tom shuffled into the living room, where Tom had been watching a documentary on air dominance in the Second World War on the Discovery Channel.

Their conversation had been short and direct. They already knew of his plans to move and, hoping to somehow put this all behind them, approved. They had always enjoyed a cordial if not familial relationship, so a quick cup of instant coffee, a few words, and hugs goodbye were all it took for John O'Rourke to cut the past with an eye to the future. After only twenty minutes he wanted to leave. After thirty minutes his former in laws made that possible. As he backed out of the driveway, he waved and mouthed "goodbye." Beth's eyes were not even directed at him as she waved in return. As he drove back towards the highway and his new life, it occurred to him that they needed him to go every bit as much as he did.

That unsavory thought and too many others were still careening inside his head two days later as he kept close watch on the taillights - dimmed by the requisite blowing snow - of the car in front of him. The driving was hazardous, but he knew that nothing lethal could happen to him at 40 kilometres an hour. There would be nothing worse than a bent fender and a sudden stop if it came to that. It was the trucks that were getting on his nerves, like usual. It never seemed to matter what the road conditions dictated; the trucks always kept up their relentless pace, regardless of who was in their way and how much snow and slush blasted on to smaller cars in their wake. Sometimes too often, really - to keep out of the deeper snow building up on the outside passing lanes, the truckers would inch closer to the middle of the two-lane highway forcing already nervous motorists closer to the shoulder on their side, where the build-up of wet, heavy snow would be enough to grab hold of a tire and pull the entire car into the ditch. John hated them for their callous recklessness.

The dashboard clock read 5:47 p.m. He had planned on making Thunder Bay by this time, but instead found himself hours behind schedule, inching his way towards Kenora when the traffic slowed to a stop. John knew Kenora didn't have much going for it in the winter if you weren't a ski-doo enthusiast or a masochist who got off on snow and freezing toes. Situated northwest of Lake Superior on the Trans-Canada Highway, the small city of 16,000 hardy residents offered outdoorsmen plenty of lakes and bush, but for John it was little more than a necessary timely stop along the way. Northern Ontario was well and truly in the north, even though it was only about 14 hours driving from Toronto. "Okay, might as well relax and try to find something on the radio other than Paul Harvey coming in from the States," he whispered." After listening to annoying static most of the way up the dial, he found a country music station that was received clearly. He hated country music, but it was the only show in town, it seemed.

"That was Travis Tritt on the station that brings you the real country, CFOX 940 am. Before Travis, we heard Brooks and Dunn, and leading the way into this half hour of commercial-free music was Canada's own Shania Twain. Just before we get back to the tunes, be advised that there's a heavy snow and high-wind advisory out there. Police are asking anybody who doesn't really need to drive to stay off the roads. And this just in: There's been a multi-car accident on the 17 eastbound where it meets 71 south. All we know so far is that a truck has overturned and cars are backed up for miles. Stay tuned and stay warm, country fans and we'll see you on the flip side of these messages."

John swore softly under his breath at the truck driver who he knew must have been driving like an idiot. Son of a bitch probably ran up the backside of some innocent guy just trying to get home to his kids through this shit. He checked the mostly full gas gauge and settled in for a long wait. The heater was working well, the wipers were clearing away the onslaught of wet, heavy snow, crappy country music was on the radio and what looked like a sign for a Best Western - sanctuary! - a few hundred yards up the road. He smiled at the thought of a warm bed. That would be it for this day, he thought. "Okay, baby, one more kilometre (less than a mile) and we'll get you off the road. You weren't made for this."

That short distance, covered in less than a minute under normal conditions, took a frustrating forty-five minutes before John could slide his way up the off-ramp towards the hotel. To his great surprise, no other car could be seen in his rear-view mirror. After checking in and finding his room for a quick but relaxing hot shower, he made his way to the hotel bar inconveniently located across the snow-swept parking lot. He caught the Mazda out of the corner of his eye, discouraged at the thick blanket of snow already layered a couple of inches deep on the little car. He figured the bar would be teeming with other lost, exhausted travelers like himself, but found instead that he was the only patron against a staff of four or five.

"Come on in," a pretty, young girl called as he peered in from the door. "As you can see, you have your choice of seats at the bar or a table." A rerun of some prime time soap - he didn't know which one - was flickering across the giant-screen TV against the far wall. The bar was typical of inexpensive hotel drink joints, though this one was more of a roadhouse than lounge. "Here," the girl added, passing John the remote, "feel free to put on whatever you want. It looks like you're it, at least for now."

A man with a white apron wrapped around his waist appeared from the kitchen behind the bar. He was also young, maybe a couple of years older than the girl, who John had guessed was the bartender. He was carrying a hot dog in each hand and held one out for the new customer. "We were supposed to have a big promotion tonight for Dry Ice beer, but I think the weather's gonna kill that."

"The beer's still half price all night long, though," the girl chirped.

"The dogs are free, as many as you want," added the man, who had placed the usual condiments on the table beside John. "Oh, and have a Dry Ice T-shirt. They're free, too. You want a few?"

John felt overwhelmed with the remote in one hand and a hot dog in the other surrounded by staff with little else to do but mother him.

Chirpy girl smiled, proud of herself. "See? Your own wife couldn't treat you this well."

"You're right," John answered, rubbing the finger that once wore a ring.

He looked at the brown bottle on the table in front of him, beads of condensation slowly trickling down to its base where a ring of moisture had soaked through the cardboard coaster. A jolting panic, a sudden terror like a boy waking from a nightmare, gripped John with ice-cold talons. He didn't know why he had come to this bar instead of relaxing in his room. He hadn't touched alcohol since he passed out in the bathroom at the wake for his family. Now, a free shirt, free food, a beer in front of him, and a staff whose soul task was to keep him happy made a quick exit unlikely and embarrassing. He suddenly, desperately wanted to be back in his car fighting the snow and trucks and his past. His father, who had been identified thanks to his wedding ring on a detached hand strewn among the other limbless, headless monsters in the field, often told him to swallow down fear, sadness and hurt. "Never let it get to you, be a good soldier. Keep your pecker up." So he did. He got raving drunk for one day, then got up and went to work the next. Work. Monday, Tuesday, Wednesday, Thursday, Friday, keep busy, keep busy, one-two-three-four-five. He didn't know how he was doing it, but he knew it was just what his dead father would've expected of him.

Now what? Why was he dwelling on all this in a bar in the north of Canada six months later? He felt the warmth of perspiration welling up under his arms. Where was this coming from? The lights were too bright, spots danced in front of his eyes. Hold on, hold on, this will pass, Johnny-boy.

"Everything okay?" It was chirpy girl. She looked confused and concerned. "Is there something wrong with the beer?"

John shook his head quickly, grabbed the beer and downed a huge mouthful. "Sorry, just daydreaming," he quickly answered. The beer was cold in his mouth, down his throat, and into the pit of his stomach, where it sat there waiting for more. Swallow it, don't let it out. That's it, keep it down and it'll get easier. He took another swig and it was easier. At the bar stood a cook, a dishwasher, and two servers watching him guzzle his beer.

"Tell you what," he said to the girl who had taken it upon herself to find a hockey game on TV for the guest of honour. "How about you all make yourselves comfortable here with me. It's really no fun sitting by myself. We'll get a bunch of hot dogs and some beer and shoot the breeze for a while."

Chirpy gave a furtive glance towards the bar, then back at John with concern and an adorably furrowed brow that made her appear to be no more than sixteen. "That would be a lot of fun, but we're not supposed to drink while we're on duty," she pouted. "I'd love to if I could." The sad look in her customer's face, though, persuaded her to relay the request to her manager, who frowned at first, then relented. The snow had intensified, there were no headlights in sight and the chances of any of them getting home were dwindling by the minute. The cook bounded into the kitchen for the dogs, the dishwasher untied his greasy apron and a few extra chairs were dragged over to John's table. Chirpy sat down with a beer for herself and another for John.

"I really hate hockey, but we sure don't get to do this very often, so it's worth it," she bubbled. "My name is Katie. This is Ron, Annie, Tracy and in the kitchen is my brother Mick."

John nodded at each of them as he heard their names, noticing he was the eldest by a good ten years or so. "I'm John, and thanks for joining me. I was beginning to feel sorry for myself all alone here."

Katie smiled warmly and looked into his eyes. "We can't have that now, can we?"

John swallowed the last of his first beer and felt the cold again as he took hold of his second. "We certainly can't," he answered.

*****

John O'Rourke and his new friend stumbled drunkenly towards the bed in his hotel room. Because it was prohibited to fraternize with the guests, Katie McGill had offered to close the bar herself, under the pretense of letting the others go home early. The snow had finally lightened and plows already were clearing lanes, first on the highways, then as the night progressed, the major streets in town. The others cheerfully said their goodnights, pleased their time hadn't been wasted and thankful for John's generosity of making sure they all received at least a little something for their friendly company, and trudged out to sweep the small mountains of glistening snow off of their cars. Only Kate's brother Mick had an idea of what she was up to.

"I'll help you," he had said. "Then you can leave your car here and I'll drive you home."

"I'll be fine," she replied with a warm, knowing smile as she kissed him tenderly on the cheek.

He stared at her for a long while.

"Really," she added. "You have nothing to worry about."

"I'm not so sure, Kate. That's why I . . ."

"Goodnight, Mick. See you tomorrow."

"You just met him. This isn't like you."

Kate smiled at her brother. He was younger by two years, but had always been the serious yin to her bouncy, breezy yang. He had been seeing the same girl for almost three years and frowned on casual sex. While Katie would never be considered slutty, neither would John be her first one-night stand. "Drive carefully, Mick," she smiled.

There hadn't been much to do. With John the only customer, the staff had been given the time to clean as they went, even while taking turns sitting and watching TV. Katie gave the bar a last look, decided it was up to snuff, and bounced toward Room 308 hoping the good-looking man hadn't yet passed out. She took the stairs as a precaution - now was not the time to be seen - and only felt a twinge in her stomach as she opened the door to the third floor. She tapped lightly just below the peephole and tried to listen for movement. She did hear a squeak from the bed and giggled in spite of herself that she should report the minor flaw to management. How would she know that, they would ask . "Because the other night when I fucked this stranger I thought was attractive and a little troubled, I heard it over and over again," she would answer. Yeah, that would work. She giggled again as the door opened revealing O'Rourke in a different pair of faded Levis and a black T-shirt. She noticed he was wearing no socks, something she liked for a reason she couldn't understand, and his hair was messy, a look she really thought became this man. She sighed quietly and John smiled. "Would you like to come in or should I order something from you?" he joked.

"Bar's closed, big guy," she replied, surprised at how cool she was acting. In truth, her stomach was somewhere else on a roller coaster careening out of control.

"Then I guess you better come in. The weather outside is frightful, you know."

"So I heard. Some guy in the bar tonight told me so. But I do come baring gifts," she smiled as she pulled two bottles of inexpensive red wine from a plastic bag. She would pay the bar back the next day for what she had taken, but figured the wine might be a good idea in case they became nervous and quiet.

She crossed the threshold and entered into a room she would never forget, even years later after she was married, after her hair began to turn gray, after she moved hundreds of miles away.

The room itself was typical of a medium-priced hotel. There was a queen-size bed; a desk and chair near the window; a TV set in a small wooden wall unit; a small, uncomfortable looking couch; a bedside table with a lamp on top and inside the drawer a Bible courtesy of the Gideons. The bathroom light was on, and Kate noticed from toothpaste in the sink that John had brushed his teeth. She smiled again. He couldn't be too bad if he was considerate enough to worry about his breath, she thought. John kissed her cheek softly and motioned to the couch. "Care to sit down with me?" he asked. There was no hint of anxiety in his voice, just a quiet confidence and warmth that came from a bottle or ten. She knew then that if it was going to happen it wasn't going to be immediate and clumsy. He would take his time to seduce her, though she'd be ready and willing once that time did come.

Two glasses of wine later, after the obligatory small talk about histories and families, and Katie felt she still new nothing about this man. Sure, she had done most of the talking, but when she did ask questions he deflected them and asked her more about herself. She began to think that maybe he was married. Why hadn't that already occurred to her, she wondered, though she wasn't prepared to leave even if he had a wife. She hadn't thought to look for a ring, silly girl that she was. But now she was getting drunk and the time for rational thought had passed with Mick's red taillights dimming in the white distance. Her head was swimming, her curiosity growing, so she figured she'd just ask him. "Do you have anybody back home, John?"

"Anybody? Anybody like who?"

"How about anybody like a wife or a girlfriend? Not that it matters to me right now," she leered with glassy eyes.

O'Rourke's face darkened and his hand moved from her knee back to his own. Then just as quickly it was back and he smiled again, though this smile did not reach his eyes. "No, I don't have anybody."

Oh, but I think you do, Katie thought. But she nodded anyway. Even so, what was one night? She'd never see him again. He would only be a pleasant memory of a snowy evening at a time when no one else in her sleepy town interested her. They had been thrown together by fate, she reasoned, and who was she to argue with fate? Plus, he was hot and it had been a while. Even her trusty vibrator, Mr. Pink, had become boring and predictable. She leaned over and kissed him, first with her lips closed, then with a hungry tongue that felt warm and smooth and wanting to John. He returned her kiss with one of his own. It was a long, deep one, but surprisingly rough to young Katie. She was the first woman he had been this close to since the day of the accident, and he was beginning to feel very anxious.

The last time had been the day of the accident, hadn't it? The very day the plane went down. One hand began massaging her breast, though he wasn't conscious of it doing so. Katie sighed and moved her own hand up his thigh stopping just before his balls. She kneeled down in front of John and unbuttoned his jeans. Then she slid the zipper down and gently pulled his penis out. Oh, yeah, she thought, I remember what you guys look like. She placed it in her mouth and slowly began to suck it, first from the top, then down its length and back up again. Her tongue lightly circled the head while her hands massaged the shaft and his balls. She heard John moan, but his cock wasn't hardening. She bobbed her head faster, snaking her tongue up and around the head then lapping at his balls. He moaned again, this time louder and full of passion. The sound excited her and she held him in her mouth while she undid her own pants allowing one hand to caress herself in the process. Still, there was little life in his cock. Had he drank too much, she wondered? Damn, she hoped not. By now she was halfway to orgasm on her own and she needed to be fucked good and hard by this man. She sucked with a fury she didn't know she had, fingering her cunt at the same time.

"Oh God!" John screamed.

"That's it, baby, feel me sucking your cock." Maybe a little dirty talk would do the trick.

"Oh God!' he screamed again, but this time his cry sounded different somehow. Katie felt his stomach heaving. In fact, his entire body seemed to be convulsing. He couldn't be coming because he still wasn't even hard. She stopped playing with herself, though she did continue sucking. That was when she heard it. It was crying. No, it was more than that. It was sobbing. A deep, guttural sobbing that frightened her. She brought her head up to look at John and saw that his face was streaked with tears. His eyes were closed and his hands were cupping his head in agony.

Katie's heart jumped and she tried to stand, but instead tripped over her pants which had fallen to the floor and fell on her behind. "What? What is it? Did I hurt you or something? What's the matter?" she pleaded. She didn't feel unsafe, but she did want to leave. Something had gone terribly wrong with a man she didn't know and she wanted to leave, to be back in Mick's car, to be home in her own bed and covered tightly.

O'Rourke's body convulsed violently, his cries desperate.

"Okay, John, maybe you should be alone. I'm sorry for whatever I did to you, but I think I should go." She pulled her pants back up quickly entirely forgetting how close she had been and looked for her jacket, which was lying across the foot of the bed.

"Oh God!" John cried again.

"WHAT?" Katie screamed, afraid of her own fear. "WHAT DID I DO?!"

John finally opened his eyes. They were red, puffy and oozing pain. "It wasn't because of work. It wasn't because of fucking work!"

"What? What wasn't because of work?" Katie McGill was now very afraid of this man, who appeared to be breaking down in front of her. She had made it to the door and opened it almost halfway, but she hadn't yet left. "What are you talking about, John?"

He looked at her with nothing but despair in his face. She let the door close again. "There was a plane crash six months ago near Vancouver," he began, his voice hoarse and unsteady. "Everyone died . . ."

Katie's mouth opened.

"Everyone on it died."

"I remember that," she whispered, as much to herself as to him.

"My wife, my son, she was pregnant with another . . ."

"Oh, my God, John. I'm sorry." She walked slowly towards him, now unafraid that he would hurt her. "Am I the first since . . ."

"It wasn't work."

"What do you mean, John? What are you trying to say? It's okay. I'm your friend and it's going to be okay." But she was very uncertain that it would be.

"It wasn't work. I wasn't at work when it went down, when it crashed and killed everybody I wasn't at work."

"I don't understand."

He began sobbing again. "I skipped the flight because I said I had to fucking work. It was a vacation and I said I'd fly the next day because I had to work."

"Then what happened? What do you mean?"

John's head dropped almost into his lap and Kate could see his back shaking. He said something, but she couldn't hear what it was.

"John, tell me again, please. I can't hear you."

"I lied, Katie, can't you see? I lied to my wife and my child and now they're all dead because of it."

"John . . . ?"

"There was another woman," he mumbled through trembling lips. "There was another woman and I wanted to have an entire day and night with her, so I told my wife that I had to finish an assignment and that I'd be along the next day. I was in bed with another woman at the very moment they all died. At the very fucking moment."

"Oh, John. . ."

"The last thing my wife ever heard from me was a lie."

Katie McGill slowly sat down on the bed, close enough to feel heat emanating from John's heaving body.

"People have affairs, John. How could you have known? It's not your fault."

He dropped his head down and began sobbing again. Kate waited for him to stop, but John O'Rourke never did stop. The last thing she heard as she quietly left the room was, "Don't you see. It should have been me. Oh, God, I'm so sorry . . ."

******

John spent a sleepless night drinking what was left of the wine as tears fell from his face. After he became drunk enough, his fragile emotions turned to suicide. He thought of hanging himself, but there was nothing to hang from. He thought of plugging the clock radio into an outlet in the bathroom, but electrocuting himself sounded too painful and very long. He might've jumped, if he hadn't been on the second floor. "Goddamn it!" he shouted, though deep down he knew he didn't have the balls to successfully do himself in anyway. Having to be carted out of the room on a stretcher with Chirpy Girl looking down at him in silent pity was too much to bear. Still, he picked up and examined the plastic bag she had used for the bottles of wine, trying to fit it over his head just to see if he could do it. When that proved to be impossible without tearing it, he looked for something else. There was his belt, but for the life of him he couldn't figure out what to do with that other than tie it tightly around his neck. The fact there were no holes that far up the belt was that idea's undoing. Trying to figure out how to die served the ironic purpose of taking his mind off why he wanted to die, for a while at least. When those thoughts did return, they made him feel stupid and addled. Images of the crash site caromed through his memory. He recalled seeing blackened shards of machinery strewn everywhere, twisted, endless and grotesque. Black, choking smoke plumed in the air, as fire scorched cloth, wires and flesh. He envisioned the somber but perfectly made-up TV newscaster describing body parts, some as small as fingertips, being collected by crash-site examiners. John tried to remember exactly what his son's fingertip looked like, but he kept seeing it as bloodied and detached, and he ran to the bathroom to violently throw up before passing out on the cool bathroom floor.

Chapter Five

As he was checking out the next morning, still slightly drunk and unsteady on his feet, John felt he was without direction, like a jellyfish bobbing along in the ocean with only the tide to push it one way or another. His own existence no longer served a purpose - if it ever really did - and he gave himself up to the currents of fate not knowing where he would stop next and not caring. Driving through the hills and valleys of the serpentine, icy Northern Ontario highway, as he passed snow-covered farmhouses, he yearned for the safety he believed the people in them must feel enclosed in their small worlds. He desperately wanted to hide in one of them, to sleep for days in a soft bed under heavy blankets with no responsibilities or commitments. Another car passed him and his stomach turned as a boy, not unlike his own dead son, smiled and waved from the back seat. He began to return the wave, then stopped abruptly for no other reason than he simply didn't want to. "I don't have to pretend to be nice anymore," he mumbled.

John pulled into a small diner just off the highway near North Bay as the sun began to set behind him in the west. Uncle Zach's was a typical greasy spoon in an equally typical

Northern Ontario town with the obligatory tourist crap for sale. T-shirts that said Uncle Zach is my hero and I got stuffed at Uncle Zach's sat folded alongside pennants and other assorted overpriced junk on shelves behind the cash register, while red, vinyl-covered booths lined the far wall against the windows. Miniature jukeboxes full of country tunes (three for a quarter!) and paper napkins had their place as well. Twirling stools were lined in formation in front of the counter, where, if you cared to, you could watch a large black man and a scrawny white kid with a serious acne problem cook your meal. The floor was tiled black and white like a chessboard and the clientele was clearly of the trucker persuasion. Hungry, tired and with no fight in him, John decided to forget about his misgivings towards the drivers, though he did make a point of remembering to spit on one of the rigs on his way out.

    He took a booth and absent-mindedly flipped the pages of the mini-jukebox while waiting for a menu. No Beethoven in there, that's for sure. Lots of Patsy Cline and Willie Nelson and Garth Brooks, even some AC/DC and the Rolling Stones, but nothing he cared to spend any money on. A waitress, as wide as she was short in a black and white uniform, came by with a glass of tepid water and took John's order of a burger, fries and a beer, which he drank before the food came. He asked for another cold one and sunk into a newspaper while he ate. Sickly full and still a little hungover, he made the decision to give up for the day and find a room somewhere. He remembered passing a small motel minutes before stopping so he turned around and drove back to see if it looked hospitable enough for the night. The Welcome Motor Lodge was a two-story building that rented rooms by the week as well as the night. It was where locals lived when marriages broke apart and where hunters stayed during moose season in the summer. There was nothing attractive about it, but it was clean, warm and his room contained everything he would need, including cable TV and a small fridge for the six-pack of beer he bought for himself.

As he began to feel the buzz on beer number four (six if you include the two at the diner), John got restless. The last thing he needed was to be alone with his thoughts because those thoughts had become dark and hopeless. His meltdown the previous night in front of that poor girl hadn't done him any good at all. He wondered why he didn't feel better. Wasn't letting it all out supposed to be good for you? He admitted his guilt to someone - he had unloaded it. In time, he hoped, he would feel better. The guilt would always be there, but he still hoped that one day life might return to normal, whatever the hell that was supposed to be. All he knew at this time, though, was that he felt anything but normal and his own company wasn't helping matters. At least Elizabeth had stopped calling him. The woman he was fucking when the plane crashed had done him the favour of steering clear of the funerals, but she had insisted on seeing John even when he couldn't stomach the thought of being near her. She had her own guilt to ease, and felt talking would help them both. To John, though, she was the instrument of his own mistaken survival, the reason he was alive, a constant reminder of the careless, selfish bastard he was. After a month of unanswered phone calls, closed doors and cold shoulders, Liz finally gave up. A last message on his home answering machine suggesting he deserved to feel pain because he was such a prick was the last he heard of that woman, as she had come to be known inside his head. At least no one else knew about the affair, though that proved to be a double-edged sword for him. The avalanche of sympathy he received might have been more tolerable if it had come with a side order of recrimination and scorn. For six months he had swallowed the beast whole, but now it was finding its way out. And it was pissed.

Chapter Six

John found his way to Hurricane's, a seedy, disheveled joint that - like most rundown bars of its kind - had a core of rundown regulars who went almost every night, talked about the same things and laughed at the same jokes. Heads turned whenever someone who wasn't a cast member walked in, though that person usually walked out again right away. For John, though, this was exactly what he was looking for. His opinion of himself matched the bar's look and he took a seat under quiet stares. He nodded at one of them, offered a half-smile and asked the bartender for a double-vodka with soda. Conversation had risen to a murmur again, but John could still feel eyes crawling over him.

"Cheers," he said to the closest patron, a guy wearing an oil-stained jacket with hands, face, and hair to match. Taken by surprise, the man nodded then turned his back on John and shrugged his shoulders at his friends, a group that included two younger men - also grease soaked - and a skinny middle-aged woman wearing too much make-up and perfume. John wondered what the place smelled like when she wasn't there and decided he was lucky she had shown up, gallon of cheap eau de toilet and all. In a past life, John O'Rourke would've never been seen in such a rat hole in the first place. He most certainly wouldn't have spoken to anybody, and it would've taken an act of God for him to stay and challenge the gang to pool, which he found himself doing after a few more drinks for himself and a shooter he bought for the bar. He had sized up his competition early. The tallest guy with red hair was a lousy player who thought he was good. The greasy man he had said cheers to was quiet, a little dark in his manner and someone John decided he didn't want to anger. Although he was shorter and a little thinner than John, he carried himself with a certain edge. John's instinct told him to watch his step with this man. The other two appeared to be a couple and were harmless, but John guessed that they probably had epic fights, as many couples who drink too much, too often together do. He had heard them talking earlier when she made a joke about his weight. The man had laughed, but John could see anger and hurt in his eyes and figured that comment would come back to haunt her when they got home to the trailer park or wherever they lived. He envisioned seeing them on Cops and laughed softly to himself.

The shot he bought hadn't endeared him to the foursome as much as he hoped it would have, but it was enough to get him on the old pool table for a quick game. The protocol to play at Hurricane's, as it is and always has been in most bars, requires players to line quarters up on the rim of the pool table. When yours comes up, you pump them in the slot and take on the previous game's winner. The red-haired guy, who they actually did call Red, had just beaten Bill (or as John preferred, Chubby), who had sunk the eight ball by mistake and stumbled grumbling back to his seat with his woman. John still didn't know her name, but he did know that Chubby was not having the best of evenings. John didn't want to appear brazen, so he allowed Red to fumble along for longer than he should have. While he wasn't a shark by any stretch of the imagination, John was easily better than Red, who was almost tragically inept. Finally, John gave in and finished off the table for the victory.

"Nice game," he said, getting a nod and an easy pat on the back in return.

"You're a pretty good player," Red remarked. "Are you a pro?"

John laughed in spite of himself, then immediately wished he hadn't. But Red hadn't been insulted; he really wanted to know. "I wish I was good enough to be a pro, but I'm just learning the game."

"Well, we ain't gonna play you for no money, mister. Got that?" It was the first guy he had spoken to - the one that made him a little uneasy raising his voice from across the bar.

"No problem, friend, I'm not looking for any trouble. I just thought a game of pool would be some fun."

"Uh-huh. Where ya from, anyway? You don't look like you're from around here."

"I'm in the midst of moving from Vancouver to Montreal and I thought . . ."

"He's in the midst, everyone. In the midst, whatever the hell that means. He's a goddamn gorilla in the midst!"

John gripped his pool cue tighter and felt his stomach turn over as cackling laughter filled the room. "Like I said, I don't want any trouble."

"You ain't gonna get no trouble, friend, but I'll be damned if I'm gonna sit here and watch you make a fool out of ol' Bill there."

John was scared and confused, but he had also quaffed enough drinks to feel anger as his face reddened. "What are you talking about?" he asked in a calm, deeper voice.

The man rose from his chair and took a couple of steps towards John. "You come in here with your fancy clothes and your wad of money and you think you own the place. You think you're better than we are."

It was only then that John noticed he had slipped on a casual sports jacket before leaving his room.

"My boss wears a suit and I hate my boss," the man continued.

"C'mon, Randy, let him be. He ain't done nothin' wrong." It was Red, though there was no sound of alarm in his voice. John looked at the bartender, who was oblivious while deep in concentration cutting limes with a large carving knife.

"Aw, shit, I'm just kiddin', buddy," Randy said with a cunning smile. "I'm just messin' with ya. C'mon, Lou, set us up on me," he called to the barkeep.

John stood in the middle of the floor, hand still holding the cue in a death grip, wondering just what the hell had happened when Red quietly sidled up to him and put his hand on one of John's shoulders. "Don't worry about Randy," he said. "He just likes to have fun. We're miners, so we work in dirt all day long. When we're done, this is all there is to do in this shit-hole town. So when you walked in tonight I knew he'd yank your chain a bit, but he didn't mean any real harm." John wondered what real harm meant.

"Don't get me wrong, Randy can be a first-class dick, but I could tell he was in a good mood tonight. Let's go have that drink, buddy. At least he bought one for you, too."

John suddenly felt very drunk and wobbly, but he wasn't going to show that weakness to the hungry jackals. He downed his Jack Daniels, then ordered another round. While he found his new companions to be crude and uneducated, he felt a need to pull his weight in the joke department. Sadly, he was no match for the miners, who, he figured, spent their identical day after day after day refining their routines. One after another the jokes and the shots came in rapid-fire succession. By the time Lou told them it was last call, John was saturated with booze. As he left the bar at close to two in the morning, he gazed pensively at his car. The windows had frosted over and it was parked unevenly, the result of the warm-up beers he had drank in his room before deciding to venture out to the bar. He had always been good about taking cabs on the odd occasions when he would stop for a few too many drinks back home. A drunk driver had killed a friend's daughter, and he never wanted his pal to know that he had been driving under the influence himself.

PASSING THROUGH OBLIVION

But he was drunk, it was cold, an early morning departure beckoned, and the thought of wasting time waiting for a taxi soured him. The motel wasn't much more than five minutes away on a very straight road, anyway. Giving his head a shake to loosen the cobwebs, he unlocked the door - a trickier task than he had anticipated - and slid into the front seat, which was hard from the cold. "Okay, baby, start nice and we'll take it slow," he whispered. As the engine warmed up, John O'Rourke pulled his weary bones back out and circled the car making sure all the lights worked. That would be a stupid reason to get caught, he figured. He scraped the frost off the windows, took a long look up and down the main road through town, and cautiously began on his way. "Come on now, stay alert," he said to himself as he looked into the rearview mirror for headlights. His heart jumped as a car pulled out of a darkened parking lot just as he passed it and settled in behind him. "Oh, Jesus," he whispered again. "What the hell is that?" His fingers tightened on the steering wheel as he double-checked his speed while staring into the mirror to see what kind of fucking car was behind him. "Please, don't be a cop," he pleaded.

He made sure he was driving in a straight line, but knew that if the cop wanted to stop him because it was two o'clock and he was the only other car on the road, no amount of good conduct would save him. "Shit, why did I do this?" he asked himself. "And why can't I see if you're a cop or not?" A few nervous beads of sweat popped up on his forehead even though the interior of the car was still freezing. John could feel his eyes reddening against his will and he could smell his own alcohol-soaked breath, which was beginning to fog the windshield. How many had he drunk, he wondered. No, now was not the time to figure that out, asshole. Check your speed again. Look in the rearview. Is he getting closer? Damn, he is getting closer! John hoped against hope that he would find an all-night doughnut joint open so he could pull off the road and escape this stupid cop - if that's what he was. Maybe he wasn't, though. Maybe he was also just another guy heading home, checking his own speed and looking in the mirror for cops. In the distance, John could see the motel's sign lit up against the black horizon. Like every building in town, steam billowed out of a chimney. Just as he sighed with relief, the police car's lights splashed red and blue in his mirror. "Oh, shit," he whispered over his heart, which had leapt through his throat. "Oh, no." For a quick moment, John O'Rourke thought of making a run for the motel with the plan of fleeing from the car to his room, but in resignation he moved his left hand from the steering wheel to the turn indicator as he slowed down to pull to the side of the road. He would have to hope for the best and trust that he could talk his way out of trouble, a remote possibility to be sure. The police car sped up until its headlights flooded John's mirrors with blinding terror. He veered slowly into a vacant parking lot, deathly afraid of how his life was about to change once again, but the police car, with its siren and lights cutting through John's head, kept on speeding down the road.

"Jesus Christ," he sighed, at once angry with the cop for scaring him so much and furious at himself for being in that position in the first place. Still unsure he was in the clear, he obediently stayed in the lot for almost three minutes waiting for the flashing blue and red lights to return in case there had been some sort of mistake. Once he was fairly certain it had all been an awful coincidence, John left his car, locked the door and stumbled the final few hundred yards to the motel, his sweat-soaked hair freezing solid into thin icicles in the early-morning cold of this barren town he couldn't wait to leave. Safely in his room, he threw up and spent another night trying unsuccessfully to sleep. Exhausted and hungover, he fetched his car in the morning and began the final leg of his journey to Montreal, where, he hoped, the ghosts would not be able to find him. But ghosts, of course, can be anywhere. They migrate with people from cold to hot, nation to nation, wherever they go. You can run from them, as Joe Louis once said, but you cannot hide.

Chapter Seven

John had signed a lease for a small, furnished apartment - sight unseen - before he had departed. Searching the Internet, he had found what sounded like a decent place to live in Montreal's West End. Notre Dame de Grace, or NDG as everyone knew it, had been recommended by a friend who had once lived there. Multicultural, it had a vibrancy and warmth that attracted John all the way from the West Coast. His pal had described the area as safe and accessible with everything one would need within walking distance. There were dozens of restaurants and small, cozy bars and pubs dotting both sides of Sherbrooke Street, and independent specialty grocery stores coexisted with Indian, Thai, Greek and other delicacies. His apartment stood on the border of Westmount, Quebec's wealthiest city where towering mansions sit majestically on hills overlooking those below. It was where those who were almost making it or about to make it lived before proudly crossing the line to the upper crust. His wife's life insurance money allowed him to cross that line, but John was only too happy to be living on the edge.

By the time he finally arrived, almost two days later, his mood had soured and he felt as miserable as the frozen, dark winter. It was as if he'd moved to a foreign country, much less a province. The signs were all in French; most of the people spoke French; asking for directions was useless; even the architecture was from another era. It occurred to him that he had lived a sheltered life out west, rarely venturing far from home unless it was to spend a sun-soaked week drinking daiquiris and getting burned with Wendy. Even then, everyone spoke English and all the comforts of a resort were at their fingertips. Such a lifestyle could hardly be considered roughing it. But Quebec was a different world. "Deux et trente-cinq" meant two dollars and thirty-five cents, while "Est-ce que je peux vous aider?" translated into "Can I help you?" John finished unpacking his suitcase and the few small boxes of personal possessions he decided to keep. On a windowsill in the living room went a silver beer stein Will had given him at his bachelor party, along with a picture of John and Will - arm-in-arm and appearing very drunk - at the same event, a party that had rolled on to the early morning hours even without the stripper Wendy had vehemently vetoed. Will had been particularly proud of the obscenities and the Mexican moustache he had drawn on the intended groom with a black magic marker after he had passed out at his friend's home. The memory of that night made him smile even as he gazed solemnly at his new, unfamiliar surroundings. The move, he thought, was a bad idea borne from a desire to run away from a past he could never escape. They would always be dead and unless he found some real courage he would always be alive. With such maudlin thoughts filling his head, he decided to check out the little bar that he had spotted right around the corner. Although it was nearly midnight, he needed a diversion from the voices and a victory drink for at least making it this far. He was in Montreal alone and depressed. Where else should he have been but at a bar?

The first thing John noticed when he went to Matty's was how short the bar itself was. There were a number of small two-chair tables against the walls, which surrounded a busy pool table, and he could see a couple of booths in the far corners near the windows. There was room for a patio outdoors on the sidewalk, but the bar itself held enough room for only eight chairs. The second thing that caught his eye, right after he grabbed an end stool nearest the TV, was the bathroom. John had ordered a beer from a tall, good looking barmaid who called herself Tania, then he went to the bathroom once the bottle had been placed in front of him to signify someone was sitting there. It was the only seat, after all, and he didn't want to lose it.

It was a hell of a nice bathroom as bathrooms go. Of course, John had pissed in a few before, but nothing had ever caught his eye enough to make him sit back and take a good look at what a fine john he was really in. Up on the wall to the left of the toilet was an ink drawing of a nude - all shady and mysterious. Above the toilet hung a very large painting of a proud conquistador, rich in colour, texture, and depth and surrounded by a heavy, detailed bronze frame. John liked that painting and wondered how it had ever found its way to a bathroom in a bar. To the left of the door - if you happen to be sitting down and facing it - was a cherry wood table with cabinets beneath that John found to be locked shut. On the top, left-hand corner of the table stood a lamp about a foot and a half tall with a glass lampshade that made the mirror on the wall beside it sparkle. Of course, there was a sink and taps to wash with and the tiling on the floor was a little old, but overall John graded it as the Martha Stewart of bar johns. Another thing that was distinctive compared to most others was the amount of cocaine done in there. John didn't know it yet, but the conquistador was guarding quite a stash behind him.

The regulars dominated the bar seating most evenings, and all of them snorted coke to some extent. Thus, they were a symphony of sniffing, one after the other trying but failing to discreetly use tissues to wipe their runny noses. At first, before he knew any better, John wondered how they could keep giving each other the same cold and he silently wished they'd all be quarantined together somewhere else.

The main core of the gang consisted of the Doctor (so called because he was a college science teacher), Doc's girlfriend Janine, Sally, Sam and Celia. Celia was an Irish woman five years older than John, who would one day prove to him that she had a hell of a time trying to figure out when to go home. Her pals called her Westcoast because there was always at least a three-hour difference between when she'd say she was leaving for home and her actual departure. They got together as most bar clans do - by stopping by one night after work for a quick drink and enjoying themselves enough to return. That's the way it always begins with bar types. They sit down after a hard day for no other reason than to enjoy a refreshing beer and warm ambiance to shrug the cold and problems from their bones. Because they quickly feel better, the thought of stopping by again is an attractive one. Should the good feeling occur again the next time, the bar becomes a place they frequent and they begin to exchange nods with the regulars who were already there. A quick hello, a laugh or two, and you're one of them. You are a regular. The staff greets you by name, they know your drink of choice, and if they see through the window that you're on your way in they have that drink at the ready before the door even opens. The lighting is familiar, as is the scent. Any bar worth your time has its own smell - good or otherwise -and regulars learn to find comfort in that security blanket. Eventually, life stories are swapped, histories revealed, bonds forged. People talk to you about their jobs, their wives, their kids and all other things great and meaningless. You tend to know them better than their spouses do because the bar is the secret society where everything said stays within those walls and few people are judges as long as they're quick with a laugh and the occasional drink. A barmaid will seek moral support over a bitter custody battle with an ex who abused her; the guy who sits near you and smells like bourbon even as he first arrives grousing about his lousy boss who's always busting his balls. Everyone has secrets, and sooner or later alcohol breaks down barriers, and truth is blended so thoroughly with fiction that one becomes the other.

John's introduction to that merry band of barflies occurred much the same way. After dropping by enough times, they became familiar enough with each other to nod, then shortly thereafter say hello and become friendly. By the time a few weeks had passed, John knew most everyone and most everyone knew him. Still, something made him feel like an outsider, like the new kid on the block that he was. So one evening as John was in the passion of another frantic backgammon game with Doc, the question was posed. The evening had grown old and they were among the last to leave Matty's that night. Backgammon had become a favourite pursuit for the two of them. Both equally skilled and competitive, they enjoyed watching what the other would do then compare it to what their own move would've been. Most times they were one and the same. Their games were creative, quick and full of strategy and they drew a pretty good crowd when they really got going. Celia always wanted to play the winner, but one of them would beat quickly and without too much effort. She wasn't very good, but craved the attention that being part of the action garnered, so they'd let her play every once in a while. Cee also had a habit of buying rounds of Jagrmeister for everyone of the regulars.

If you've never had the pleasure, Jagrmeister tastes just like awful cough medicine, though its medicinal effects are not to be trifled with. It's just got that awful taste, but Cee loved the stuff and everyone drank it because she bought it. John had to give her some reluctant credit, even if he wasn't overly fond of her. She was a good-looking woman for forty-four. She told John she had once trained as a gymnast when she was younger back in Ireland, and he had no reason to disbelieve her. Her body was firm, lithe and devoid of almost any fat. Her long blond hair was dyed not for colour but to eliminate the increasing gray, and she possessed incredible stamina considering how little sleep she allowed herself.

The only real clue to her age was her face, which could look either handsome, as they say about women of a certain age, or tired and lined depending on her mood or health. Doc, who had spent the occasional night with her, said she looked much like Keith Richards the morning after the late night before.

But on that evening, there was only Doc and John seated at the bar, the trusty backgammon game surrounded by ashtrays, a glass of beer and a vodka and soda - tall, loads of ice, no fruit. John, who had not been a smoker, took the habit of with enthusiasm and was pleased smoking was allowed indoors in Quebec at the time.

"Hey, Doc, I have to ask you something," John began.

"Go ahead," Doc answered as he rolled the die. "Damn! Five. Can't get you."

"Well, I don't consider myself stupid . . ."

"I'd say not."

"I've been coming around here for a few months now, much to the occasional chagrin of my editor who would no doubt like to see a more cheerful, re-energized writer after a supposedly good night's sleep, and I've noticed a few things."

"Such as?" the doctor asked, his attention momentarily diverted from the board in front of him.

"Well, tell me if I'm straying into something that's none of my business, but I'm only asking because I feel we've become friends."

Doc sat silently waiting for the question. "Go ahead," he finally said.

"Well, I was wondering if you knew if I could get something besides liquor in here." There, he had said it.

"Like what?"

Doc's evasiveness surprised John, who wished he hadn't brought the subject up. These were still his only friends after a couple of months of living in Montreal and he had come to rely on them and the bar for all his social activities. The job was going well enough because he was doing much the same thing he had done in Vancouver, but the guilt that had attached itself to him and grown like ivy on an old southern mansion only ebbed when he had a belly full of booze and the company of his new friends to distract him. John wasn't even sure why he was asking except for the hope he would be trusted with that secret, and with that knowledge become fully entrenched as one of them. He didn't know it then, but he needed them as much as he had ever needed anyone.

. "Look, Doc, I'm not a naïve kid now, if I ever was one. I want to know if I can get anything else in here besides drinks. I'd like something . . . more fun, let's say."

"What colour do you want?" John asked comfortably.

"What colour do I want?" John repeated, taken off guard by the direct question.

"You want green? Brown? White, maybe?"

Bingo! That was the colour John was curious about. He had tried coke almost fifteen years earlier, but only at a couple of parties and only in ineffectually small amounts. Now, the effort of outrunning the ghosts had become almost unbearable. By the time he made it to the bar most evenings after work, he felt as though he had been beaten with a lead pipe all day. Yet the others were all chipper and full of lightning. They came in looking like hell, but were laughing and barking out jokes and stories shortly thereafter. Even if he wouldn't do it often, John yearned to be trusted enough to know what the others were up to.

"Yeah, Doc, I'd like some white. Can you help me?"

Doc stared into John's eyes. He appeared to be very serious about something. "You know a lot of people could be in a lot of trouble if the wrong person was to say something. We all know what you do for a living."

John nodded as earnestly as he could.

"Give me your cigarette package," Doc whispered.

John's eyes fell to Doc's nearly full package of Players Light, but he did as he was told and handed his own across the backgammon board. The doctor took a cigarette out, lit it with his own matches, then, like a magician, slid a different book of matches he had palmed into John's cigarette pack and handed them back. Do you need a bill, too?" he inquired as calmly as if he was asking if they should have another drink.

John sat motionless for a long moment unsure of how to answer.

"It's in the match pack," Doc smiled. "Do you need a bill to roll for when you go to the bathroom?"

John felt a jolting rush of excitement. He actually now owned cocaine and it was lying right in front of him for the taking! It wasn't the promise of what the drug would do to him that caused his heart to accelerate, it was the fact that he had been trusted and the knowledge that he could now get it whenever he wanted it. He had been promoted from acquaintance to friend and the door had been opened for him to become part of their secret life, one that he had to admit looked like a hell of a lot of fun. John never failed to notice Doc's simple trick of handing out matches to others after that.

"Well, then, I guess I have to go to the bathroom," he smiled.

"Get to it, man. I'm in the middle of kicking your ass and nothing can get in the way of that," Doc winked.

"Yeah, this must be a first for you, but don't get used to it because it won't happen again," John hollered back as he closed the bathroom door. A new life he could never have envisioned waited for him as he gazed upon the majestic conquistador on the wall. He carved a small line on the counter, noticing for the first time the powdery residue of others who had come before. He turned to the painting.

"Here we go, my friend, cheers," he whispered as he carefully inserted a rolled twenty-dollar bill in his left nostril. While most made its way to his bloodstream almost at once, a little caught in his throat and he grimaced from the harsh taste. As dreadful as it tasted, though, John still was careful to wet a finger and run it over the leftover on the white counter. He licked the coke off his finger and felt a small portion of his tongue go numb. He stood perfectly rigid and gazed into the mirror to see if he could spot any difference in his appearance. He was disappointed when he couldn't and briefly wondered if he should do more, but decided to wait and see what that one would do first before snorting any more.

He rejoined his friend at the bar after double-checking to make sure he had left nothing out for anyone else to see.

"Everything good?" Doc asked him.

"So far, so good, but I don't really feel anything yet," John admitted before beginning a story that really went nowhere and took fifteen minutes to complete, during which he smoked four cigarettes and ordered two more drinks without ever once throwing the die.

"I think I'm going to try just a little bit more to see if it'll hit me this time," he said as he finished.

Doc motioned the way to the bathroom. "If you think it'll help," he laughed. Then he whispered again: "Oh, and it was $40 worth when you get the time, brother."

John returned Doc's smile realizing that the narcotic had affected him much more than he had known. "Okay, give me a minute to organize myself in there. And aren't you supposed to give me the first one for free so I get hooked?"

"Only in the movies, my friend. This stuff isn't cheap, you know. Take your pack and just put the money inside for me. I'll take it out while we're playing."

John gave himself a slightly larger dose the second time, sure to remember to hide Doc's money before returning. This time he shivered involuntarily as it entered his system. "Whoa, that's the stuff," he smiled to the conquistador. "You really should try it sometime."

John and Doc played three more spirited games before Janine came by for a nightcap and to drag her boyfriend home.

"Guess what John did tonight?" Doc asked Janine.

"Whipped you at backgammon?" she guessed.

"Ha! He wishes he was that good. No, our new friend John has discovered he likes treats."

Janine thought for a second, then stared at John. "Really? I wouldn't have guessed. You look so straight."

"What the hell do I look like?" Doc complained, who, we must remember, was a college teacher at the time.

Janine bellowed laughter like a large man. Anyone short of the deaf could hear her thunderous guffaws from blocks away. "You look like my man and I want my man home."

For the first time, Doc and John shook hands as they parted. "I'm trusting you." Doc said.

"You have nothing to worry about," John promised. "We're friends and I enjoy my time with you too much to screw anything up. It all stays right here."

"I know. Want one more for the road before I leave? I might not be here tomorrow evening. Janine insists on dinner out somewhere that isn't here," he winked.

"Fucking right," she laughed.

John fished in his pocket, but it held only the one bill he had been using as a straw. "I'd have to go to the bank first," he said.

John slid another pack of matches along the bar. "Give it to me when I see you next," he smiled, as he and Janine walked through the door into the cool Montreal darkness.

By the time they made him leave at 2:30 in the morning, John was a ball of electricity. He had smoked his pack empty and had spent the previous hour bumming them off Tania, the bartender he had come to know and like. He wasn't sure, but he thought he might have even had a crush on her.

Tania was the usual bartender - a darling, John thought, if there ever was one. Although she was almost six feet tall with long auburn hair and bangs down to her eyes, and a full, curvaceous body that was built for sex, Tania's most unique feature was her laugh. The actual laugh part - that's to say the Ha! Ha! Ha! part when she exhaled - was loud and rich, but it was when she was breathing in that heads really turned. That's when she sounded like she was fighting a horrific case of asthma while choking on a chicken bone at the same time. It was someone being strangled. It was loud, startling and hilarious and it scared strangers and amused friends. John liked Tania for her wickedly funny sense of the absurd and the way she could will a subdued crowd to have fun, but mostly he liked her because he'd been given a glimpse on rare occasions behind the facade of the happy bartender. He had seen her tired, worried about everyday problems and in need of a hug. "Oh, John," she whispered softly one night when the last few stragglers of the evening were walking towards the door, "I am so tired. I just need to go home and get into bed."

John reached across the bar to place his hand on hers. "Want some company?" he teased, his mind racing furiously from the coke.

"My husband might object," she answered.

"Let him find his own girl," John laughed.

"He probably already has." Tania smiled, but there was no joy in her eyes. "I don't know how much longer I can do this, Johnny. I mean, look at me. I'm almost forty. I'm getting too old to keep up with these crazy fucking hours."

She didn't look forty - far from it - but in the dead of night it was obvious the work was taking it's toll on her. "I'll be back in a second," she said. "Will you stick around until I close? I'd like the company, if you're not too tired."

John was clearly not too tired for anything, and it being a very early Saturday morning with no work to confront when he finally did wake up, he was more than happy to stay.

"Great," Tania smiled as she poured John a drink on the house. "I'll be right back."

And when she did return, Tania was far more awake than she had been minutes before. "Here," she said, sliding a small package across the bar to her only customer. "This should keep you happy until I'm done."

John wasn't sure how to react. Tania smiled and took his hand in hers. "Don't think I don't notice what goes on here," she said softly. "Consider this my appreciation for keeping me company."

John thanked her and eagerly trotted off to the bathroom to visit the conquistador once again

Chapter Eight

John O'Rourke stared wildly at himself in his apartment's bathroom mirror amazed and excited by his appearance. His heart was a jackhammer and his eyes bugged out like two eggs painted blue in the middle and his hair was sweaty and matted to his head. Small pearls of perspiration dotted his forehead and face even though he had just arrived from the cold early morning darkness. His knuckles were white, both hands securely clamped on to the sink like an eagle's talons gripping its prey. His mouth opened as if to shriek in pain, but no sound came out. He noticed one foot tapping the floor incessantly, tried to stop it, then realizing it to be impossible took his toothbrush and pounded the sink to keep the beat until it broke in two, the longer end bouncing off the mirror and narrowly missing his right eye. "Okay, John, we might have had a little much tonight, a little much, I say," he told the maniac in the mirror. "I know," it answered, "don't you think I know that. Look at us. I don't even recognize that guy. Yeah, but it's cool, though, isn't it? I've never seen us look like this, no, no, no, never like this." John threw his head back and laughed like a mad man. "Holy shit! So this is what this stuff is supposed to do to you." Suddenly aware he might have really had too much, he checked his pulse against the second hand of the living room clock. Unable to calculate its rate the first time, he tried again and found it to be somewhere around a hundred and forty beats per minute. "That can't be good," he thought, walking back into the bathroom to look at his contorted face again. "I . . . am . . . on . . . COKE!!!" he sang. "Former mild-mannered reporter John O'Rourke, now invincible superhero Cokeman," he laughed, proud that he knew people who did it and sold it to him. Until that time, his affair was the craziest thing he had done, and that had not ended well. No, it hadn't gone well at all, had it? Fuck off, stop thinking about it! Sure, he used to go out for drinks with some of the guys from the paper, and once in a while he'd have too much and still drive home. He and Wendy had friends who furnished the occasional joint, but Wendy had soured on that after the kids were born. John had tried a little speed and twice popped acid when he was a teen, but any thoughts of living fast and dangerously had died along with his youth after he and Wendy got married. After that big event, Wendy had suggested he focus more on saving his money for a house and the children she wanted and less on having fun with his pals and other "stupid things." She urged him to grow up now that he was married and look toward the future she wanted to have with him and the kids she thought he wanted as well. For a time, he made himself believe that was the life for him, but as the years passed Wendy's mostly unfulfilled material desires made him feel inadequate even though he was a well-respected if underpaid columnist for a major newspaper. The loving attention she paid to him was a fleeting shadow of what Henry received. It wasn't that he was miserable, he simply wasn't happy, and that was something he could ignore for only so long before feeling compelled to do something just for himself. And then, as if in direct response to his adultery, his family was gone.

"But we're all right now, aren't we?" he whispered to the grimace staring back from the mirror as his toes continued to tap the tiled floor. After an hour of pacing across the apartment, he felt settled enough to watch TV, which he did by flipping from one channel to another for two hours before finally falling into a fitful sleep that lasted until he awoke sore and dazed just after one o'clock in the afternoon. He tried to eat but the thought of food sickened him further, so he waited a couple of hours then dragged himself back to the bar for a little hair of the dog and to see if any of the gang was there already.

"Seriously, the weather has got to get better soon," John said to the doctor as they played their fourth game of backgammon of the evening. A hockey game was on TV above the bar, full that night mostly because people didn't have the ambition to go anywhere else further as they impatiently waited for a spring that so far was refusing to show itself.

"I miss the patio," Celia chimed in. She was looking more attractive than usual in a slinky black dress that contrasted nicely with her long, blond hair. It was nearing the end of March, but outside Matty's it could have been January. The temperature hovered around zero and wisps of snow and freezing rain blew almost horizontally in the biting wind. Celia looked as though she was trying to will the warmth to come so she could lounge outside and lazily watch the people go by, but nature was having none of it.

"I'm bloody tired of sitting in here every night."

Doc and John looked at each other and smiled. Inside or out, Westcoast would have been sitting somewhere nearby almost every night regardless of what the weather was like. Perhaps aware of their silent mockery, she sidled up close to John purposefully brushing a breast against his shoulder. "Time for a shot?" she purred. She was either very wealthy or very foolish, John thought, but there was also something about her that he was beginning to find attractive. A vulnerability or maybe some kind of self-destructive tendencies that subtly cried for someone to save her may have been it, but he was getting too drunk to pursue that thinking any further. She pressed into him again, and this time he could see that the doctor noticed.

"One for all of us?" he asked.

"I was thinking one just for the two of us," she answered with a smile that said far more than her words.

"We can't leave the doc out, can we?" John said, as said doc smiled broadly.

Celia put her hands on her hips and tilted her head just enough to look sexy. "And would you bring him home with us if we left together one night?"

"There it is!" Doc cried. "It was only a matter of time."

"Shut up, you!" Celia retorted.

"There what is?" John asked confused.

"Nothing," Celia answered.

"Put your seatbelt on, it's going to be a bumpy ride," Doc laughed.

"Fuck you!"

"Just that one time, darling," Doc said with a smile.

"Shit, where are those shots?" John muttered.

"Do you want one or not, sweetheart?" Celia asked as her left arm snaked around John's neck.

John had to admit to himself that it felt warm and exciting to feel her that close. On drugs, everything felt exciting. John had been thinking recently that it would have been a far different evening with that waitress if he had been stoned. But that had occurred one life before this one and one life after the first one. "Oh, yeah," he whispered seductively.

"Oh, no," Doc said shaking his head from side to side.

"Two Jagermeisters, darling," Celia called to Tania, who looked over and laughed her laugh when she spotted Celia with John. "Why don't you all fuck off?" Celia smiled while her pale blue eyes danced with John's.

"Be careful, old man," the doc said, as Westcoast bounded for the bathroom. "If you're not, she'll take you out at the knees."

John looked puzzled at his friend.

"All I'm saying is you're a big boy, but make sure you know what you're doing." He arched an eyebrow for emphasis and rolled a double-six causing John to groan.

"Shit," John spat.

"You're about to find out, son," Doc countered.

John worried about the friendly group dynamic he was enjoying and whether that might change if he were to get involved with Celia. To John, they were a lifeline to some semblance of sanity and normalcy, and he was terrified to give that up for a woman he wasn't sure he wanted in the first place.

"I'm going to the washroom," Celia said to John, "so decide what you want to do by the time I get back because I want to go home and I want you to come with me." Those last words were said louder than the rest and were as much for Doc's benefit as they were for John.

"What do you think?" John asked his friend, who appeared to want nothing to do with the debate.

"I've been there," he whispered out of earshot of Janine, who was wobbling slightly but noticeably in her chair while she attempted to hold a conversation with a woman who's friends had just deserted her for fast food down the street . "As I said, you're a big boy, but she can be a real mean piece of work. Caveat emptor, my friend."

That helped to make John's mind up; it wouldn't just be a fuck, it would be a challenge. He, too, trotted off to see the conquistador, returning with a renewed sense of purpose and vitality. "Ready?" he asked Celia, holding his arm out for her to take.

She smiled brightly if unsteadily. "Really?"

John nodded and arched his eyebrows seductively. "We're wasting time here. Let's go."

As the door closed behind them leaving Doc alone with the backgammon set, Janine thought she heard someone say, "That's gonna be trouble."

And sure enough, John O'Rourke's newfound happily irresponsible existence was about to be visited by more dark clouds. And this time they wouldn't be so easy to escape.

Chapter Nine

To his great surprise, the sex with Celia came off without a hitch. Whenever he felt that he was about to slide down into Memory Lane via Guilt Avenue, he offered or was offered another fat line to keep his spirits up, so to speak. Blissfully oblivious of reality, he explored Celia's body from top to bottom, pausing here and there where he wanted to play for a while, and thanks to the combination of liquor and drugs in his body, was able to achieve an erection without ever coming. Celia, who had experienced her fair share of one-night stands, climaxed three times with John and once on her own just so he could watch.

Without ever getting to sleep, Celia drove John home a little before noon. Their eyes were glassy and baggy with dark, ugly circles framing them from underneath, and his hair was lunging in all directions as if it was trying to escape his head. He felt too unfamiliar to use her toothbrush, leaving his mouth tasting like he had dined on a rancid carcass the night before. Doc would've said he had. As Celia's Toyota sped east along the highway, then south onto the Decarie Expressway, John wanted nothing more than to get inside his apartment away from the blinding sun that threatened to burn holes through his eyes. But he was also riding a wave of relief that he might not have to spend the rest of his days asexual, afraid of being with a woman. If nothing else, Celia gave him his manhood back and he felt a certain warmth towards her because of it. "Want to go for a coffee before I go home," he asked with a voice full of gravel from smoking too much.

Celia looked surprised, but pleased. "Sure," she answered with as much enthusiasm as she could muster under the circumstances. She was happily surprised John had asked, but her aging body was buckling under the strain of the all-night drug binge. It begged for more artificial stimulation if it was to keep going.

They settled on the Second Cup across from Matty's, which, much to their unbalanced chagrin and relief, was opening again. A table far from the magnifying glass of a window was chosen and they began to sip their steaming coffees while making feeble attempts at small talk.

"So, what now?" Celia asked when she could take no more vapidity.

John's stomach clenched in response to this question he knew and feared would come. "Ah, well, maybe keep it as it is," he mumbled into his mug.

Celia laughed in spite of herself. "So it's a wham-bam thank you, ma'am? I have to admit I expected a little more out of you than that," she smiled. "I mean, what do we do about last night?"

John felt his bowels begin to loosen, but knew that escape to the bathroom, regardless of his pain, would be seen as cowardice.

"Did you enjoy yourself?" she asked.

"You know I did," he answered grudgingly.

"Then we should do it again sometime, maybe," she offered.

"Yeah, could be," John said into his mug. "Let's go have a drink," he suggested. "It's not that I need one to answer you, but I may need one to survive. Could we do that?"

Celia nodded knowingly. "I can't see how that could hurt," she said beginning to laugh again. John laughed too, and felt some warmth return. "I have to go to work tomorrow, okay?"

"You can leave whenever you want to, can't you?"

John hung his head in mock resignation. "I'm not sure anymore. My editor said I smelled like a distillery one morning last week. I have to play a little safer, so just a couple to ward off the dogs and then home."

"Whose home?" Celia whispered closely into John's ear, but her toothpaste had lost the battle and he pulled quickly away from the sour odor.

He gave her a plastic smile. "My home, darling, alone and asleep."

Celia retreated at once. She had heard words like these too often before and she half-expected John to promise to call her, which, of course, he would not do. She decided to tread lightly and allow him to dictate how their day would unfold.

People sauntering by for a nice Sunday coffee had been ogling the couple as they entered the coffeehouse. At first, John's ego allowed him to think it was because his picture was in the paper four times a week, but those stares weren't inviting; rather they were contemptuous. John took a good look at Celia, startled himself, then rushed to the bathroom to see what kind of condition he was in. When he returned to Keith Richards, he told her to get up and follow him to the bar now. To his shock and dismay, they looked like they had been awake for more than 24 hours drinking and doing drugs. He needed his sanctuary, the one just across the street with the dim lights.

The door swung open to a darkened bar. After the glare outside, it took a few moments for them to see anything. But there was no stopping the sound of Tania's laughter coming from somewhere in the darkness.

Three hours later, the doctor arrived to thunderous applause from the couple at the bar playing backgammon and dabbing at their noses.

"Doctor!" John called.

"Whatsizname!" Celia added with good-natured cheer.

Doc paused at the sight of the couple, reconsidered his plans for a moment, then proceeded to a stool beside John. "So this is the way it's going to be," he said with faint annoyance in his breath.

"I guess we're seeing each other," Celia stated with little conviction. She then slapped an arm around her new man. "I love him!" she squeeled.

Doc laughed heartily at John's face, which looked much like that of a dog that has crapped on the living room rug. He, too, wrapped an arm around John, softly and with genuine friendship. "If this is what you want, my man, all power to you. I'm happy for the both of you. Have you chosen a china pattern yet?"

"That's enough out of you," John sneered. "And there will be no china patterns," he added in a tone that told Celia there would likely be no anything.

"You look pretty spry for a guy that was . . . up all night," John laughed, obviously relishing the moment.

"Got some from Tania," John answered, "but it was just enough to prop us up. Care to do some business with your old pal John?"

Doc scoured the room to make sure it was empty. Satisfied it was, he stood from his seat. "To the Bat Cave, Robin."

"I'll be back," John bellowed back to Celia.

"You better or I'll come looking for you."

"Jesus," Doc muttered.

"I doubt he's here," John laughed.

"Hang tight, my friend, you may just find him after you try what I have for you."

"Oh, good, I have some questions for him."

"I bet he has some of his own for us, too."

Chapter Ten

John awoke dazed and defused amid the carnage that was his apartment. He grimly tried to go back to sleep, but something was agitating him enough to keep him in that confusing twilight zone between peaceful slumber and unwanted consciousness. For a few minutes, he lazed spread-eagled on his bed that had gone far too long without its sheets being laundered, but the slight odor unreasonably comforted him. He remembered he was a little late on the rent and hoped no one would knock on his door before he pulled himself together. Dirty dishes, almost two weeks in the sink, had begun to attract tiny fruit flies, as did spaghetti sauce stains on the faux-wood counter. Garbage that had fallen from those same counters was attracting its own wildlife on the kitchen floor and reams of newspapers - some piled by the door, others strewn with reckless abandon across the living room and bedroom floors - were threatening to become a new carpet. "Man, I really have to clean today," he whispered to himself through dry, cracking lips. And then it hit him like a kick in the stomach. It was not Sunday at all. Sunday was a blur of drinking, drugging and laughing all the way from early afternoon through to early morning. Sunday had not been a day of rest at all following his sleepless Saturday night. With mounting panic, he slowly turned to look at the time on his clock radio - the one Wendy had given him. When he saw the red numbers he threw his pillow against the wall, sending the Monet print crashing to the floor. It was 10:39 a.m. and John O'Rourke was already thirty-nine minutes late for a meeting with his boss, who also happened to be the editor of the Tribune. Walter Higgins was not a man to rile, especially when others were already questioning your character and, more importantly, your performance. John was mired in the dilemma of whether to call Walt with some lame excuse or to fly in as quickly as possible with an entirely different flimsy story about a flat tire or a bad car battery. The one thing John couldn't reason in his suddenly aching head was why he would only be calling now. He did have a cell phone, naturally, so now he had to come up with a reason for not using it. "Okay, John, think about this," he said to himself, as if rehearsing what he would say. "You ran out of gas on the expressway and forgot the phone at home. You had to wait for a tow truck, then you had to go back to the garage where they fixed a dead battery. Or a fuel problem. Come on, think!" His lack of understanding about the mechanics of cars had finally crippled him. It would have to be a tire or a battery or he might sink himself, unable to answer even the rudimentary of questions. He quickly dressed in clothes off of the floor that he felt were clean enough, cracking his head against the wall after losing his balance trying to put his right sock on. "Shit!" he cursed as the pain shot down his spine. A new panic gripped him and he whirled to see if Celia was anywhere to be found. Thankfully, she was not.

Of course, John had little to worry about. Even in the brief time he'd been there, he'd developed an audience that liked his style - his unique everyman way that his readers had come to enjoy every couple of days. As opposed to many of the writers, he had found a way to connect with his readers as one of their own. Though he didn't know it at the time, he had found his calling. An audience of free-spirited

Montrealers that loved the laisez-faire style that epitomized the city better than any other writer could do at the time. There was one, a few years before, who could grab the city like no one else. Nick Auf der Maur even had an ally named after him for a drunken evening when he had taken a leak against a stone wall and had been arrested for it. The public outcry over such a beloved figure being shackled for pissing in public had led to a smirk and a grin as Montreal officials curried favour by naming the very same ally after the pissoir. Since then - especially since Auf der Maur's death - John had wondered what it might be like to hold such public affection in a city so ready to offer it. He had no idea that circling the drain with drugs and alcohol would do it, as long as you had a column in a major metropolitan daily to play cool with and a public persona within which hide.

Although he was a very small, scared man inside, he strode into the paper that morning like he owned the place, even though he knew he was in for a pretty good wrist slapping again. Of course, this was something he was getting used to. He had been ostracized by some in Vancouver for his image - the playboy with the patient wife who got away with murder - but his gritty writing had captivated a city and cemented his reputation as a must read, whether you loved or hated him. He was known, he was needed, and he would be despised after a long enough time under the lights of local fame.

As he headed toward's Walt's office, there were looks that would've never spooked him before, but which now made him feel like he had strolled happily into a lion's den of hatred. Co-workers he had happily dismissed as too boring to bother with now looked down upon him.

> People are strange
> When you're a stranger

What the hell was happening?

Shirt half-untucked, hair matted against his head, white crust embedded in the corners of his mouth, the journalist who imagined himself as the Great Canadian Writer looked nothing more than some drunk off the street in need of a cleaning and a warm cup of coffee. He tried to smile, but a rather nasty contemptuous, crooked grin greeted his colleagues. He felt out of place - out of his comfort zone of happy, irresponsible drunkenness. What happened then as he struggled to compose himself in front of people he truly did want to be a part of was legendary.

Nadia from design approached John cautiously, slowly, like predator does to prey when it's unsure if its victim still has some fight in it. She was the only person at the paper he had taken the time to know, though he never understood why. Others stared for a moment or two, then turned away and pretended to continue working. The corner of everyone's eyes were glued to the man they had heard of but rarely seen. Muffled curses wafted here and there as phones rang and had to be answered, diverting the attention of those involved. The publisher, Roland (Duffy) Dufresne himself, paused on his way to a meeting to eye his city columnist from head to toe. His face contorted judgment, and the verdict was guilty. John O'Rourke icily felt as though he was about to lose his job.

Nadia inched closer and reached a tentative hand toward John when she was no more than a foot or two away. She could smell the booze seeping from his pores, but she felt no anger nor did she pity John. As her wheelchair stopped directly in front of him, she whispered something that would never leave him.

"It's okay, John. Sometimes it's harder to be perfect than to be broken. I forgave the drunk that did this to me because he has the rest of his life to think about it. Maybe you need to forgive yourself. You also have the rest of your life to live. Are you sure this is how you want to live it?"

And then John O'Rourke, man-about-town, friend to the common man, and blossoming addict did something he never would've believed he could do. Weeks later, he barely remembered doing it. Instead, he would think back on it as if it had been a dream, out of focus and with a little of this and that missing. He took Nadia's hand, fell to his knees, dropped his head into her numb lap, and began to cry. He sobbed as he did that night with Chirpy Girl in the hotel room, with great, heaving cries and uncontrolled shaking. He begged forgiveness in front of these strangers, who would phone, e-mail and speak of what had happened to everyone they knew. Although he never actually clarified what he needed forgiveness for, Nadia stroked his dirty hair, bent over and kissed his cheek, and told him he was loved.

John rose unsteadily from her grasp suddenly ashamed of himself and his condition. Surprisingly, it mattered to him that he was letting her down, and her compassion further shamed him. He was only comfortable now with the doctor and his nightly prescriptions. It stunned him that he was in an office in the daytime, smelling sour and old and barely able to keep upright. The lights were beaming ever brighter and they were burning his skin, or perhaps it was the stares that were doing that. He didn't know, he didn't care. John O'Rourke only knew that he was about to go mad if he didn't get the hell out of that building as quickly as his unsteady feet could carry him, if they could at all. He wanted to scream, to growl and bite and escape the cage he found himself in.

"No," he stammered, "no, this isn't right. I don't deserve this. I have to go. I'm sorry," he breathed to Nadia. "I have to go."

He then took Nadia's hand and gently squeezed it. "I don't believe in God or absolution or redemption or heaven or hell," he stammered again. "I'm a little lost right now, but I'll right the ship. I always right the ship, don't I?" He looked at Duffy Dufresne with a crooked, unnerving smile. "I'm sorry, but I really have to go." John tried to say more, but his lips did nothing more than form the words his brain was trying to get him to say. He felt helpless and panicked. "I guess I quit," he whispered before unsteadily turning to leave.

John shuffled out with the little dignity he thought remained. As the double-glass doors closed behind him, he thought he heard Dufresne's baritone voice. He thought he heard the word "no."

Chapter Eleven

It had been an embarrassing evening, one that left John in a dark mood and feeling sorry for himself. Back among friends in the bar that felt like home, he unwound with a few drinks, then wound himself back up again with some coke, the see-saw of his emotions rising and falling depending upon which substance was entering his body at that moment. It had been a month since the episode within the walls of the Trib, a month in which John did his best to curtail his intake of drugs and drink, something the doctor applauded because "It's something we all have to do once in a while. You were going pretty hard at it, so a little time off won't hurt." John still went to Matty's a few nights a week and he still allowed himself the odd treat, but he had pulled himself together, more or less, and spent a long morning talking to Walter Higgins about his strange behavior, which he blamed on flashbacks of grief for his family. He admitted to drinking too much - he had to admit something to deflect the real problem - and told Walt that he had identified the problem and the reason for it. He asked for forgiveness, which Walt was happy to give, and if he could bypass the office for a while because of his embarrassment over the scene he had caused. Of course, my boy, Walt had said, take all the time you like. John promised to re-energize himself and his columns, which, to be honest, had been less than crisp lately, replaced by meandering thoughts on this and that. Walt was a grizzled old man, who climbed the ranks in the days when editors kept bottles of bourbon in their desk drawer and chain-smoked in their office. To him, this wasn't anything more than a little youthful mistake that anyone could make. Hell, he enjoyed tying one on as much as the next guy, though he had to admit that he had never come into the office tanked like John had done.

After a few weeks he called John to see how he was doing. Satisfied that his star columnist sounded like a new man, he told John about a promo the paper would like to do. It involved a bar, Walt said, so if that was a problem John could simply decline the opportunity and they'd go with the sports guy. But John did feel better and although he had increased his frequency at Matty's over the past week and had allowed Doc to prescribe a little more medicine again, he thought he would be strong enough to be a celebrity bartender at a fundraiser for breast cancer on trendy Crescent Street. He did enjoy being in the spotlight sometimes, he had to admit, and it had been a while since he actually got out and met new people.

He told no one at Matty's of the personal appearance just to be sure they wouldn't show up unannounced. That, he knew, would be too much. There was to be press coverage not only from his own paper, but English and French TV and radio were going to be there as well.

He began the evening nervous, but clever, witty and very charming. He could see a few of the female guests catching his eye and smiling, while the older ones told him what a good job he was doing. At about nine o'clock, when the auction began and most of the guests were sitting rather than standing at his bar, John served himself a drink. The first one led quickly to a second, which naturally gave way to a third. He was funny and attractive, he told himself, and why shouldn't he get into the swing of things for a little while if everyone was busy with something else? It had been a month, after all, and he was doing much better so why not have a drink or two and have some fun? It worked for a while, but as is the case with most drunks, he went from zero to sixty in less than half an hour as he began to pour stiffer drinks, which he swallowed in gulps. The auction ended and the guests flooded back to the bar for their wine spritzers and Perrier and champagne. They were smiling, John was smiling, the entire room was glowing. And then he said it.

"Oh, come on, come on!" he slurred to the stunned crowd. "We're all friends here. We're having a good time. We can joke about this because we're doing something about it. Come on, and have a laugh at yourselves," he added, as he slowly listed to the left and then the right like a nicked bowling pin. The stares were ones of disbelief, hurt and anger. Telling a joke about faulty breast implants at a breast cancer fundraiser had sucked the air out of the atmosphere as the well-to-do throng, including many survivors, couldn't believe their ears. With little warning, the booze he had been chugging down did its job, as did the frightful eyes boring through him, and John threw up a spectacular tsunami of half-digested food all over the red dress and white pearls of the matronly organizer of the event as cameras recorded every second and sound. As Mrs. Francoise Deslauriers shrieked; as people around her shoved others to get out of the line of fire; and as creamy vomit ran down the celebrity bartender's chin, John simply threw up again, this time missing innocent bystanders as it hit the floor almost five feet away with an audible splash.

As if on a sinking cruise ship, many of the guests frantically scratched and clawed to escape through the only door, while others tried to suppress their own gag reflexes as the stench of half-digested fettuccini primavera wafted heavily in the small bar. The unlucky ones with weak stomachs added to the chaos, as Mrs. Deslauriers and other slipped and fell in puddles, one unlucky woman breaking her wrist. The image the world would see for years on YouTube and blooper shows was that of Mrs. Deslauriers herself struggling unsteadily to her feet, a look of sheer terror on her partially vomit-covered face, as she realized at the last second that she was about to throw up right into the lens of the CTV cameraman, who dropped his camera to the wet floor before puking himself. On New Year's Eve, that was named the Number One news image of the year, beating out a week-long mine rescue in Russia and an earthquake in Japan that cameras caught leveling a sports arena that, fortunately, had been empty.

Terrified, John lurched back to the bar, where he found a towel and wiped his face clean. Amazingly, he had spilled very little of his own vomit on himself. Reasonably straightened up, he steadied himself for a run at the door - and freedom. The crowd that was attempting to exit the bar parted for him, as he staggered closer like a zombie in an old B-movie, hands outstretched and throat gurgling. Some made contemptuous remarks as he went by, a woman screamed, but John didn't hear them. His only goal was to escape and get as far away as quickly as possible. He zigged and zagged down Crescent Street desperately hoping it was still early enough to find a Metro - a subway to the rest of North America - to take him home.

Fortunately, it wasn't yet 11 o'clock, and the further he walked, the more settled his head and stomach became. By the time he found a train, he was barely weaving, though humiliation cascaded upon him as the numbness wore off.

Almost twenty minutes later, John emerged from the stale depths of the metro station into the thick, humid air of downtown Montreal in summer, the sudden heat blanketing his body and tickling his gag reflex. Christ, it's almost midnight, John thought. How could it still be so hot? Regardless - or perhaps because of - what had occurred earlier, he needed a drink or three. He picked up the pace as he spotted Matty's two blocks down the road.

"Jesus, John, what's up with you tonight?" Doc finally asked. In the hour they had been sitting together in the half-empty bar, John had spoken no more than a sentence or two with a few one-word answers thrown in for good measure. He'd also turned the good doctor down three times for backgammon, ordered four vodka sodas and had stumbled off to see the conquistador three times as well. He looked pale, clammy and unsteady on his feet. "You don't look all that great. Maybe we should call it an early night and head home. Even Janine didn't want to come out tonight. Hey, I thought you weren't coming out tonight either, come to think of it. Didn't you have some sort of thing you had to go to?" John moved only his eyes to look at his companion. The look told Doc all he needed to know. "Whoa, it didn't go well, did it?" John's eyes narrowed menacingly. Causing Doc to whistle softly. "Okay we're not going to talk about it right now, are we? That's fine because I've always said to people that you can be my best friend in the bar, but don't tell me your problems. I've got my own."

"I appreciate it," John mumbled as he slid a pack of matches with a couple of folded twenties inside of it.

"You sure?" Doc asked, again looking closely at John's pasty face. "We could leave and take this up again tomorrow."

"Thanks for your concern, but I'll be fine," John interrupted. "I'll just do a little more and then I'll come out and tell you all about the fucking horrible evening I had before you read about it in the paper tomorrow."

"Whatever happened, your paper would print it?"

"Maybe not them out of sheer embarrassment, but the French ones will be jerking each other off over this."

Doc's face contorted as he tried in vain to stop a grin.

"Fuck off," John smiled.

"Oh boy," laughed Doc, "I can't wait to hear about this! Tania, darling, could we have a couple more, two Wild Turkey shooters and a couple of seatbelts. This is going to be a bumpy night."

In the bathroom, John's head was spinning as he chopped up some of the cocaine with a credit card. He could see himself swaying in the mirror, small droplets of perspiration forming beneath his eyes and on his upper lip. He felt like he was dying of thirst, so he turned a tap on for some cold water. He snorted the large line while the water was running, then cupped his hands and drank deeply. The coke worked quickly turning John's stomach, as it sometimes did. This time, though, he gave in to the sick feeling and threw up for the second time that night. He cupped more water and cleaned his mouth out then splashed more in his face. The room was tilting slowly as if he was playing a part in an art house film in which the camera is being tilted this way and that for effect. He felt for the doorknob, found it and turned it slowly. He had used too much coke, he knew, and now he was feeling it.

"There he is!" Doc called, the drinks lined in front of him and at the ready. John carefully navigated the 20 feet from the bathroom door to his barstool, fearful of tripping over an unseen barrier and falling flat on his face. As he placed his right hand on an empty stool to keep his balance, John noticed it shaking slightly. Way too much damn coke, he thought. He could see Doc's face tilt, almost like a dog's does, as he tried to make out what was wrong with his friend. John didn't know it, but he began to soak sweat through his shirt. He was also taking an extraordinarily long time to walk the 20 feet. The nauseous wave returned, this time faster and more ferocious than a few minutes earlier. He lifted his index finger as if to tell Doc he would be another minute, then wheeled around and ran for the toilet. He slammed the door shut with no time even to lock it and puked violently into and around the bowl. "Jesus," he laughed breathlessly to himself, "I am leaving my mark everywhere tonight." He cleaned his mess on the tile floor with toilet paper, then cleaned himself for the third time that evening, before making his way back to Doc, this time walking a little quicker to his stool.

"You okay?" Doc asked with genuine concern.

"My friend, I have never been more not okay, okay? I am going to drink these drinks with you and get the hell home."

PASSING THROUGH OBLIVION

Forgetting that a good story was supposed to be told, Doc agreed. He would discover his pal's secret soon enough, anyway. "Bottoms up, boy. Time to go."

Chapter Twelve

John could feel his heart drumming as he halfheartedly slapped Doc on the back and waved goodbye. The heat again suffocated him, pouring sweat into his eyes, which could only see a kaleidoscope of colour and movement surrounding him. He knew he was just stoned, but he'd never felt so incapacitated. Outside of Matty's, John's world blurred as if he was standing in the middle of the track of a Formula One race. People raced by him so quickly he could barely make out their faces. Large beads of perspiration snaked their way down his forehead and into his eyes, as he tried to regain control over his senses. Desperate to be safely home, he stumbled left when he should've gone right, and as he lurched left again down the next street he found himself inexplicably lost a block and a half from where he lived. To top it off, the contents of his stomach were sloshing from one side of it to the other threatening to explode upwards yet again at any moment. The trees lining both sides of the street appeared menacing to John as the sweat continued to pour into his eyes and down his chest and back and balls. It reminded him of nightmares he used to have as a young boy, in which nothing seemed familiar, even his own back yard. Those dreams had always terrified him the most because he thought if you can't trust your home to be a safe place, what can you trust? John scrambled wildly left again, then right, each step taking him further away from home. It was very late and very dark and few people were roaming the usually well-traveled streets, much less the quiet, tree-lined residential one he found himself on. Spotting a single light in a window a block away, he staggered his way towards it hoping to call for a taxi. A cab driver would know where he lived, he reasoned. But the light he had seen was one that was left on all the time, as much for safety as to act as a beacon for those in search of spirituality and comfort. "A fucking church," John mumbled angrily. "A fucking church." He tried to recall where he had seen a church nearby before. If he could remember where it was, he would be able to find his way home, but time was running out for John O'Rourke. His stomach was heaving and his head was spinning with equal ferocity. He pulled on the large oaken door and was shocked when it began to open. It took all of John's strength to pry the heavy door open, and as it opened John fell through it onto the floor face first, where he began to vomit and choke. He tried to push himself up with his arms, but they never moved from his sides. He felt paralyzed as he puked, then choked again on it, his face planted in the growing puddle of liquids and semi-solids. His entire body had quit on him at the time he needed it most, and as he began to lose consciousness he understood that he might be in some real trouble.

    John O'Rourke grudgingly opened his eyes, just enough at first for his eyelids to tremble, then with surprising difficulty he opened them all the way to see that he could not see much of anything at all. It was pitch dark and he could see no walls, no ceiling, no pews, nor anything else for that matter.

    He was still lyingprone on his front, his arms and legs splayed out in all directions like a broken doll. A shiver raced up his spine tickling the back of his head before making the return trip back down to the small of his back. He no longer wanted to throw up, but the dizziness was still present and he was as cold as he had been hot. He tried to push himself up with his arms, but he was too weak to raise himself more than an inch or two so he decided to give himself more time while he completed a systems check.

Okay, he could breathe, think fairly clearly, he could move his arms and legs and swivel his head from side to side, and he could feel very cold.

"Are you gonna get up, man?" he heard a faint voice ask.

"What? Who's there?" John whispered. He was terrified because of his vulnerability and he tried unsuccessfully again to lift himself up before falling face first onto the floor.

"Yeah, don't worry, take your time, but we do have to go soon, okay?" the voice said.

"Go where? Who are you?" John tried to sound tough, but there was no mistaking the tremble in his voice.

"Aw, man, I'm not here to hurt you. They always think I'm there to hurt them- except that guy in Oregon. He seemed to know exactly what was going on. That was really spooky."

John was still working at getting up, but managed only to roll over.

"See? There you go, man. It won't be long now."

"What won't be long?" John asked. "Who are you? How do you know me? Do you work for the church? Show yourself, damnit!"

The voice laughed. It sounded closer now and John thought he could see a shape move through the darkness. "Yeah, I kinda work for the church," it replied chuckling. "Well, not the church you're familiar with, but it's like a church. I don't know. I always have trouble answering that one. Almost everyone asks that, though, so you'd think I would've come up with a good answer by now, but it's not all that cut and dry, you know."

John's eyes flashed open as the thought crossed his mind. "I get it! You're a drug hallucination. I knew I took too much. Jesus, I hope I'm not dying."

"You may well be, my friend. Try again to get up. We have a long way to go."

"What the hell does that mean, I'm really dying?" John spat. "If I can move and speak and hear and get pissed off at some stranger for playing games with a person who could use some help, I am decidedly not dying."

"Have it your way," the voice drawled. Whoever it was had a California surfer or hippy way of speaking. It was slow, almost as if he was stoned on pot, John thought. "Hey, are you stoned on pot?" he asked.

"That would be sweet," the voice replied, "but those days are sadly over just as yours are. Was that cocaine good? Was it worth all this? Damn, I miss it sometimes, dude."

John had managed to struggle to a seating position, but he still couldn't see where the stranger was. The church was dark and cold and seemingly vast and empty. He felt sand or gravel on the floor instead of carpet or wood and was confused by everything. Nothing smelled as it should and, well, nothing felt as it should. "Fucking drugs," he muttered.

"You have no idea," the voice responded.

"Okay, enough of this shit," John said. "Either come here and give me a hand or get lost. I don't need an audience, asshole."

"You could be a little nicer, you know," it said. "We're gonna spend sometime together so chill a little, man. Oh, sorry, I didn't mean that. You're already freezing, aren't you?" he laughed.

"Who the fuck are you?" John shouted.

The voice sighed. "You have to get up now, man. I'm not really good at these confrontational things."

"I'll say it once more: Show yourself or I go nowhere with you, jackass!"

Another sigh wafted through the emptiness. In front of John a figure silently appeared. He was about John's height, but he was very slim, bearded and he had long, dirty-blond hair tied in a ponytail. His clothes were old, baggy white pants, a yellow T-shirt that had passed its best-before date and battered Converse running shoes that John figured had been bought during the Nixon administration. He reminded John of the hippies he'd seen as a child or maybe that guy Jeff Bridges played in the movies, the Big Lebowski.

"Happy now, dude? Look, we have to get going, we sincerely do. This is my job, man, so I have to bring you now."

"Your job? What's your job, pissing me off with riddles? Hell of a job."

"You don't know the half of it, man. I didn't choose this job, but I have to do it."

"Why don't you just quit if you hate it so much?"

The man smiled sadly and answered very softly. "You don't quit this job, man. You just don't quit."

"What? You have to do this your entire life?" John asked as he rose unsteadily to his feet.

"If it were only that long, compadre. Now come on, you're up and ready to roll. I have lots to tell you and we've got a really bitchin' walk ahead of us. You gonna wear those clothes?"

John shook his head. "Oh, all knowing entity, do we not need clothes where we're going? (you fruit fly)" he whispered under his breath.

"Of course we do, man, it's still civilized here, but I thought you might want to wear something with a little less vomit on it."

John looked down at himself and saw that he had thrown up all over his clothes. "Whoa," he said. "I guess this is silly to ask, but do you have something I could change into?"

"Never thought you'd ask, man. The smell was getting kind of rank, to be honest with you." The man handed over some clothes he seemingly plucked out of mid-air. John took them and looked them over. He had been given a pair of brown sandals, a pair of white linen pants and a long white shirt with black buttons.

"Nice," he smiled. "Not really my style, but at least I'll be comfortable. Now where's the way out of this place? You'd think they'd leave a light on at night.

"Yeah, run to the light, man, run to the light!" the man laughed.

"Oh no, you're not some sort of Ghost of Christmas Past here to show me the errors of my ways, are you?"

"Did you know Dickens wrote that story after nearly dying and seeing someone like me?"

"He did? And what does 'someone like me mean?'"

The hippy voice laughed again. "No, I'm just messing with you. I wasn't even born when he died. Besides, even if you do go back, you don't remember this."

John shook his head slowly. "Seriously, what's going on? And who are you really? Do you have a name?"

"You can call me whatever you want to call me, man, but most people call me Ziggy."

"Okay," John said, "I'll call you Ziggy, too. How's that with you?"

That's cool with me, man. You could've called me Brad. I hate being called Brad."

"Why do you hate that name so much?" John asked.

"Because my old lady ran off with a Brad and that's what made me get drunk enough to fall off my boat."

"And seeing as you say we're dead, I take it you drowned?"

"No, dude, do I look like I drowned? I fell on the dock."

"Oh, and you hit your head and died."

"No, dude! I was eating some pizza and the crust got stuck in my throat when I landed on my back."

John stared at Ziggy for a long moment afraid to say a word.

"And that's what killed me, man!" Ziggy cried. "Pizza stuck in the throat.Oh, and I had a ton of Valium in me at the time too."

I see," John said. "So I really am dead?"

"Do you want to be?"

John thought the question over for a short time, then nodded his head. "I think I do," he whispered.

"Then you're in the right place," Ziggy said. "Time to go, man."

John and Ziggy walked for some time, neither saying a word. It was still very dark, which was why light coloured clothes were the attire of choice, Ziggy explained. It was easier to see everybody. "Why do you think those few who come this far and make it back believe everyone in heaven wears white? They can remember what they saw only in the most remote way, like an out-of-focus snapshot from an almost forgotten dream. And so, they remember a light, white clothing, and sometimes seeing dead relatives."

"Will I see . . . my . . . relatives?" John asked softly, afraid that no answer would comfort him.

"No, man, you won't see your family," Ziggy replied as he placed a hand on John's shoulder. He was silent for a long, empty moment, then said: "Stick with your pal Ziggy. Maybe you'll see the light, too."

"Yeah, just what I want to see," John grunted. "How magic."

"You never know, man. Now come on, they're going to have to give me time and a half if we keep moving so slowly."

"Where are we going?" John complained.

"To the Promised Land, my friend, to the Promised Land. If we're lucky, that is."

"That's nice, Ziggy, but what does that mean? How long will it take? Where will I be when we get there?"

"It's kind of like a journey through your life that lasts an eternity, give or take an eon. The select few that survive and go back just remember it as a blur, if they remember it at all. Hey, you know that joke I made about running to the light? Listen to this, it's really cool. People who go back say they saw a light, right? I mean, they get all mystical and religious about it and they tell everyone, right? Man, that's just the doctor opening their eyelids and shining his pen light in to see if their pupils will dilate." His raucous laughter shook him. "Their brains register that, you know? So when they go back they remember the light and think God was calling them just like how they think angels wear white. Man, can you believe it?"

John shook his head and tried to look through the lightening darkness. "Nope," he said, "I sure as hell can't."

What's the end going to be like?" John asked as they continued making their way. "I mean, is there a heaven - or a hell, for that matter? You have to admit, this is a lot to take in all at once. Tell me where you're leading me, will you?"

The light eventually began to grow brighter, luminescent in oranges and yellows forcing

John to shield his eyes that had already become so accustomed to the darkness.

Beside him Ziggy smiled as he picked up the pace. "This is, like, my favourite part, man," he said.

John thought he could hear . . . people. He thought he could hear many people and believed, just for a moment, that he had indeed fallen into a drug-induced hallucination that he was now coming out of, and the voices he was hearing were those of the paramedics and bystanders. His heart leapt and fell again in the small crevice between hope and reality, and he was surprised to discover how much he still did want to live. Ziggy glimpsed his charge from the corner of an eye and knew what John had felt. He gently rested a hand on John's back, subtly pushing him forward. "Look, dude, this part can be fun, you know. Just go out there and try to have a sense of humour about it all. It may get uncomfortable sometimes, but these people are on your side. They want you to do well."

"What the hell are you talking about?" John asked, jolted back from his foolish hopes.

"See her?" Ziggy asked, pointing to a pretty young woman carrying a makeup bag.

"What about her? John asked."

"You've got to go see her, man. She'll straighten you out and make you look pretty for the cameras."

John stopped dead. "The what?" he demanded.

"I told you, have some fun with it. Everybody has to do something at this stage. Some people do this, others kind of ride an assembly line from one person to the other, a few unlucky ones are turned into dogs and other old family pets. If you ask me, this is the best of the bunch. You should be happy."

"Well, who wouldn't be? I just died. That would make anybody happy and jolly."

"There you go!" clapped Ziggy, ignoring John's sarcasm. "It's just that sort of thing that'll make it a great show."

"A great what?"

The makeup girl, whose name was Melissa, turned to look at him, annoyance in her face. "Hey, come on, you're late. We have to hurry, okay? Why do you always bring them here so late?" she asked of Ziggy, who smiled broadly and shrugged his thin shoulders.

"He didn't want to come," he replied simply.

"None of them want to come, that's the point. That's why you bring them here in the first place."

John looked at Ziggy, then at Melissa, who was growing more impatient by the second. "What the hell?" he whispered.

"Ten minutes, everybody!" an unseen voice called.

"Come on, come on!" Melissa implored.

Ziggy gave John another gentle push and Melissa ran over the rest of the way, grabbing John's hand and pulling him towards a chair placed in front of a bright mirror framed by sixteen small light bulbs.

"You're a young one," she said happily once John was firmly seated.

"Usually, I have to make up older men and women, but every once in a while I get a good looking man I can really do something with. Must be my lucky day."

John jerked his head around and glared. "Oh, sorry," Melissa relented, "I guess it wasn't yours."

"Aw, that's all right," John grumbled. "I just don't know what the hell is going on here. I didn't expect death to be anything like this."

"Nobody does, honey, but to be honest you're not quite dead. You're only mostly dead," she said giggling.

"That's from The Princess Bride," John answered. "It's one of my favourite movies of all time. How did you know that?"

"I see everyyy-thinnngg, whooooo!" Melissa giggled.

"Well, you're not quite the ghoul I'd expect to see if I were dead and could see something," he smiled.

"You should see me in the morning, honey," she replied.

"So what does mostly dead mean around here?"

Melissa added another touch of powder to John's forehead, then stood back to appraise her work. "You know how people say that you see your life flash through your head as you begin to die?"

John nodded.

"Well, this is where you go to see it."

"How?" John asked, curious to know which part he was going to see and how he would see it. "You mean to say this is something like Judgement Day?"

"Not really," Melissa said. "Most of who you become and the life you live was determined when you were born. This is just kind of a recap to see how you lived with what was given to you."

"I can't believe my life was preordained," John whispered.

"I'm not supposed to say too much," Melissa countered, "just go out there and try to have some fun with it."

"Why does everyone tell me to have fun? What fun will I have?"

"Were you a really good person when you were um, you?" Melissa asked.

John's eyes lowered as he inhaled slowly and deeply. "Not really," he whispered. "I guess that's why I lived the way I did. The good ol' rock n' roll lifestyle that put me here in the end."

Melissa stopped fussing around John's face and crinkled her forehead in serious thought. "Hmm, this might be interesting, then. Don't forget to read the cards. That's very, very important."

"Read what cards? Am I a guest on some ghoul's death show or something?"

"Melissa laughed a pretty, melodic laugh. "No, silly, you are the ghoul and it's your show, the Whatever-your-name-is Show."

"Places!" screamed the unseen voice.

"And you're on, tiger. Have fun and good luck with your guests."

John was being pulled away again, this time by a burly man wearing a communications headset. "My guests?" he called to Melissa.

"Have fun!" she shouted in return. "Death doesn't have to be all tears and decomposition!"

John was placed behind a giant red curtain, and as music began the audience howled its approval. He was sure he would crap his pants except for the fact that such things seemingly didn't occur anymore at all.

"John Ooooooooooo'ROURKE!!" bellowed a deep voice.

"Out ya go, precious," laughed the man in the headset as he shoved John through the curtain.

John stumbled onto the gleaming wood stage blinded by the fiercely bright lights and stunned by how close the audience and it's thunderous applause sounded to him. John was terrified as he looked left, then right hopelessly trying to find the cards Melissa had told him about. He'd seen enough talk shows to know that if this was to be his ultimate fate that he could at least pull it off if someone told him what to say, but the notion of him being a talk show host through eternity seemed too absurd to believe. Even David Letterman couldn't do that. This can't be the true afterlife, he thought. Almost hidden in the pool of light was a silhouette of a tall man with long hair and a beard waving to John. It was Ziggy, and he was guiding his eyes to the cue cards he so desperately needed. The audience had quieted enough for John to hear Ziggy stage whispering, "Here, man, look here."

As the lights went dark one after the other leaving a single spotlight on the host, John could see the card and also the crowd, all of who were in differing degrees of decomposition. So far, everyone John had come across had looked normal, but the audience for some reason did not. Or maybe they were normal and everybody else looked strange. Either way, it spooked the hell out of him. Regardless of their deteriorating condition, they were all dressed in tuxedos and top hats and evening gowns and jewels, bottles of champagne were being passed from one to another and they all appeared to be having a hell of a good time. It was like everyone in The Great Gatsby had risen from their graves, cleaned themselves off, got dressed in their finest and organized a party directly in front of him.

"Come on, man, get with the program," Ziggy whispered with frustration. John forced himself to look away from the studio full of corpses so he could read.

"Good evening, ladies and gentleman," he began nervously, as beads of sweat began to trickle down his forehead and upper lip like small snowballs gathering steam and size as they roll down a hill. It was only then that he realized he was also in a black tuxedo he couldn't recall putting on himself. "*We're not in Kansas anymore*," he thought before continuing on with the cue card. "You're here on a special evening, as you know (great applause). It's our final show after a run of more than 40 years and we have some very special guests that many of you will remember from the past. They've brought clips that you'll enjoy, though I'm not sure I will (mild laughter), but it promises to be interesting and perhaps even a little emotional. Let's get started, shall we, with a clip the staff here found in the archives."

The spotlight dimmed as a screen rose from behind John. While his common sense told him that he should be in a state of shock, or at least heavy denial, he had begun to accept that death wasn't what he thought it would be - a revelation that made hosting a talk show in front of carousing cadavers almost seem fitting. He turned to see what was playing on the screen.

The clip was quick, but memorable. It began with a teenaged John sitting with his tenth-grade English teacher,

Mrs. Thomas. She was a woman of about fifty, John estimated at the time, but she was attractive. Matronly would be an apt but insulting description and she possessed an obvious love of literature and the language itself, which she called a "living thing, ever-changing." This day she had asked John to stay behind after class to talk to him about his seating arrangements. "You know," she began, "I believe you have some potential, John. Your essays are a cut above the others and you appear to have talent as a writer."

"Thank you," teenaged John replied. "Can I - "

"I'm not finished yet," Mrs. Thomas interrupted. "The problem is that you sit next to Max. Max is a twit. He's a happy twit, but he's a twit nonetheless and he is slowing you down. I want you to sit as far away from him as you can for the next class. Is that clear?"

John watched his younger version nod his head and promise to do just that before being dismissed and darting into the hall in search of the twit himself.

Out of nowhere a huge, deep voice startled him enough to make him jump in fright. He swung around to see what manner of being possessed a voice that reverberated through his very soul.

The audience of corpses howled wildly and swung champagne bottles over their heads as The Voice egged them on.

"A CROSSROADS, EVERONE!" it bellowed. The only time John had heard such a voice was when the wizard was admonishing Dorothy and her pals when they went to see him in The Emerald City. "WHAT WILL HE DO?" it asked. "A CARING TEACHER WITH A GOOD HEART SEES SOMETHING IN THIS YOUNG MAN. SHE WANTS TO STEER HIM IN THE RIGHT DIRECTION BECAUSE HE HAS TALENT, BUT HE IS YOUNG AND UNFOCUSED. SHE IS WILLING TO BECOME A MENTOR AND A FRIEND, TO TAKE HIM UNDER HER WING IF ONLY HE WILL SACRIFICE SOME FUN TIMES TO WORK A LITTLE HARDER. WHAT DOES HE DO??"

PASSING THROUGH OBLIVION

The crowd shrieked and hollered, bony, tattered hands thrusting through the air, each one hoping for the correct answer to the question. The sound they made reminded John of that one summer on his uncle's farm when he was twelve years old. One day he and Uncle Leo herded the pigs into the back of the truck to take them to be slaughtered. He never saw anything, but the sound they made as they were electrocuted, hung upside down from a hook and sliced open from stem to stern never left him, especially at night when he would wake up sweat-soaked, screaming in terror. After that, his mother labeled him her sensitive child and never let him return to the farm, not even for a visit.

John took the opportunity to run over to where Ziggy was standing with the cards. "What the hell is going on now?" he yelled.

"It's kind of a game show, too, man. It's like a talk/game show. Well, it's more of a talk show because there's so much talking, if you get my drift."

John stared at his guide much like how a dog crooks its head when it's confused or thinks it might understand something it's master is saying, but isn't quite sure what.

Ziggy took a deep, understanding breath. "Okay. You see the audience, right?" John looked out at the sea of skeletons and nodded. "They come here time after time because they get to play the game. They guess what the host did in the clips they see and the one with the most points at the end of the show wins."

"What do they win," John asked.

Ziggy moved closer and stared deeply into John's eyes. "They win life, dude."

John gasped as a shiver raced up and down his spine. "Life? What do you mean life? How do they come back after everyone knows they died? Do they go back in time or something?"

"Whoa, Mr. Einstein, slow down and don't over-think it. I mean they get to be born again, man. They get another shot at life."

"You mean like reincarnation?" John asked. He marveled over how this was something he never would've believed in before this day, but considering he was almost dead anything seemed plausible. He found a spiritual advisor who was a hippy named Ziggy; he was the host of a talk show in front of an audience of cadavers in top hats and tails; and it appeared that the voice of God was John's announcer. Yep, he was ready to believe anything.

"No, man," Ziggy said shaking his head slowly. "You have to be here at least forty or fifty years before it can happen, but when you go, you go back pretty much as the person you were before. You just don't know it. Not really, anyway."

"What do you mean when you say not really. Either you know or you don't, right?"

"You ever hear of déjà vu, man?" Ziggy smiled.

John sighed, knowing he was about to be let in on another of life's - or death's - little secrets. While he did enjoy learning about how the world worked, at the same time it was making him feel that he was that much closer to permanent death, as though he was now one of them, a confidante of the dead. "Yeah, of course I have."

Ziggy threw his hands in the air, unconsciously mimicking the audience. "Well, there it is, man!"

"There what is?" John shouted back.

"Think about it," Ziggy yelled pointing a finger at his head, but his words were drowned out by the audience whooping and cheering.

"I can't hear."

"AND WE'RE READY TO SEE WHAT HAPPENED!" The Voice said, once again shaking John's insides with its power.

Images on the screen began to move again as the emaciated audience fell silent. A young John O'Rourke, slim, tanned, with blue eyes sparkling with fun walked quickly to where he knew his friend would be. English class was the last one scheduled before lunch, so John figured he could catch up with Max in the cafeteria.

PASSING THROUGH OBLIVION

As he neared, John accidentally inhaled the nearly noxious odors of cheap, greasy hamburgers, watery minestrone soup and rubbery hot dogs. The smell was awful, but it still made him hungry. As a teenager, he could eat almost anything and still enjoy it, even Mrs. Grubb's famous (or was it infamous?) meatloaf, known throughout the school as the perfect remedy for constipation a full one hundred per cent of the time. Sneaking up from behind, he slapped Max's back hard enough for a partly chewed mouthful of burger to be propelled across the table and onto Jaime Bonner's plate of fries. Not a regular member of John's group of friends, Jaime was kept around only because he had an old car, a prize no one else had yet to achieve. Still, he knew better than to whine, so he gave both Max and John an exasperated look and pushed his plastic tray aside.

"What the fuck?" Max mumbled through the food in his mouth that had survived the slap.

"Sorry, sir, I'm not allowed to talk to you because (and he paused right there for full dramatic effect) you're a twit!"

The rest of the gang at the table was still roaring with laughter at the sight of the airborne mystery meat when Max asked his friend just what the hell he meant by that now.

"Mrs. Thomas took me aside after class and told me that I should move away from you because you're a twit."

Max looked stunned as he chewed and finally swallowed his remaining mouthful. "That bitch!" he spat.

"Well, she did say you're a happy twit, if that makes any difference," John laughed.

"Hey, twit," Jaime said, pointing a finger at Max, who had become visibly angry.

"Fuck off, you ass bandit!" Max replied. "Go sit somewhere else with your bum buddies."

Jaime looked around the table for support, but like all the other times he had pissed someone in the gang off, he found none. He looked once more at Dean, the unspoken leader, who simply shrugged his shoulders and subtly crooked his head as if to tell Jaime he was no longer wanted at that moment. Jaime was often not wanted until they needed a ride, but he knew his place and slowly got up from his seat, disappointed that he had once again been banished.

In the studio, the cadaver crowd was getting restless; they wanted an answer to see which of them would win points.

"So are you going to do it?" Max asked after an appropriate pause to restore his dignity in front of his pals.

"Yeah," John replied to raucous cheering from a portion of the audience, "but only for one day, then I'm coming back to sit with you. You know, just to let her think I listened at least a bit."

With that, a small portion of the audience cursed and fell back to their seats, while the majority shrieked with satisfaction for choosing the correct outcome and winning the available points. The slaughtered pigs squealed again. In a flash, Michelle was at John's side touching up his face, which, John feared, was decomposing as he stood there. "You're doing great," she smiled. "But you should've moved away from Max."

"What the hell is happening?" John asked. "Who's going to be here?" Dead or not, he was scared.

"Easy, dude, it's all good, so far," Ziggy whispered as he came up beside John. "There's more, so try to relax and understand."

"Understand what? Look, I still believe dead is dead, so what the fuck is this?"

"Who said you were dead, man? You're on the way to being dead."

"Remember, you're mostly dead," Michelle giggled, as she dabbed a little this on a lot of that.

Chapter Thirteen

"TEN SECONDS!" The Voice warned.

"What do I do?" John asked frantically.

Ziggy had already taken up his station with the cards, but Michelle pointed to the desk, which was beside the obligatory chair beside the ubiquitous couch. "Go and sit at the desk," she pointed, "and read the cards!"

John stumbled over to his seat beneath the lights that happily blinded him to his skeletal audience. He could only see Ziggy holding and pointing at the cue cards. Ziggy counted down the last few seconds with his fingers, then pointed at John when the time was right. "And welcome back," he said with surprising confidence. "We've got a long way to go, so let's get started. My first guest is someone from the distant past, but someone who never really left me either." John's mind was spinning trying to figure out who he was about to meet again, and why. Then he said her name. "Please welcome Judy Hill."

The audience, which seemed to know a little bit about Judy Hill, whooped in appreciation. An exploded cork from a champagne bottle arced over the first few rows and landed on the stage, rolling only a few feet from where John was sitting. That seemed to only encourage the crowd to raise the dead, so to speak. But John also knew a lot about Judy Hill. He stood from his chair and took an involuntary step back as she slowly came through the curtains looking as if she was just as reluctant to see her high school boyfriend again as he was to see her. A talk show fan, John knew that he should greet his guest as she approached the interview area, but he found himself glued to his spot, unable to move or say anything. Judy hesitated forward, one tentative step at a time, until she came to her seat beside the large desk. Her appearance had aged appropriately, and John was at least thankful that she looked nothing like his audience, but she had none of the girlish innocence he remembered. She was still attractive but she had hardened, like how once-beautiful women who have spent too many years in bars get that world-weary, seen-it-all visage. She looked resolute more than pretty, far tougher than her years would suggest. John finally thought to sit down, but could think of nothing appropriate to say to this woman, who had become his first love. He stole a glance in Ziggy's direction, but he was nowhere to be found. There were no cards to read, no words given to him to speak, there was just him, Judy Hill and a deathly quiet audience silently awaiting what might come next.

And so his first question was, "Are you dead, too?"

"All these years and that's the first thing you can think of to say to me?" she replied. "Are you dead, too?"

A wave of laughter swept over John, who felt as if he was going to throw up. "I'm sorry," he stammered, "how have you been?"

"I've been better, thanks all the same," she answered. "I thought dreaming of you had ended a long time ago, but I guess this is my lucky day - or night. You know, I got good enough to be able to wake myself up when you appeared in a dream. After a while, I would know it's a dream and wake myself up. I don't know why it isn't happening this time. It's a dream! Wake up, Judy!" she screamed, but she remained far more in this world than her own. "Fine, not this time," she said clapping her hands together once out of frustration.

"That's okay. My other dreams haven't been so hot either, so why not a little you to break the monotony? So, Johnny, how have you been? Life been good to you since we last saw each other? I'd like to say it's good to see you, but seeing as you've been the star of so many lousy dreams I'll reserve such kindness, if you don't mind too much."

John felt the black stares of many empty eye sockets as he searched for the right thing to say. There was, of course, no right thing to say to this woman. "I've always wondered what happened to you since we saw each other last," he tried.

"Have you now? Well, the last time we saw each other we had been a couple for the final three years of high school. We had talked about getting married after college and then you knocked me up before the prom. Do you remember those happy days together, Johnny? Weren't they just sweet?"

"We were young and -"

"Yes, I was young. I was sixteen years old and pregnant. And I had a boyfriend who swore he'd stick with me, no matter what I chose to do. Do you remember saying that? You stuck with me right until I had the abortion, then what happened, huh? Fuck, I hate these fucking dreams!"

John's eyes darted everywhere hoping to spot Ziggy and one of his cards. He desperately needed someone to tell him what to say! But everything was dark except for Judy Hill, who sat stone-faced in front of him, his personal judge and jury. Seeing her took him back to that time of youthful stupidity when he was called to become a man, but instead stayed a boy. Judy had lost a part of herself after the abortion. Her eyes had lost their innocence, her face sagged under the guilt she carried, even though she believed her decision to be the best one for all concerned, except, perhaps, for the baby she had given up.

"I can't believe I'm doing this again," Judy cried. "I must be getting immune to the meds. It's been so long, though."

In that moment, John could see the entire consequences of his decision to dump his high school sweetheart a month after her abortion; not only what such a betrayal had taken from her, but the tumor of guilt it had grown in him.

"So where the hell is this?" she asked herself. Squinting through the lights at the audience, Judy recoiled but quickly recomposed herself, this dream only scarier than the others, but no less common. "Fuck, the meds must've gone bad. Remember to call your doctor in the morning," she whispered, again to herself. "And throw out those fucking pills. Now, go away from the dream. This is a dream. Wake up. Wake up!"

But this time she did not manage to wake herself up, as she had learned to do a long time ago. For the first time in years, she knew she would have to ride this one out. "Gonna be tired in the morning," she muttered.

"You actually have dreams like this?" John asked with genuine surprise.

"You should know," she answered, "you're always in them."

The crowd whooped.

Judy and John met when they were both 15 years old. John had fallen in love with the cute, perky blonde on sight, and he believed because that had happened, she must be the one for him. He'd heard people talk about the pretty new girl, though no one seemed to know much about her. She liked wearing faded Levis and a tight top and her hair was usually tied up in a ponytail that bounced jauntily when she walked. On the day they met, someone must have told her something funny just before she swung around the corner in the hall near the cafeteria because she was giggling. And that's what did it for John, that giggle. And the bouncy ponytail. And the fact she saw him watching her as she was giggling and she didn't stop and look down at her books in embarrassment or seem to feel self-conscious at all. In fact, John had been the startled one. She had looked his way and he'd tried a quick smile in return, but the strength of his attraction to this girl he'd never seen before portrayed the fearsome grimace of an unfrozen dental patient more than a flirting smile. Still, she had breezed by him without cowering in terror, so maybe there was a chance he hadn't embarrassed himself too badly.

So Johnny O'Rourke, aged 15 years and nine months, did what any kid in his position would do. He casually told somebody who knew Judy that he liked her, knowing this news would reach her in minutes, which, under the strict Law of Teenagers, meant she had to indicate one way or the other that she either did or did not like him back. He soon got his answer when only a day later she asked him between classes if he would like to sit at her table for lunch. The problem was Judy's table consisted only of her girlfriends - and one empty seat - while John's usual table held his pals who were waving at him to join them - as he did every day. He knew if he sat with the girls, they'd be checking him out for her and whispering to each other about him and giggling, and he wouldn't like that kind of giggling. There was the very real chance he would be reduced to a squashed bug on a windshield if he made a mistake like talking about sports or something. No, he'd have to feign interest in whatever they talked about, which would be tough because he was pretty certain that whatever they discussed would drive him crazy with boredom. He recognized only a few by name, so there would be no half-ass camaraderie, no oasis in the desert of strange girls, no one to turn to if he needed encouragement. On the other hand, if he said he had promised to sit with his friends, he would slowly die inside believing he had blown his opportunity with Judy. He swallowed hard and waded into the feminine mystique with the crushing sound of laughter coming from across the room.

"Hi!" she chirped as he approached the table. "I didn't think you'd come."

"Oh, yeah, well, you know, I wanted to," he stuttered as three of the girls began to titter.

"That's a lot of food," the skinny one with braces remarked. "Is it all for you?" This time all the girls laughed. John was almost blind with panic.

"I looove you!" Max squealed from his table. "Joooodeeee, I loooove yooooo!" that fucking . . . twit screamed again. The girls covered their mouths and giggled more as John's face whitened.

"Would you like to go for a walk with me after we eat?" Judy asked sweetly. "Maybe this was a bad idea. I feel we're being watched."

John fell in love with her at that second. What was strange was not that he knew he had fallen for her, it was that she seemed to know.

"I'd really like to," he smiled. And that, as they say, was that.

"Bye-byeeeeee!" Max hollered, as John subtly gave him the finger from behind his back as they walked out of the cafeteria.

"You seem to be pretty popular," Judy said.

"I used to be," John smiled, but the electricity of her arm brushing against his as they stepped though the door told him all he needed to know about the decision he had just made. Before their walk was over and they reluctantly separated for their own classes, she had kissed him on his cheek. John would never forget that kiss. Years later, John could feel that kiss.

She wasn't kissing him or giggling now, though. Now, she was staring him down, daring him to say something. What she was waiting for was a hell of a mystery to John, though. He quickly felt like he did on those late nights when he was driving home to Wendy with a good excuse percolating on his lips. Would this sound right? Would that? Why not? It worked every time regardless of what he said. The current dilemma John faced, that he well knew, was that Judy most decidedly did not love him and therefore did not blindly trust him as his wife had. This woman wouldn't accept a halfhearted excuse and close her eyes to what was becoming more obvious all the time as Wendy had done. John cringed as he thought Wendy might still be alive if she had been less trusting. Or, at least, he would be dead with her and not hallucinating a talk show from the crypt.

Judy continued to wait, so John decided to take the offensive.

"You know, Judy, I'm very sorry, but it's been a long time, don't you think?" he asked.

Judy Hill's eyes narrowed, exposing the deeply lined crow's nests partially camouflaged under too much make-up. "I stopped being hurt and traumatized by you a long, long time ago," she stated. "But as time passed, I became angrier as I thought of what kind of a happy girl I was before I met you and what you made me become. I'm not angry; I'm ripped off. You stole my happy girl and left a mistrusting woman."

John looked alarmed and confused. "I'm sorry, I . . ." was all he could mutter.

"You stole the child out of me." She could see that John was beginning to understand. "John! I was a girl, a young girl, pretty and happy and in love with who I thought was the greatest guy in the world. I would've done anything for you, John. I did do anything for you, if you recall, and then you left me for another girl after I became pregnant with your baby. I had the abortion and it hallowed me and then you felt - what did you say then - weird about it. You felt weird about it. I never really did get that, John. What did you feel weird about? That I had to go through the sucking of it out of my body while you were nowhere to be seen? What would I have done if my Aunt Lynda hadn't have gone with me? Do you think my mom would've done that? Do you think my dad would've let you live? I lied to them over and over just for you - for us! And to thank me for being your good soldier, you left me."

John fidgeted with a pencil while he recalled why he had stopped being attracted to his girlfriend. Out of the corner of an eye, he could see that Judy had resumed that stare, the one that demanded an answer, but this time tears were welling in her battle-hardened eyes. "I don't know, I really can't remember what happened," he said.

"Don't lie to me, you son of a bitch!"

"Whoooooooo!!!!!" the audience erupted.

John thought back to those endless days when he was wrestling with breaking up with Judy. The debate consumed him, the indecision torture. He thought of how he would've been so much happier if they had both fallen out of love with each other at the same time. As it was, though, he had fallen out of love because she had been pregnant with his baby and that was too much real life for his shallow mind. And that made him responsible for killing the baby, and the guilt from that weighed too heavily on his shoulders. So as a teenage boy with less than adequate maturity, he had done what came naturally: He went camping with his pals, got drunk and nailed a girl from a nearby tent. He thought often over the years that his roll with that girl had been no more than a dog shaking the water off of itself after a long walk in the rain. He had fucked someone else, shaken the wet off his body and was cleansed to return to Judy a new man. The only fly in that plan's ointment was a fellow by the name of Gary Hughes, who happened to like Judy Hill very much, which meant that although he was a part of the constant gang, he hated Johnny O'Rourke and would do almost anything to shove it to him. It turned out to be a massive shove. Within minutes of returning home, Gary Hughes called Judy and told her what that prick of a boyfriend had done to her. And it wasn't the first time, he added, even though it had been. Gary Hughes promised to be there for her, told her that she could do so much better and that he would be happy to take her out just to get her mind off of things. After he hung up, confident that he would be there to pick up the pieces, he took a long warm shower and jerked off.

Judy's reaction was sudden. She called Johnny and asked him directly if he had cheated on her. His stammering and pausing and accusations of his own convinced her that Gary had been telling the truth. She hung up on the boy she loved - had loved! - and fell to her knees, sobbing hysterically and gagging until she was afraid she couldn't get enough air in for all that was pouring out if her.

John, for his part, half-believed that Judy would either think Hughes was trying something stupid or she would at least be mad for a while then forgive him.

He was wrong as could be on both counts.

By the next day, Judy had engaged in quick sex with Craig Donner, a friend of John's, in a secluded field on the hard, cold grass surrounded by bare, grey trees under a cold fall sky. Then she phoned Gary Hughes.

"Just tell him that someone knows me - in every way - as much as he does now. Have you got that, Gary?" she cried. "Make sure you tell him that."

Jealous Gary only wanted to know who had screwed his girl, but she wouldn't say, so he transferred his anger the only way he knew how. He called Johnny O'Rourke to dutifully tell him the news.

"Get off the phone, you fucking cocksucker!" John screamed. He thought it was true and he knew why Gary was the one to tell him. "The next time I see you, you're dead!"

"Don't blame me, John," Gary whispered. "Blame yourself." And he slammed the phone down mortally afraid of the beating he knew he would get now that his betrayal had been discovered.

John was left listening to the dial tone, lost in a tornado of emotions far too complex for his maturity level to process. He decided he would kill Craig Donner as slowly and as painfully as he could, as only a teenage boy who had been betrayed by a friend would think. This he would do by standing outside Donner's house first thing in the morning because Donner had to go to school. There would be no way out for him. He had to walk out that door and he had to come out to the sidewalk because this was where the bus picked him to go to school. The simple logic floored John, who still refused to believe that Judy would leave him, especially after all they had just been through. So he walked the extra five blocks from where he would normally catch his bus to the stop eight yards and four feet from the right edge of

Donner's driveway. He arrived there 45 minutes before the bus was scheduled to arrive to be sure that he would be there when that sack of shit opened his door. He wanted to see the look on that prick's face when he saw him standing there waiting like he had all the time in the world. As he watched the seconds tick away on his watch, John wasted time by picturing in his mind exactly how it would happen. The first scenario had Donner striding out through the front door lost in space, oblivious to his menacing presence. John would stand there salivating while the poor, little weasel wasn't paying attention. His mind drifted to those animal shows he liked, in which the lion (or tiger, or cheetah, take your pick) runs down a defenseless animal and devours it like it may be the last damn dinner it ever had. John was three inches taller than Craig Donner and he outweighed him by a solid 30 pounds, so the image of the strong lion tearing into the weak prey tickled him. The next scenario was Hughes seeing him right away, but being unable to run away before John was on him. But in this one, John made him squirm; maybe even wet himself. Donner would plead, of course, even try to bargain his way out of his punishment, but he would get what's coming to him in the end.

"Johnny! Johnny! I'm sorry, man. I didn't mean to tell her. It just slipped out! Really! I'm fucking sorry! I'll tell her I was lying. Come on, man, let me up and I'll do whatever it takes to make this better. Please!"

There was no way to make this better, though. There was nothing anyone could do to make John O'Rourke forgive this piece of shit. And then he would beat him as hard and as long as he would ever abuse his punching bag hanging in the garage, the object of his anger so often before. But not this time. This time he would abuse Craig Donner like the filth he was.

Then, the impossible happened. Craig did not walk through the door, oblivious to what was waiting for him. He didn't even come out, see John and run like a coward. The bus was in the distance but rolling quickly his way, and Hughes was nowhere to be seen. His dad's car was in the driveway, so John knew Craig's parents must be home. Then he reasoned that if Craig's parents were at home, they would either tell him to get the hell to school or - and this is the one John believed - Donner had told his parents what had happened and that the big kid standing near the driveway was there to beat him up. In his mind, John saw the police screeching to a stop, lights flashing, guns drawn, every neighbour on the street on their front porches to see what the commotion was about. He saw Craig's father, an enormous man who had spawned such a spindly kid, rumbling down the stairs, mayhem in his eyes meaning to teach John a lesson about bullying. Suddenly, the bus couldn't come fast enough for him. He swiveled his head right, left, then back again looking at the bus and for incoming terror. The bus pulled up agonizingly slowly, finally stopping in front of a petrified teenage boy who already had the fight knocked out of him. By the time he reached school, the knot in John's stomach had loosened enough for him to be angry all over again. Still, his gut told him not to get excited, that he could be suspended if he fought in the school. The screaming in his head had been replaced by scheming. If he saw Donner in school, he would do no more than look at him in such a way that Donner would damn well know that John was going to kill him. John might even wait days to get him if the uncertainty seemed to be eating away at him. During this long period of feeding his inner vengeance, John only thought of how Judy was feeling in passing. If he had thought of asking, he would've discovered that she was thinking of forgiving him if he would just look her in the eyes, admit his mistake, and promise it would never happen again. He would have to convince her of that, but if he could she would try so hard to forgive him. However, John was on a personal mission to make himself feel better by beating up the guy who had blabbed what had happened to his girlfriend, who he believed still must love him. He just had something to take care of first, then he would make things better with Judy. He thought he knew how to do that, too.

John never did beat Craig Donner up. The gang considered Craig a turncoat, a two-faced prick they couldn't trust with their own various indiscretions and drunken revelry, so he was banished as a squealer. There was no reason to pound on him anymore. By that time, though, Judy was moving on with alarming enthusiasm. Almost every guy knew of her sudden vulnerability, and all of them were more than happy to be the shoulder she cried on because she shed a lot more than tears with them.

Days before, when Judy had come up with her plan for revenge, the epiphany had hit her so hard she nearly fell to the floor. For three days, she had thrown up every ounce of food that her parents had forced her to eat, slept not a minute and stayed curled in the fetal position for hours at a time. Her father had sympathized with her, talked to her, ordered her, then finally raged at her before the moment he resigned the fight and considered calling a psychiatrist for help. Her mother, who had felt the sting of her own husband's unfaithfulness years before, would at times enter Judy's room and lie spooned with her on the bed, but more often would size up that no good husband of hers as the snake he really was. Judy's pain became hers all over again. A short time had passed when Judy Hill's epiphany occurred, but everything in her life had irreversibly changed.

The vision that came to her in that twilight of hunger and fatigue, when her father had broken down and her mother had stopped loving him, was as stark as falling through the lake ice near her home. In an instant, it was glued in her head and the clock began to tick on Johnny's bomb. Judy had been a virgin before Johnny, something he was proud to tell anyone who asked. He was ecstatic that he would be the only guy who had ever, ever touched his wife. There would be no stories, no comparisons, no twinkle in her eye placed there by anybody but him. He said it so often that Judy had wished there had been someone else just so he would shut up about it. And like that, her plan was hatched. That evening, as dinner was being ignored by her suddenly silent parents, she bounded down the stairs sporting a wide smile with the appetite of a thoroughbred. The next morning, after a long, sound sleep, Judy Hill left her house in loose jeans and a bulky sweater, still smiling that same smile. When she arrived at school, she darted for the bathroom and tore off the jeans and sweater. Underneath, she had been wearing a sexy short skirt and a tight tank top. In her backpack was a pair of flirty heels and makeup. The Judy who had been cheated on by her most trusted angel was dead. From her ashes, Jude had been born. Judy had been the victim, but Jude was an entirely different woman. Jude would never let that happen to her.

The new Jude knew Sean Mallory's parents both worked and that he always went home for lunch by himself. He was no prize, but she had to start somewhere. Besides, he was someone John picked on, so why not give the poor guy a break? She spied him in the hall just before homeroom. She could hear the muffled buzz in the hall as she strode towards him, see the hunger in the boys' eyes as she bounced and jiggled for their amusement. Sean Mallory had his back turned trying to stuff his sneakers into his backpack along with some textbooks and the lunch his mom made him take to school every day just in case he decided to stay rather than come home. Because he had no friends, though, that rarely happened. What Sean did have was an empty house and, if he was put together properly, a penis. He jumped when she tapped him on the back and purred a soft "Hi." Flustered to see who had talked to- and more importantly - touched him, Sean just smiled awkwardly. Jude was relieved to see that his acne wasn't as angry as it usually was.

"You're Sean Mallory, right?" Jude smiled.

"Uh, yeah, I guess so," he replied.

"Well, my name is Jude and I forgot my lunch at home," she spoke confidently through her smiling disguise. Judy would've been mortified blatantly hitting on this boy for sex, but Jude was determined to see it through. If she couldn't go through with the first one, how would she be able to do the others, she figured.

"Oh, wow, that's too bad. Do you want mine?" he asked, holding forth his wrinkled, brown paper bag.

For a brief moment, she thought he was cute and her heart warmed, but then the reborn Jude took charge again. "That's really sweet of you, but I thought we could maybe go back to your place and you could, you know, give me something there."

Sean's eyes darted back and forth in a comedic synchronized dance of confusion. His breathing had increased noticeably, but he laughed out loud when "What do you want me to give you?" leaked out of his mouth, which had been a big secret to his brain until that second. Jude placed a hand over his mouth to stifle him. "Shh, you can tell anyone you want after, but not before. Do you understand, Sean? If you say anything to anyone before, it's not going to happen. I'm not kidding. We'll have fun together at your place at lunch as long as you don't breathe a word of it. Promise me."

Sean began to feel like he was being set up, but he had never seen Judy Hill dressed like that before and the people he knew who knew her had heard she was really nice. Sean couldn't understand why she would set him up for ridicule - even if her simpleton boyfriend teased him - but neither could he figure out why she might want him. Still, one part of him didn't want to dismiss the notion entirely, and that was the part he always liked to listen to. "I promise," he heard himself say.

"Where do you live?" she asked as she pulled a notebook from her backpack.

Sean Mallory gave Jude Hill his address, though he wouldn't really remember doing it just ten minutes later.

"Good! Then I'll meet you outside your house right at lunch, okay?" She whirled around and began to speed down the hall for her first class. "Remember, don't tell anyone. And be there!" she called.

A very distracted Sean Mallory drifted through the morning's four classes like mist over a vacant field. So much of him wanted it to be true, not just for the first time he would ever have sex with someone else present, but to validate what he had always seen in himself, even if everyone else thought he was wasted space. If Judy Hill wanted to have sex with him so badly she didn't even need about ten dates, flowers, and lots of alcohol, then he must be all right; maybe even better than all right. If Judy Hill would be outside his home at noon ready for him to shove his boner into her, then he must be pretty fucking great. Only one girl had ever shown any real interest in having sex with him, and she had even been too ugly even for him. "It's not a trick," he thought, "it's not a trick. It's Judy Hill and she's major pissed at her boyfriend for cheating on her and she wants to get him back and that's all right because she wants to do it with me." In second-period math class, Sean had to think of showering with those bastards after gym class to stop his penis from getting hard in anticipation of what lay ahead.

In her second class of the day, Judy - now Jude - Hill felt as if she had swallowed a jagged rock. She spent most of the class fighting back waves of tears and nausea thinking of what she was about to do. What kept her vigilant was the thought that one day she would be out of high school and living somewhere else. No one who knew her and what she did would be anywhere near where she was going. She would be allowed to forget about the whole thing, but Johnny would feel it for the rest of his life. He would never forget what she had done to him, and the vicious sin he had committed to ask for it. She would have a loving husband who would always treat her right, but Johnny would be suspicious of women his entire life. "Look what we're capable of, you bastard," she painfully tried to project to him through thought and about sixty-five feet of hallway. "I hope you can feel this because I want you to know what's about to happen. Have a nice life, bastard." Still, that intense nausea wouldn't go away. She had been so happy, she thought, so carefree. And within a few months she had become pregnant, she had aborted her baby, and she had been cheated on for it. Yes,

Jude Hill was pissed right off and she was going to do something about it. So when the bell rang to end her final class of the morning, she knew what she was going to do. She stood up from her desk, straightened the few clothes she was wearing, made sure she was exiting the school far from where Johnny would probably be, and strode towards Sean Mallory's house with what her father would describe as "a purpose." Sean had pedaled his bike as quickly as he could so he would beat her there. The thousand deaths he would die if she left because he was a few minutes late kept his chubby legs pumping the entire way. He was nearly suffocating when the clock hit five past twelve and she had still not arrived, but walking (almost running!) down the sidewalk towards HIS HOUSE was Judy Hill, blond hair bouncing in time with her breasts - which he was about to see! He opened the door almost hyperventilating from the excitement as she bounded up the driveway. She really had come!

"Get inside, Sean," she barked. Of course, Sean retreated on command.

"Hi Judy."

"Hi Sean. Let's do this quickly. Do you have a condom?"

All of Sean's veins constricted in fear. "Uh, no," he mumbled.

"Didn't think you would. Here, take this one and put it on properly."

Sean looked at the condom package in one hand, then peered at Jude as if his best friend had just died. "I'm not really sure," he whispered. "Aren't we going to kiss or something first?"

Jude pulled the white tank top over her head and quickly unclasped her bra, revealing round, taut sixteen-year-old tits begging to be touched. "Are you still worried about kissing?" Jude asked. "Then kiss these."

Sean did as he was told, willing one foot to go forth after the other, all of eight inches at a time while his knees threatened to give out at any moment. Judy reached and took Sean's right wrist in her left hand. "Come on, tiger, put it right here."

He was touching a naked breast! It was a real naked breast! His cock strained against his baggy jeans. "Mmm, that's nice," Jude purred. Touch the other one, too." Sean did as he was told as the pain began throbbing in his balls. Jude could feel him against her and dropped one of her hands down to make sure he was hard. She didn't want this to last any longer than it had to. On the way down, she changed her tactic and - after a little fumbling - found the button to his brown corduroys, undid it, and unzipped his fly. Then she snuck her hand inside his white briefs and found his cock.

"Oh my God!" she yelped.

Having only known Johnny's penis in her life, she thought they were all like that, but Sean Mallory's penis was not the same at all. Sean Mallory's penis was much bigger than Johnny's was. She reached further, and then further, until she reached the base; Base Camp, she would later name it.

"What? What?" Sean cried. He hadn't done something wrong already, had he?

Jude was laughing as if the secret of life and been given to her.

"What?!"

"Nothing, I'm just -"

"You're what?!"

Jude kissed him deeply and roughly. "Let's get these off you and see what you're all about," she giggled.

The entire event lasted less than five minutes, but both received everything they were hoping from it. With permission, Sean told everyone he knew and became, for a while at least, a very popular guy. Jude was immediately tabbed a slut and was thus able to continue her plan through fruition. Johnny beat the hell out of Sean, but never did feel better. And Sean grew, got into shape, and made millions as a television psychologist. They said people loved him because it seemed as if he knew where they were coming from. It was like he was one of them; the lonely, the flawed, those just looking for a break to show what they really could do.

Back in the studio, about half the audience howled and danced, as the rest of them - the one's who had bet that Judy would not have sex with Sean - sat down in skeletal disgust.

"Hurry up and wrap it up," a voice whispered from the darkness. "We have to go to commercial in two minutes."

John turned to Judy, his eyes asking the questions of almost thirty years in the making, but with not a sound exiting his quivering mouth. He tried to say something, but it was a lost cause.

"It's over now, Johnny," Judy Hill said softly. "We were children and we didn't know any better. I'm sorry for what I did, and I'm sorry for what you did. I think we both changed after that, and not for the better. Even my shrink thinks I'm obsessive about that time in my life. I hate to say it, but I think he's right. I've used it as a crutch for every failure I ever had. I think, Johnny, this may be the last dream I have of you."

John's mouth remained open and silent as he heard someone say "And we're on break." His eyes welled up with tears as Judy was whisked off stage. "Judy!" he called. She stopped for a moment. "I'm sorry, I really, truly am sorry," he cried.

"I know. I am too. And it's past time I forgive both of us. Be good to yourself, Johnny," she smiled sadly. And then, she was gone.

Chapter Fourteen

Michelle scooted over to John and began patting him down again. "Come on, honey," she said. "You're sweating like a Teamster in July. Sit still for me for a second."

"What the hell are you people doing to me? I want out of here now!" John growled helplessly. If they let him out, where the hell would he go?

"Be careful what you wish for, dude, you might just get it." Ziggy said, as if reading John's mind. "If we're still here, and it looks like we are, then things are going all right. She forgave you, man. That's pretty cool because no one saw that coming. I mean, everyone thought she was going to flip you the bird or something, man."

John slumped down into his chair. "I hope you'll excuse me at this particular moment if I don't know what to think," he moaned.

"Well, you can start by thinking how lucky you are to be on this side of the desk - at this moment - instead of being one of them," Ziggy said, pointing at the audience. "And you can be happy for how Judy's going to feel when she wakes up."

"Will she be okay?" John asked.

"She's going to have ups and downs like everyone does," Ziggy answered, "but she's going to be able to deal with everything much better now. She's going to smell spring again and enjoy sunsets and thunderstorms."

"She was always afraid of thunderstorms," John smiled ruefully. "She used to hold me so tightly when lightning would flash. I wish we would've had more time to talk."

"Dude, there was nothing more to say. Not a single relationship has worked out for her because she couldn't trust those men, sometimes rightfully so. For a time, she felt as if she had raped herself in high school. She didn't want to have sex with all those boys, but she forced herself to do it. She felt victimized and she didn't know who to blame or how to get help. Finally, she saw a psychologist - who, by the way, is going to have a field day dissecting this trippy dream of hers - and talking began to make things better. She's going to find someone who will make her feel safe during thunderstorms again, dude. She's going to be okay."

John sighed deeply. "Good. What's next, Ziggy, that cat I accidentally ran over when I was eighteen?"

"No," Ziggy laughed, "there were too many other things to choose from. Besides, cat's can't talk, not even here."

"Ten seconds!"

Ziggy scurried back to the cue cards and motioned for John to read them again. John's stomach quaked, a result of either his fear of what was next or the drugs killing him slowly. He didn't know which option to hope for the least. Ziggy's fingers again counted down the seconds as John squinted to see the card he was supposed to follow. Ziggy pointed and John began read.

"Welcome back, everybody, there's a lot more to come." A lot more to come?! "My next guest is another graduate of Lawrence Patterson High School. He has a secret to share, something we'll all hear about, and after the first five minutes of the interview, you, the audience, will have a chance to guess what that secret is. Please welcome Blair Higgins."

Blair Higgins! Who the hell is Blair Higgins? John wondered. The name was familiar, but he couldn't remember who he was. Before he had time to search his memory, a tall, good-looking man slipped through the curtains, hand extended in front of a wide smile. He must have been at least six-and-a-half-feet tall, but he was slim, almost skinny. As he neared, John took his hand and shook it softly; very unsure as to which dark direction he was about to be taken this time.

"Johnny, so good to see you again," Blair Higgins said with a warm hug that took O'Rourke by surprise. "It's been a long time. I never expected to see you again."

John involuntarily backed away from the hug. "It's, ah, good to see you, too."

Blair laughed as he discovered John couldn't remember him. "Let's sit down, Johnny - or is it just John now?"

"I've been John since university."

"No worries, it's perfectly acceptable if you can't remember who I am."

John searched for Ziggy, but like the last time the only lights in the studio were on him and his guest. He had been left to fend for himself again. He studied Blair's face for anything recognizable like a scar or unique abnormality, but nothing rang a bell. He tried to remember who had been tall and good looking in school, but no one came to mind. There had been some towering kids, but he hadn't known any of them very well and he was pretty sure he couldn't have had any kind of an impact on their lives just because of that.

"ONE MINUTE GONE!" announced The Voice. The audience roared their disapproval, having learned nothing at all about why this guest was here. They shrieked for more talk, for more clues as to how it would end.

"Okay, okay," Blair laughed at John, "I'll try to give you some hints, but I'm not even sure hints will help you out."

"I can't hide it, Blair. I don't remember who you are? Did you grow a lot or something after school?"

"I grew a lot during school and it was all thanks to you."

"Hmmmmm . . . ." came from the audience, the tuxedoed cadavers having heard their first hint stroked their bony chins and whispered quietly to each other.

"Thanks to me?" John exclaimed, shaking his head. "What role did I play in your life? I don't even think I know you."

"To be honest with you, we never formally met."

"Well, then how . . ."

"All in good time. Hey, did you hear about Sean Mallory? Isn't it weird that the two people from our class who became famous turned out to be you and him? Well, Sean mostly, but you're kind of famous in your own way, too. I mean, he's on TV and has that bestseller and all, but you've done all right yourself. Does it eat at you that he's a beloved TV star? I think it would slowly kill me to have to see his face and hear his name every day after what happened. How do you feel about it?"

John examined Blair's deep, brown eyes and perfectly white smile. He thought he could see something familiar about him for a moment, but then it was gone. "I never really blamed him for what happened with Judy. I always saw him as the innocent bystander who did just what I would've done if the tables had been turned."

"Then why did you beat him up?" Blair asked.

"I was out of my head with anger and I couldn't pound Judy, though that's what I wanted to do. Like I said, Sean was the innocent bystander caught in the middle of a hail of bullets during a bank robbery. He got it, but it wasn't his fault. He called me about two years ago, you know, to ask if I'd go on his show."

This news seemed to surprise even Blair Higgins, who to that point had known everything. "What did you say?" he asked, awestruck by the drama of the confrontation.

"First of all, I told him that what had happened was a long time ago and that we were now adults, so why bring it up again?"

"What did he say?"

"TWO MINUTES GONE!" The Voice called, scaring both of them.

"He told me that Judy and him had become friends over the years, mostly because he was the only guy who didn't consider her a slut for what she had done. He said they often spoke about everything under the sun, especially those days."

"Ah, his first patient," Blair whispered.

"Yes, that's why he included a stanza from "Hey Jude" on the acknowledgment page of his first book. Remember what it said?"

Blair slowly shook his head. "I thought I knew it, but I can't think of it now. What did it say?"

"The line was: 'Hey Jude, don't let me down, take a sad song and make it better.' He told me that was for her because she never stopped trying to be happy and he never stopped trying to help."

"Oh my god," Blair quivered. "I really should've known that, but I didn't."

"Yeah," John continued, "so he asked me to be on that Dr. Sean thing he does on TV. I asked him why after all this time and he told me Judy was going to be there, too, as long as I agreed to appear."

"So what happened?"

"What happened was -"

"THREE MINUTES GONE!"

"What happened was I saw no possible positive thing that could come from that disaster. I would've gone on TV for everyone to see what a prick I was. No good could have come from that, none at all."

"Well, not for you, but maybe for them, or her. Did you think of that?"

John had to admit that he had, but she would be crying and he would be left wriggling in his chair as a lonely nation turned its eyes to the idiot box and condemned him. That wasn't the kind of publicity a city columnist courts, though neither was throwing up at a charitable event he had to admit.

"Look, we're here to find out the story about you and I (the audience roared), not more about those two. It would've been nice to help her back then, but it just didn't work out, okay? What about you? What did I do that was so good for you because I could use a little good news right about now. This has been a very long day."

Blair was still smiling, but now the happy smile had been replaced by something that radiated sympathy and understanding. "Of course, shall I tell my story now?"

"If you'd be good enough," John countered.

Blair put a finger up and made no sound.

"What are you waiting for?" John asked.

"Just a second . . ."

"FOUR MINUTES GONE!"

"Okay, that's what I was waiting for. I hate being interrupted, especially by that. I went to the same high school, as you now know, but we never really talked. You did, however, often talk about me."

John shook his head, as Blair paused, as if to say he still couldn't remember.

"Your friends used to make fun of me, sometimes right to my face. Does that jog your memory at all?"

John quickly rattled off a list of the students they had picked on or otherwise insulted. There was the skinny Greek kid, who had pissed them off enough to be hung from one of the goalposts by his underwear. There was that computer geek; the foreign student the girls gushed over; any guy with braces; a few races; and ugly girls. John didn't know where to begin.

"Come on, think back and you'll get it. Think of who I wanted to bring to the graduation dance. Do you remember why I couldn't bring a date, John?"

"Blair Higgins! I do remember you now. You were the guy that -"

"TIME IS UP! PLACE YOUR BETS NOW!"

Shrieking erupted from the audience as they madly stabbed buttons with hard fingers. Ziggy was back in formation at the side of the stage with his index finger held up to his lips, warning John to be quiet while the wagering took place.

"Good looking crowd," Blair whispered.

"Thanks, I've come to love them," John smiled. "Hey, how come you're not all fouled up over what's happening? Don't you think this is a strange dream, too?"

"I'll tell you later," Blair replied.

Ziggy pointed at John and mouthed the word "Go."

"Okay, we're back with Blair Higgins, who I think I do know after all."

"Guess away!" Blair cheerily encouraged.

"You didn't go to the grad dance because they wouldn't let you bring a guy as your date!"

"That's me," Blair said.

"You're the Ass Bandit! Oh, God, I'm sorry. I didn't mean it."

Blair offered a warm smile in return. "That's okay, I know you didn't mean to call me an ass bandit."

"But I don't understand why you're here. How could I have had any influence on your life? I don't recall even teasing you or anything, so why are you here?"

Blair sat back in the plush chair, crossed his legs and began his story. "High school was hell for me. Almost everyone was merciless after I came out in Grade 11, whereas before they only made fun of me for not having a girlfriend and for sounding like a fruit. When I told people I was gay, my life became a dartboard. Everyone had something to say and everyone thought they were the first ones to say it. Teenagers are a cruel species, brother."

John tried but still failed to think what word or action could be linked to Blair Higgins. "Was I really bad to you, Blair?" he asked.

"You were in the very beginning, but I could see that as time passed and the same jokes and insults flew that you began to question what was happening."

John sat blankly, transported back to his final year in high school. He remembered the day word spread like a tornado picking up everyone in its path. That was all anyone could talk about, and everyone wondered what was going to come next.

"My parents, God love them, didn't know what to do or how to feel themselves, so coming home and telling them I was being bullied would have screwed them up further. Every day I was called names. Ass Bandit, like you said, was one of them."

John winced in embarrassment.

"They called me a cocksucker, a fag, they said I liked the Hershey Highway and that I was a freak of nature. I used to vomit every morning after breakfast terrorized over what would happen to me that day. I was desperate for an ally, anyone who would give me the slightest inclination that I wasn't alone. It became so awful that I thought of killing myself. I thought that if that was the way I was going to have to live for the next fifty years, I wanted no part of that world. I was all alone and being crushed to death by everybody else. It was the most afraid I've ever been. I needed a quiet place where no one would hate me, so I chose the night my parents would be at their support group meeting. There was a full bottle of sleeping pills in the medicine cabinet and I would have about two hours to swallow as many as I could. That day, which was to be my last, was the same as all the others. I was abused and no one would do anything about it. By that time, I figured I was the freak and they were right to pummel me with insults. You and your friends were about ten feet down the hall as a nameless student I had never met passed me and called me a fag. I didn't even know who he was, and he didn't know me. He just knew of me, but that was enough to make him go out of his way to insult me. I began to cry, which made everything worse because I had promised myself I wouldn't let those fuckers see me broken. It was then you and your gang came my way. One guy, I think his name was Max, pantomimed wiping tears from his eyes like a baby. Another guy simply swore in contempt. You were the last one in line, and as you walked by me, you slowed and placed your hand on my shoulder, patted it once, then you quickly took it back, hoping no one would notice. But I noticed it as if I'd been struck by lightning. That fast, simple gesture let me know that someone cared about me and felt bad for what was going on. It made me believe that if there was one person like that, there may be another and then I wouldn't be alone anymore."

John sat dumbfounded for the second time, mouth agape like the sucker on the tentacle of an octopus. "I remember that day," he breathed. "I remember doing that."

Blair nodded and gently rested his hand on John's shoulder. "It meant so much," he said.

John continued: "I thought it was funny at first because we'd never seen a fag before. Most of the kids were mean, but we could be meaner. That day, everyone was making fun of you, as if the principal had ordered everyone to do so. I don't know why I noticed that time and not the others, but you looked so . . . beaten. You looked beaten like an abused dog. I didn't know what else to do, but I wanted you to know that I felt bad for what everyone was doing to you."

"I went home after school and waited for my parents to leave so that I could take the pills. But I knew even before they left that I wasn't going to do it. That single act of kindness, as random as it was, opened the door just a crack so that a little light could come in and give me hope. I didn't kill myself the next night or the night after that, so, thank you for my life, which was a very good one."

John grinned broadly, happy for the first time in, well, a hell of a long time. "That was so great to hear, Blair. I'm ashamed now that I didn't have the courage to do more."

"You still don't know what you did, do you? You don't know how important you were to someone's life."

"I didn't think I had ever really been much good for anyone's life," John said softly. "I'm not sure how to react to this. His head turned up and he locked eyes with his guest. "What do you mean you're life was a good one?" he asked without blinking. "Why did you say it that way?"

Blair sighed, but smiled again. "Because, Johnny, I'm dead."

"No."

"I'm afraid so," he said solemnly.

"How? Why? I mean, you look so damn good." John hung his head. "Ah, shit," he muttered.

"It happened about a year before you came to join us here. It was March in Calgary, where I was living then, and I was jogging along the lakeshore when I heard someone scream. At first I thought it was just one kid screaming at another, but as I rounded a bend I saw a young boy down by the water and he was waving his hands in the air like he was trying to catch the attention of a plane. I actually looked up for a second to see what he was waving at. Then I realized it was me. He was trying to wave me down. That's when I swung my head to the left and saw the hole in the ice."

"Oh, you tried to save him and you fell through the ice, too?" John asked. "Wow, you died a hero."

Blair sat back and motioned with both hands for John to be quiet. "That's not exactly how it happened," he stated. "Now, I did run down onto the ice and I took my Jacket off and held on to one sleeve while I tossed the other towards the hole. I could see the boy, I recognized him from the neighbourhood. It was Kevin Milhouse. His family lived about a block from me. He was pasty white and his lips were blue and he was terrified and shaking violently. The sleeve was close enough for him to grab, but he couldn't close his fingers around it. He began to sink, John, so I slid along the ice on my belly until I reached the hole. I was about twenty feet from shore and I could hear the ice cracking beneath me, but it was still holding. There was no way to grab him and haul him out because I had no leverage. The ice was coming apart at the seems, it was pretty damn slippery and Kevin must have weighed over a hundred pounds with his winter clothes being soaked."

"Well, what did you do?" John asked.

"The only thing I could do, I dropped myself through the ice and into the water. I wrapped my arms around Kevin's legs and kicked and lurched as hard as I could trying to push him up and onto the ice. The water froze me almost instantly, but I still had the strength to try once more before it took me down. This time, I sunk down to my ears and then shot up with everything I had, and at the apex I shoved and screamed and Kevin slid about two feet towards the shore."

"My god! You saved his life! Oh," he said. "You died doing it. Oh, man, you're a true hero. I don't think I've ever known anyone who performed such a great, selfless act of courage."

"I'm not done yet," Blair interrupted. "An elderly woman living across the street saw everything happen and she called 9-1-1. The firemen showed up just as I was pushing Kevin out. Once they got him to the ambulance, they came back and formed a chain from shore. The guy closest to me threw me a rope and they pulled me out, saved my life and one of them told me his name was Paul. Isn't that romantic?"

A confused John nodded blankly.

"So, Kevin survived and the newspapers all called me and everyone interviewed me, even on the TV, and my phone didn't stop ringing all night. They wanted to come and see me and take my picture. The next morning, after precious little sleep, I went for my run again and as I was passing the bend where it had all happened the morning before, a car coming the other way lost traction on the slick road and slid right into me and then me and the car slid smack into a tree. That was it for me."

"You were killed in the same spot the very next day?" John gasped.

"Yeah, it kind of boggles the mind when you think about it, so I try not to do that too often."

John nodded in empathy. "I guess not," he said earnestly. "I have to ask you, though, what are you doing here?"

Blair's face washed from serious to silly in an instant. "Oh, I'm an appraiser," he laughed. "I get to say where all these poor souls go."

"You get to, like, pick them?" John asked with awe, as if God himself was standing before him.

"No, no, no," Blair laughed again. "That happens way before me, but thank you for thinking I have that power. I get the undecided ones. It's not really more than a percent of the population that dies, but if you ask me, they're the most interesting. Take you, for example. You should've seen my face when I saw you on the list."

"So, I am dead," John moped.

"I see you don't understand what I'm saying. Okay, this is easy to explain. Step one: People die. Step two: Most go this way, some go that way. You don't want to go that way. You'll probably see one or two that have taken the wrong path before you're done with us. Stay away from them at all costs, John. Step three: The undecideds come here."

"So those unsure of whether they're going to heaven or hell," John proposed, hoping he was at least within the ballpark.

"Not really," Blair replied. " There's no real heaven or hell. I help to set up the scenario which the Undecideds go to. For example, you and your talk show and what happens after that."

John was properly awed. "Do you - do you decide who lives and who dies?" he asked.

Blair knew where John was headed, and he bowed his head in sincerity. "No, I don't get to do that. I'm sorry, but I'm kind of glad I don't have to do that. The responsibility would kill me, pardon the pun."

"Then what do you do?" John asked.

Blair's face softened at the question. "I told you. I'm like a creative director of a TV show. I come up with story lines that both decides the character's destiny, but also what could happen along the way that could satisfy our audience, which, in case you hadn't noticed, is a little cold."

"So you could make this easier for me, at least," John offered. "You could at least help me win this and survive."

Blair lurched backwards, his eyes threatening to escape their sockets. "NO!" he pounded on the desk. "I can't and I wouldn't do that!" His face contorted in fear. "If I were to tell you, they'd send me to Decomposition, or something worse, if there is anything worse. But I always try to keep an open mind." It began to darken, and Blair's face had become washed and hard to see. "Remember, John, keep an open mind!"

Chapter Fifteen

And then he was gone and everything was foggy and cool like a gray fall day in Chicago. It was as thick as it had been dark before the duo reached the studio. "Hey, man, that was pretty cool, huh?" Ziggy said, trying but failing to stifle a laugh. "Man, I thought your eyes were gonna fall out."

"What the hell?" John protested. "Where the hell are we?"

"Hey, calm down, dude," Ziggy stated. "We have to go again. We still have a long way to go and time is running short."

John sighed wearily and felt a strange pressure on his chest that couldn't be determined. "How much further do we have to go?"

"Come on, man, we have to keep moving as quickly as we can."

The duo shuffled their way through the dense fog, blindly seeing nothing as they continued. "Man, this is a first for me," Ziggy said. "You must have had a very complex life. Usually, I get a pretty good sign of which road to take, but this time, it's impossible to tell."

John nodded, slowly catching on to the rules of the game. "I have a feeling we're going to find out together," he answered.

They continued on, sometimes over rising terrain, often creeping no more than a foot at a time, unsure of what might be around the next fog-shrouded bend. The air smelled like a musty gym locker and the humidity John suffered before passing out in the church was now chilling him to the bone. "Having fun yet?" John joked.

"Let's put it this way, man, I'll have a lot to tell the guys back at the cabin," Ziggy shrugged.

"Do you ever get involved with the people you're, ah, escorting?" John asked.

Ziggy shook his head. "They're usually not people, at least not . . . put together like you are," he answered. "I've had suicides and even the accidental overdose, man, but I've never had this sort of walk. They've always been over pretty quickly."

John stopped and held Ziggy's shoulder tightly. Concern was painted across his face. "Don't lie to me. What's going to happen?"

"I wish I knew, man," Ziggy said. "I wish I knew. One thing I do know is that we have a long way to go. No one magically told me this; it's kind of a feeling. No, wait, it's more like a . . . . craving to keep going. I just know we're supposed to keep walking. This is not a good place for us."

John loosened his grip on Ziggy's shoulder, but left his hand there. "Then, I guess we should keep moving," he said.

Ziggy nodded and began to walk slowly. "Hey, Blair was cool, huh? You gotta love a guy with a positive outlook like that."

John began to walk again, shuffling inch by inch. "Lot of good it did him," he sulked.

Before long, they began to drift into their own worlds. The fog promoted the use of other senses, the macabre surroundings warping them so that neither knew for sure if they were moving in a straight line or in circles. They marched in unison, one tentative step after another neither hearing nor seeing a thing. John expected to see some sort of light almost immediately, and though he was reluctant to meet his destiny, he was hooked on discovering what it might be. There had been one good experience and one bad one. Correction, his brain whispered, There had been one very bad one and a less bad one. Let's not minimize what happened, he thought. This is not a good place to be. He slowed to a stop and bent over holding his hands at his waist, like a runner after a grueling sprint.

"What's wrong?" Ziggy asked. "Are you hurt?"

John, still doubled over, crooked a head at his companion. "What's happening, Ziggy?" he asked with a hint of terror.

"What do you mean, man?" Ziggy asked because for him, things were pretty much normal. "Wow," he smiled, "you look great!"

Just as John had finished speaking, light washed over them, not like a tidal wave, but more as a soft breeze beginning slowly then becoming stronger. John took form again, but this time he was dashing and handsome in a black suit, red tie and polished shoes, his hair slicked back like a stock market shark. Of course he could've had no idea, but Ziggy was beside himself. "Whoa!" he howled.

"What?" John asked.

"I've never seen this before!"

"WHAT?"

"Man, I don't know where we're going, but I think we're gonna eat well," Ziggy laughed.

John, who hadn't noticed the lightening of his world until that second, began to understand what Ziggy was on about. "We can see!" he screamed. "There's light again."

Ziggy had stopped laughing but he still had a long, winded sigh for his efforts. "Can you smell something, man?" he asked.

They passed through large, tall black doors with expensive-looking gold handles that hadn't been there even a moment before. They were inside a restaurant he never could have afforded in life and he was being beckoned by a number of arms waving in his direction. "What do I do?" he asked his guide.

Ziggy shook his head at the question. "I told you, man, I've never seen this before. I don't even know what I'm supposed to be doing, much less what's in store for you."

This did not comfort John, who smiled weakly at the table and repeatedly kicked his left heel with his right foot. "That's really comforting, Ziggy," he said.

"I guess we should go and sit down, dude," he suggested.

John snorted with disdain. "I don't think I have a choice . . . dude. Let's go and see what's playing at the drive-in tonight."

John pranced over to the table in a mawkish pantomime of a long, lost friend. "Hello, boys!" he announced. "I'm here."

Those already at the table, which comprised three men opposite three women, sat in stunned silence, superior in their stupor. "Mr. O'Rourke, I presume," the older man with the square jaw said. He sat at the head of the rectangle table, his authoritative manner worth a hardened general's four stars. "Please, sit down," he said gesturing in a manner that was both graceful and intimidating towards the only unoccupied chair. "Sir," he said to Ziggy, "your services are not needed here. Please, wait in the hallway, coffee will be served."

"Now wait a minute!" John railed.

The man took John's arm in a firm but unthreatening vice grip and rasped: "He will wait outside, sir." Stifling John's concern, he added: "He will be fine. Now, please, sit down with us. We have much to discuss."

John's chair was at the far end of the table, opposite his new friend, but, thankfully, as far away as he could be without insulting his host. "Thank you for coming," the man said. John noticed the rest of the table looked much like the man. They wore dark suits, their hair was coifed just right, but none had the gravity of the man's presence, one that reminded John of a crime boss in the movies. They were nothing more than poorly made carbon copies of the one who scared and attracted John, though one of the women who looked a little too much like the man gave him the shivers.

"Thank you," he said. "I'm happy to be here," spilled out of his mouth as he gazed around his surroundings.

"Please sit and be comfortable," the man continued. "We're here - all of us are here - because we need to find a new publisher."

The black-and-white penguins all nodded as one.

"We think you might be the one for the position, but we have to ask you a few questions, of course."

John nodded, then immediately wondered why he did so when he wanted nothing more than to go home. "Um, well, yes, let's see what this is about."

He sat down as a waitress approached to take orders.

"I'll have the rib eye, medium rare, with mashed potatoes, gravy, asparagus tips and a bottle of your best red for the table," announced the man. "Who's next?"

The young man next to The Man was no more than a kid trying to impress the boss. "That sounds good," he boasted with transparently false bravado.

"Another bottle, then?" the waitress asked.

The blond, balding young man retreated. "Well, perhaps the one bottle will be good, for now," he mumbled unsure of what the liquor and lunch protocol was.

"Next," the man said impatiently.

Everyone at the table ordered the same dish, sans wine, of course. When it came to John's turn, he hadn't so much as glanced at the menu. He was not hungry - very reasonable under these circumstances - but to not order something might be an insult, and in his position he thought insulting someone could mean the end. And so he ordered the same dish, then turned his attention to his company, all of whom had already turned their attention back to him.

"Relax, John," the man said. "We want you to feel comfortable in what we know is a most uncomfortable situation.

"We're going to ask you a few questions to get to know you, and you can respond any way you want. Does that seem fair to you?"

John, who was not picking up on this particular scenario at all, nodded and gasped "All right."

"Well, then, we're happy you decided to join us," the man said.

John swallowed hard and replied, "I'm happy to be here, I think." He turned his head side to side hoping Ziggy would be holding his cards that would tell John what to say. There would be no such luck, of course.

"Tell us a little about yourself," the man said.

John sat stunned, afraid to move. He didn't know what this guy wanted from him. "Well, he began, "I am - I was, I guess - a writer for a paper in Vancouver and then Montreal." His answer was rewarded with deep silence.

The man reached a meaty paw out to John's shoulder. "No," he whispered, "that's not what I mean. What I mean is tell us a little about who you are. Who do you think you are?" John remained silent, miserable in his ignorance. They all waited for him to speak, edging forward in their seats with each passing moment, but still John said nothing. The man tried once more, but he was clearly losing his patience. Mr. O'Rourke, if you please, we're all busy men and women. Why are you here?"

John sighed in resignation, slumping his shoulders as the stares began to burn through him like lasers. "I don't really know," he said.

The man fell back in his chair and folded his arms across his barrel chest. "That's what we were afraid you'd say," he grumbled. "What's the problem? Aren't you happy here?"

John couldn't believe what he had just heard. "No offense, because you all look like very powerful people, but no, I'm not happy here."

The man was not amused. "We've gone to a lot of trouble to see that you're happy. Do you mind telling me - us - what is troubling you? Excuse me if I don't quite understand what you're saying, but things have been set up pretty nicely for you. He opened a folder and scanned the papers inside. "It says here that we gave you a good career, an interesting life, a family, the whole ball of wax. Sorry about what happened, but we're not in charge of that. We here in Logistics, even went a little over budget for you. I'm sure you'll be happy to know that some kid who could've made the big leagues as a pitcher will instead wreck his arm in college and end up selling insurance just to even out the numbers. And he hates selling insurance!" The others at the table laughed into their hands. "So, tell me, my friend, why are you not happy?"

John gnawed on his bottom lip, The closest thing he knew to any semblance of reality was Ziggy and he was nowhere to be found. "You get to decide all that?" he asked. "How does anyone get to decide how someone's life will turn out?"

The man pulled himself forward again until his face was nearly touching John's, and he looked deeply into John's eyes. "It's not easy, let me tell you. We have to work under a fixed budget here. For every Olympic champion or billionaire businessman, there's a drug addict and a thief. Most people come out somewhere on the low end, a lot break even, but overall there's a little good and a little bad. In the end, we have to give what we can to as many as possible. After that, it's up to them to decide what to do with what we've given them. Forgive me for being so blunt, but you've been a great disappointment to all of us." The other stern members of the table nodded solemnly. "I may go so far as saying that our budget may have been better spent elsewhere. In short, you've lived a life of wasted potential." A gasp was heard from the far end of the gathering. The Man raised his hand to quiet the room. "What I say is true. I may be taking liberties, but we have to be very careful and this one was a great risk from the start."

"We thought he was worth it," barked a voice from the right side of the table. "We all voted and we thought he was worth the risk."

The man sat back slowly and fixed his hard eyes on the man who had interrupted him. Although the stares now burned him, the younger man with the dark, long hair and goatee continued. "Need I remind you there is a ratio we follow? Sixty percent of the poor and underprivileged; twenty-one percent of the lower middle class; an even ten per cent of the overwhelming middle class; nineteen percent of the upper middle class, and as much as three quarters of the affluent and beyond end up on the sunny side of the ledger. We dole out more than that, but those are the numbers that come home with smiles on their faces from an easy life. So what if this one didn't live up to what we gave him. I don't take it personally like you do."

The Man was clearly offended, but he held his tongue until the younger man was finished. "I just wanted to pick one that would really make it," he sulked. "I've been on a bit of a losing streak, if you hadn't noticed, so when I saw him," he said, pointing an elbow at John, "I thought I had one. This middle-class kid had something that should've done it for him. I can't believe I didn't see the self-destructiveness."

John instinctively backed his chair up as the argument was joined by the rest of the group. He felt himself taken back to when he was a ten-year-old boy and his parents would debate - often with great passion -- the endless saga of his potential versus his results. Back then, his father's eyes would bug out at his actual results, which, frustratingly, never matched the potential his mom never stopped believing in.

"Am I dead yet?" he asked. It was a question that muted the din at once.

The tuxedoed men and women exchanged furtive glances, one to the other, before the man spoke. "No," he said. "You're not." Then he tried to correct himself as the eyes latched onto him again. "But if you've made it this far, it's only a matter of time before you are. Anyway, we've got you down here as a suicide," he said looking at the folder again.

"I am not - I was not - a suicide!" he argued.

The man quickly regained his composure and previous stature of a Mafia Don. "Excuse me, but it says here you died from voluntarily ingesting too much narcotics. Is this a mistake, because I can tell you that we never make mistakes here."

"It's a mistake!" John railed. "No, I mean I made a mistake. I didn't mean for this to happen."

"Perhaps so," the man interrupted, "but you did voluntarily take enough narcotics to kill yourself, am I right?"

John stuttered and stammered, each story rushing out of his mouth nothing more than a simple lie too easy to be dissected. "That's not the point," he argued, as his face began to redden. "I didn't think it would kill me."

The man ruffled through some papers until he found the one he was looking for. "Ah, here it is," he said proudly. "I thought it was in here."

John tried to extend his neck to see what was on the other side of the blank pages facing him. When that failed, he thought of reading through the pages, but there were too many of them for the dimly lit room. "So what did you find?" he asked with a sharp note of sarcasm in his tone. "Was I really different than so many other people?"

The stocky man a single seat from the head of the table fielded that one. "No, not so different," he replied in a baritone voice. "The funny thing is that a lot of people who should don't, and just as many who shouldn't do it. We kind of picked you out of the litter because you had what you wanted and because you were born with a reckless streak - don't blame us - that satisfied our curiosity. I guess you could say you were our case study. People here won and lost small fortunes on your whims. Just when everyone thought you would do one thing, you'd do the other. We hated you for it, but we appreciated the tiresome effort it must have taken to be as unknown to us as you were, just as you were unknown to yourself."

John rubbed his eyes, shaking his head. "Can't I just die and go wherever dead people go?" he pleaded. "It cannot be worse that it is here."

"There it is!" exclaimed the man with dark hair and beard, pointing at the others. "There's your doubt, your self-esteem issue and your suicidal tendencies. I hate to say I told you, but . . ."

"That's enough," growled The Man. "We all made one mistake or another on this one."

John's eyes bounced from one tuxedo to the other, eager to know which would be the next in line to judge him.

"Relax," the man said. "You're not the only one, and we don't have a hand in how you're doing between the time of birth and the time you see us next, which would be about now, one way or the other, nor do we for anyone else."

John recovered his senses in time to ask the question that had until then been lodged firmly in his mouth. "What gives you the right?" he trembled.

"But what's puzzlin' you is the nature of our game," sang the youngest looking man seated at the far right of the table. The others turned and sighed.

"This is the last time," ordered the statelier of them, seated second from the left. "I'm not in the mood for this sort of thing anymore. You will be replaced if this continues."

The young man withdrew and shrunk back into his chair. "Yes, sir," he whimpered.

"I have a question," said the old man. His hair was white as snow, and its length cascaded over his shoulders, his beard following suit in perfect unison. His skin was taut for how old he actually was, yet his eyebrows remained thick and black like two large caterpillars sleeping on his forehead. "What gives you the right to waste all the gifts we gave you?" he put forth with a wave of authority. To John, he was ten-feet taller and at least five times as heavy. His eyes looked as though they had seen the history of the world causing John to flash back to when he was no more than five or six and helping his dad pick the neighbour's garbage off of their manicured lawn.

"Why doesn't he pick it up, Daddy?" Johnny had asked. Even at that tender age, he knew a little bit about right from wrong. If the scary neighbour had thrown his trash on their lawn, why were they picking it up? "Why, Daddy?"

John's dad began to scoop the chicken bones and beer cans quicker. "Because, John," he whispered, "we do it because our neighbour is a bad man and we don't want to get him mad at us."

"Why, Daddy?" John repeated.

"Keep your voice down, Johnny," he whispered, yet there was more than a touch of menace in the message and it startled the young boy.

"Because we're nice people and he's a bad man," he answered under his breath. "We don't want to get someone like him mad at us, do we, Johnny? Besides, how hard is it to do this, eh? We get a little fresh air and some time to ourselves to chat." The monster in question was just across the fence, within earshot, Johnny feared, watching them cower. He stood, arms crossed, in front of the setting sun, so that all you could see was his crazy long hair and massive form in an ecliptic silhouette. The shadow he kept left Johnny and his dad in the dark. As John's reverie ended, he could even smell the man, though he admitted to himself that it may have been the memory of the garbage they swabbed up that day. Or, he dreaded, dinner.

"Well?" the man repeated, pulling John the rest of the way back from childhood. "I asked you a question."

John said nothing as he surveyed the men in front of him. They appeared to come from all walks of life, silver spoon to homeless, captains to con artists, with a few in between to keep the scale weighted properly. "You see?" said the man. "Even now he doesn't have the spine to admit to us what he should have admitted to himself years ago."

"Fuck . . . you." John replied in a level, controlled voice that surprised even himself.

"I'm sorry, what was that you said to me?" the man sneered, as he appeared to grow larger. "I could not have heard you properly," he growled, his hot, sour breath charging into John's nostrils suffocating him.

"I said," John heaved for air, "fuck you."

"What did you say?"

"Fuck you," shot a voice from across the table.

The man spun in shock and ferocity. "Who said that?" he stormed.

"You bring a necessary attribute to the table," one said.

"A character trait we require," another continued, as the man's head swiveled from one to the next.

"Like I am Sympathy," one called.

"And I'm Humour," another followed.

"Yes, yes, and I'm Wisdom, he's Temptation and you are Fear," the oldest said with a soft Welsh accent dismissing further discussion with the wave of a hand. "You have your place here, but you mustn't make it only your place. We've spoken of this before, do you remember? And do you remember that there are countless others of your vein out there with jobs far worse than yours, and that any one them would be thrilled to splinter your bones for the right to be here?"

"Excuse me," John interjected. "What do you want from me?"

"What we want from you, Mr. O'Rourke, is an explanation, no more and no less!" The Man boomed. "You were given more than the average man and frittered it all away. We gave you a gift, sir, and you didn't appreciate it."

All eyes were squarely on John as he considered what The Man had said. He was angry, first for what he felt was a trial to justify the way he ran his life, but what he couldn't escape was the knowledge that they were right. He remembered an old car he once owned when he had been nineteen or twenty. The car had seen better days, that much was true. It had spots from front to back as if it had been shot numerous times with a gun loaded with rust and there were dents from age and poor driving, but the mechanics worked fine and it never failed to start, even in the pitch blackness of a stinging winter morning. He loved the car and appreciated its faithfulness every time the engine turned over when he just knew that it wouldn't, but he treated it shabbily, starving it for oil and tune-ups that would have extended its life long enough to be sold again. Instead, one warm spring day when everything seemed to be going John's way, the oil light flashed red. On the highway with no gas station in sight, his only alternatives were to pull over and wait for help or continue and hope that there would be one a little further down the road. He patted the dashboard and whispered: "Come on, baby, I know you're thirsty, but get me to a gas station and I'll fill you full, I promise."

No one ever got to see if that pledge would have been fulfilled because the old Buick Century began its death throes. It quickly lost power as the dry engine rattled, a sound John had never heard before coming from any car. He had been told enough times, though, what a seized engine sounded like and he was pretty sure that metal gnashing against metal was it. The dials in front of him died like a heart monitor on a patient who was crashing and the gas pedal was rendered useless. The grinding continued, though, until he brought the car to a stop on the shoulder. He tried once to turn the key, but the deed had been done. He had been given a car that had everything it needed to work, but he had wasted it with neglect.

"The cat has hold of your tongue, I believe," the older man said. "That's fine, then. I know all I need to know. Thank you for joining us. Your friend is over there," he finished, pointing a thin, crooked finger towards Ziggy, who was once again in the right place at the wrong time. He began to walk away from the table.

"You're lucky it wasn't me who's in charge," The Man sneered.

"Now, now," John heard the older man say as he approached a waiting Ziggy. "You really mustn't do that, Ego."

"Aw, hell," the man muttered.

Chapter Sixteen

Before long the pair was feeling their way through the murky fog again with outstretched hands and hesitant fingers. There was dampness in the air and a heaviness to it that blanketed the travelers, and their whispers amplified around them. "What is this place?" John quietly asked.

"Can't really tell you man," Ziggy replied, "because I've never been here myself. It's kind of freaking me out."

John nodded knowing Ziggy couldn't see it in the dark. "Yeah, me too. Why do you suppose I'm getting preferential treatment?"

"Don't know that either, man. Anyway, who said this was preferential? I wouldn't say you've had a rockin' good time so far, would you?"

This time John blindly shook his head. "No, I guess not. This day hasn't really been good to me, has it?"

"Yeah, well, what did you do for the day, man?" Ziggy asked.

John opened his mouth to answer, but nothing came out. He thought about it some more, then tried to speak again. "I don't think I did very much," he said flatly.

"Yeah, you gotta think of things that way sometimes, you know?"

John thought he did know. "You're not going to start giving life lessons, are you, Ziggy? You're not going to tell me that you're my spiritual guide, are you? Because I already figured that part out, so save your breath. Right now I'm trying to determine if there's a heaven or a hell, though the feel of wherever we are is making me think we're closer to one of them than the other. Is that what you want to tell me, that you're my Yoda and are therefore all knowledgeable? Well, if so, the first lesson was pretty lame and sounded like it came from a motivational poster."

A small pause hung in the air. "Man," Ziggy said bewilderedly, "I was just making conversation." Another pause, this slightly shorter than the first floated by. "You sure got a lot on your mind, dude."

John sighed deeply. "I sure do," he said, as his fingers continued to feel nothing. "Why do you suppose some things happen?" he asked.

"Like what things?"

"You know, why do things happen the way they happen? Why do you meet a girl and fall in love with her and not the friend she's with? Why does one person like Bruce Springsteen and another Beethoven, or why is chocolate so good? Why are some people heroes and others not? Why do people become friends, while others are foes, and . . . why do some people die and some people live?"

This time the silence wasn't broken for almost five minutes. Finally, Ziggy whispered, "You sure got a lot on your mind, dude."

John felt for Ziggy's arm, found it and gripped it firmly. "I kind of miss our old audience," he chuckled.

Ziggy returned the laugh. "That's the spirit, man," he said.

John continued to speak. "When I was a boy, my dad and I played catch every weekend. I must have been about eight or nine when we did this. He and my mom had split up when I was five, but I saw him each week and once in a while for Christmas so it wasn't all that bad. In winter, we skated and shoveled snow together, but in the summer we had baseball. I was always Brooks Robinson, who was my favourite player growing up. My dad had a place in the country with a big yard thanks to the fact he had a better lawyer than my mom and that he was a real prick when it came to the divorce. But what did I know about all that back then? I was a kid and I idolized my old man, even if my mom did call him every name in the book when I was home with her. He would throw the baseballs everywhere but where I was standing so that I would have to run, jump and dive after his pitches as if I were playing third base and spearing line drives just like my hero did. Man, he must have thought I was part dog with the way I'd fetch those balls. And I would do it for hours if he let me," he laughed again. "As we both got older, the game eventually stopped, but by then we could relate to each other on the level more as men or friends than as father and son. We always kept a good friendship, especially after my mom died. Years before, after a long talk between the two of us, he showed up on her doorstep and apologized for treating her so badly over the money. He brought a cheque worth exactly half his life savings, which was something like eight thousand dollars. It wasn't much and it was years too late, but he knocked on that door anyway."

"And when she saw what he had done, she forgave him?" Ziggy asked.

"No way," John replied, laughing even harder than he already had been. "She kicked him square in the shin, called him a lying son of a bitch because she just knew the cheque would bounce and slammed the door in his very contorted face on her way out. Not before she took the cheque from him, though. She marched straight down to the bank, which was only a few blocks from our house, presented it to the teller, and asked for cash. She then offered the entire thing to one of the top lawyers in town, who took her case and won her a house, a car, and an ungodly amount of child support and alimony every month. My dad, who had been outsmarted so badly by this woman he thought was so dim, did not get angry, believe it or not. Rather, he developed a new-found respect for her and treated her as a best friend until the day she died, in the house she had won, in the bed she had shared, beside the man she had loved, who had stayed by her side as the cancer weakened her day by day. In her last hours, I held one hand while my dad held the other."

"Wow," Ziggy whispered. "That really tells you something."

"Yeah, it taught me that there is both good and bad, and that sometimes they were in the same person, and it taught me that there could be second chances if you tried hard enough. But it also taught me in crystal clear terms that life is also random and that the best and the worst die on the same day for no good reason. Then I come here and find out that some of this shit is controlled, some of it isn't, some people get a little bit extra from those who don't get quite enough, and death isn't really death because you were never really living and now you're not really dead!"

Ziggy stopped walking and turned towards where he thought John would be standing. "What would that knowledge have done for you before this?" he asked.

"It would have changed everything," he answered softly.

"Well, if you think so, man, but I doubt it."

"Why do you say that?"

"Because this is who you are, dude. You are the guy who is here. You are you, dig it?"

John looked at Ziggy's voice in stunned silence. "What the hell does that mean?" he demanded.

"What does what mean?" Ziggy asked.

"What you just said!"

"Oh, yeah," Ziggy smiled. "What did I just say again?"

John growled and kicked the ground. "Never mind, it's not important anymore," he told the darkness. "Where do you think we're going?"

"No idea, man. Probably in circles."

They stumbled forward in silence except for the sandpaper sound of their feet shuffling along a dry road. John was lost in his thoughts and when he woke and realized it wondered if Ziggy had been lost in his own. After all, he reasoned, Ziggy had been alive, too. "What were you like?" he asked.

"What was I like?" Ziggy replied. "What was I like when?"

"You know," John mumbled, "when you were alive? What kind of person were you?"

"Oh, I was a pretty normal guy, you know? I hung out and tried to have some fun, man, just trying to make my way through it all."

"Did you have a girlfriend?"

Ziggy stopped and stared into the darkness beside him. The silence melted down on John like warm molasses. It hit him hard and fast.

"Oh!" John whistled. "Oh, I remember. I'm sorry, man. I really forgot. Brad and all that bad stuff."

Ziggy pawed out beside him searching for John's sleeve. "It's okay, dude, it happened long ago and you've had a pretty trippin' day yourself. Tell me about your mom. You told me a cool story about your dad, now tell me one about your mom, man."

John could still feel Ziggy clutching his sleeve. His initial reaction was to pull away and deflect the conversation from his mother, whom he did not enjoy speaking about under the happiest of circumstances, but he was either dead or just about to be, so he rewound his memory bank to find a story that neither hurt nor embarrassed him. He thought back to childhood and the one thing that never failed to make him laugh until he thought he would pee in his pants. His mom would always stop just at that point, as he always knew she would. "Sometimes," John began, "if I had spent a bad day at school and was moping around the house - or maybe at that point it was an apartment - she would creep up on me and grab me from behind. I thought I knew it was coming, but when she actually did grab me, I was surprised out of my wits and I'd scream my head off while she turned me over on my back on the carpet and sat on me. Then she would ask me a question, all red and laughing herself, something like who the prettiest girl in the world was. She'd wait with this great anticipatory look on her face because she knew I'd say the wrong answer. When I said it was Nanny or a movie star, she would pounce down like a panther and begin tickling me mercilessly. It only took a second or two for me to scream, "Mommy is the prettiest! Mommy is!" She would stop tickling me, and after we'd caught our breath just enough she would ask another question. It would be something like who did our dog love the most. As soon as she asked it we'd both be laughing like loons knowing I'd say it was me. She'd scream and bear down on me tickling until I thought I'd pass out or pee. In the end, she was given all the answers she was looking for and she hugged me tightly because she knew I meant them."

John stopped walking. Ziggy heard the silence and stopped as well. "Wow, she sounds pretty cool, man," Ziggy said

"Yeah, I guess she must have been at some point. I mostly remember her as old and unconsciously bitter, a woman who seemed defeated and worn because of life's short stick." John hung his head and shook it slowly. "I wonder why I thought of the tickling game now," he said.

"I bet you think of a lot of things when you're here," said Ziggy. "I've had people tell me about their first teddy bear, others remember smells like apple pie cooling in the kitchen or moth balls when they visited their grandparents. You know, you're near the end here, man, so you remember the little things that you'd forgotten because there's nothing left to think about. It's not like you have to be anywhere in a hurry."

"Yeah, I suppose," John answered weakly. "Listen, can we control where we're going or what I'm going to be doing? I mean, does it have to be random or pre-destined or whatever the drill is here? Can I choose who I want to see?"

"I don't think so, man. That's what they give you life for. You get a whole lot of choices then, but you play by their rules here. That doesn't mean you can't win, man, because you're still technically alive." The revelation seemed to stun even the man who had said it. "Wow, dude, you're still not dead. Maybe you do have a chance."

"Thanks all the same," John said, "but I think if I've gone this far my chances are slim to none."

Another endless pause in the conversation elbowed its way between them. When he could wait no longer, Ziggy said: "Well, at least you went down fighting."

"What's that supposed to mean?" John asked curtly.

"I'm just saying, man, that you're not dead yet so why not give it, you know, a little effort? You did well on your talk show with Judy, so maybe that'll work for you."

"I know what you're saying. But get this news flash: I'm dying of an overdose somewhere in Montreal, and that's why I'm here and I've had dead people as an audience and the Magnificent Seven lecture me for not appreciating what they gave me, not to mention my new best friend is a hippy-zombie-philosophy major. So forgive me if I can't see the bright side of all this."

Ziggy found John's arm again and held it tightly. "You consider me your best friend?" Ziggy smiled. "That's really cool, dude, thanks."

John stopped shuffling again. He rubbed his face with his free hand suddenly afraid that decomposing skin might tear off. When he found his face as he had left it, he breathed a small sigh of relief. "You're welcome," he said. "Ziggy, what I'm trying to say is that the dye is cast, my fate pretty much a foregone conclusion. Have you ever known anyone to reverse course and go back to be saved?"

"Well, not me personally, dude, but I've heard of it happening. You know, people talk here."

"But you've never seen it?"

"No, I've never seen it, but I know it to be true."

John didn't believe him, but he kept that heavy doubt to himself. It was beginning to look like he would have to finish this surreal journey before anything concrete could happen, so he shrugged off his rebuttal and steadfastly began to move forward again. "I hope you're right," he said.

"Who's there?!" an unfamiliar, raspy voice called from out of the darkness.

"WHAT THE HELL??" John screamed and pivoted wildly in the direction of the voice.

"It's okay," Ziggy whispered urgently into John's ear.

"What do we do?" John asked.

"We be quiet," Ziggy replied.

"I said who's there?" it asked again.

Ziggy had pulled John down into a squatting position. "I said I didn't know where we were," he whispered apologetically.

"Now what does that mean?" John hissed. He thought he could hear something sniffing the air near them.

"It's probably nothing, but please be quiet right now, dude."

This time, John was certain he heard sniffing, along with shuffling feet that were clearly getting closer with each step. For the first time since he had woken up to Ziggy, he felt his heart beating like it was being played by a coke-fuelled drummer. He winced as a bolt of electricity shot through his body at the very moment the thing brushed past him. He didn't know why he was terrified, but he was as afraid as he had ever been and the urge to scream and run was almost overwhelming. Only Ziggy's firm hand on his right shoulder kept him in place. The shuffling was moving away from them, stopping every few seconds to sniff and listen before moving on again. When it was far enough away, Ziggy relaxed his hold on John's shoulder. "I think we should move on very slowly and quietly," he said softly to John. "I'm pretty sure he's going to come back."

"What if it hears us? And what the hell is it we're hiding from?"

"I told you I've never been here before, and I also told you that people talk and you hear all sorts of things." He paused to listen, but once again there was no sound. Still, he waited another minute before continuing. "There's no absolute heaven and there's no absolute hell," he said before stopping to listen again. "But there are different levels of eternity, and the distance between one and another is pretty thin. You know how they say what a thin line there is between genius and insanity?" John nodded silently and anonymously. "That's true, by the way, man. There are no geniuses who aren't at least a little screwed up at the same time."

"Go on," John said.

"It's true, man. Some people even think I'm a little screwed up."

"No," John laughed.

"Anyway, someone told me that every once in a while one or two leave their level and end up on another by mistake, but I'm not sure if it really is by mistake, man. It's really one big flaw in the design of this whole thing, but that's the way it is and we have to live with it, so to speak. So if you mistakenly meet one of these guys they try to bring you back with them."

"Why would they try to return if it's so bad there?"

"Because they get found sooner or later and get exiled, man, just like that, so they figure they might as well bring a few back with them before they get caught."

"What for?" John asked, listening for the sound of sandpaper.

"You know that audience you had?" John nodded again. "Well, they're the good guys, man. They're dead, but they get to play Great Gatsby forever and be entertained every once in a while by a cat like you, who is also considered one of the better people. Don't forget, some of them also get another chance at life, so they're not doing too badly. But your audience somewhere else might not be as cool and - what's it called - refined."

"I'm not sure what you mean," John ventured.

"Dude, you would be their entertainment, but it would be a lot different than sitting behind a desk and talking to an ex-girlfriend."

John didn't want to hear exactly what the alternative might be, so he nudged Ziggy and whispered that maybe they should continue on. After they had crept what felt like an adequately safe distance away, John asked if they would come across another one of those along the way.

"Could be, dude, could be because I don't know if he was lost - or if we are."

John tucked that little gem of information into a little-used crevice of his mind, where he rarely visited, the place that also contained the breast cancer fiasco and a puzzling and quasi-gay experience when he and his friend Neil were no more than ten years old.

"Either way, I don't see a lot of fun ahead, Ziggy."

"Me neither, man, me neither."

Their shuffling, now pared down to nothing louder than tiptoe steps, the pair continued the journey ever vigilant for the sound of danger. Ziggy's hand never left John's shoulder and John never stopped being thankful for it. After half an hour - or it might have been days, as far as they were concerned - John felt distanced enough to speak in a satiny soft voice. "Do you think we're okay?" he breathed.

They stopped and craned their necks hoping they wouldn't here a single shuffle or sniff. The only sound they could hear was the muffled, rapid sound of their breath through clenched teeth. "I think we're good, man. I gotta tell you, I think I have a story that other beings here will talk about. I didn't just hear of one of them, I heard one of them, and I didn't flinch, dude. I fought the good fight to get keep you safe and get you there, man."

John felt his arm being jerked as Ziggy became excited at the thought of being the one who tells instead of listens and because his story would be told to generations behind him. "No one stays here forever, dude," he said to John a while back. "After a while, say like about a couple hundred years, a whole ton of us move to a different home, while others move into ours. Then, we move all over again. It's like some kind of ultimate time-share deal, man."

"What happens when there are too many people here for the number of worlds you have?" John asked as naturally as someone who is not a reporter asking how you are. "What do you do then?"

"I don't know, build another level or something, I guess," Ziggy replied, as though it was fact. "There are a lot more dead people than there are alive people, compadre. Room is always found for them here and - where else are ya gonna put dead people?" he asked triumphantly.

John smiled in appreciation of his friend's naïveté. He was new here, while Ziggy was a veteran, so who was he to tell him what was what? For all John knew, there might be a million worlds inter-changing all the time. Or, he might be in violent convulsions, writhing on the ground somewhere and hallucinating the entire thing. Even if that's all this was, he was smart enough to know how real everything felt and the importance of trying to stay out of danger. Even hallucinatory danger was real to him. "Sometimes I forget where I am and that there's a reason for everything," he said with only a touch too much friendliness in his voice.

"Okay, dude, stop trying to freak me out, okay? It works now, doesn't it?"

John laughed quietly and took hold of Ziggy's calloused hand in his own soft grip. "I'm sorry, I was simply trying to break the tension. You know, I'd feel just fine if you knew what was happening."

"Probably not as good as I would, man," Ziggy said.

"Well, I am sorry. You know, I used to play a lot of little shit-disturber games like that when I was a little kid," John said. He thought back and recalled - more as a disjointed slide show than a fluid movie - some of the stunts he would pull when he was growing up. As an only child, he hungered to break the slavish chains his well-intentioned and far-too-busy-to-care parents bound him in to discover what it was they were hiding so tirelessly day after day from him. He learned to manipulate with surprising ease those who loved him to win prizes such as chocolate as a child and love as a man. As a lion cub learns to hunt for food with its sense of smell if not its sight, John had learned to hunt for vulnerability. He breathed in heavily. "I don't really know why I did it now," he said softly.

Ziggy stiffened his grip on John's hand. "Yeah, I've felt that way, too, dude, don't knock yourself out over it. One thing about this place is that you get a lot of time to think. I mean, you get forever to think, so you might as well try to put it behind you and find something useful to do here. In a weird way, you get a sense of satisfaction doing your job here."

"Yeah, I'm sure it's very exciting," John mocked, "but I'd still like to find a way out of this place."

*****

Elsewhere, a well-dressed man smiled knowingly at his companions seated in the well-appointed restaurant.

"You see? You were wrong, again," the old man said to the other, who was working the wad of gum between his jaws as if it would come to life and attack if he didn't keep killing it.

"It's not over yet," he replied, a little more forcefully than he had intended.

"No," conceded the old man, "there's a very long way to go still."

"Why are we doing this now?" asked the skinny man, shocked he had actually asked a question.

"Why wouldn't we?" the old man answered with singular authority. "The world changes, my friend, and even we must change with it."

"It seems a little barbaric," the skinny man in the ill-fitting suit retorted, this time mortified that words had slipped their shackles and darted between his lips.

The old man turned this time to face his accuser, but he smiled warmly at the challenge, especially because it had been so weak yet so courageous. "Yes, I suppose it is, from time to time, but are even the best of us exempt from those primal urges? Even if we were, and clearly not all of us are," he said twisting his head towards the man, "we owe it to all of them, the good and the bad, our undivided attention and best intentions."

"You know what they say about the best intentions," the man began.

"Yes, I'm aware of that saying," the elder snapped back. "That's not the only thing the road to hell is paved with, my impetuous friend."

The men who had stood sat again. Order had been restored to the table once more, as it should be, as it always had been . . . more or less.

Chapter Seventeen

Things were looking up for John and Ziggy as well. There appeared a hazy, dark blue hue - a midnight blue against the black in the sky ahead. Ziggy saw it first, took John's arm and pointed it so John would know where to look. "Okay, man, follow the direction of your arm and look as hard as you can at the sky. Initially, John couldn't see a thing, but after a few moments he found it as well.

"They do say to follow the light," John laughed.

"Follow the yellow brick road, man," Ziggy replied. "At least there's a wizard at the end of that one. Don't know what's waiting for us at the end of this one, though."

The pair picked up their pace, less afraid of bumping into one of the body snatchers, as John had coined them, because they apparently never went near light. "What does wait for me at the end of this road?" he asked.

Ziggy breathed heavily and shrugged his shoulders, an act John could almost see as the sky above began to lighten to a ghostly gray/blue. "I can't tell you, dude," he said honestly and with a hint of sadness.

"You can't or you won't tell me?"

"No, man, I can't tell you. I'm only supposed to bring you so far, then I don't know what happens. All I do know is that sometimes I see them again in an audience or on a cruise ship or -"

"There's a cruise ship?"

"Yeah, but only for a few of them. Man, there are more scenarios on all the levels than you could ever imagine in your weirdest dreams." When John said nothing, Ziggy continued. "Anyway, I take them to a place, it's almost always different, and then they go off on their own and I come back to take another. There are more things in heaven and earth than are dreamt of in your philosophy, dude."

"Nice one. So you really don't know," John sighed.

"Nope. Sometimes I see them again and sometimes I don't. What happens in between is a mystery to me. Maybe someone tells you after you've been here a while, but no one's told me yet. I think I'm happy about that."

"Well, I'm not looking forward to being on my own."

"I wouldn't be either."

As the sky lightened further, John was surprised that it was blue. Although he hadn't actually thought about it beforehand, he would've figured it to be different than the one on earth. On earth! Now he was talking like a goddamn alien from another planet! He decided not to think about the sky and tried stowing it in the brain crevice that was filling quickly with the unthinkable.

"What do you think happens?" he asked.

"I try not to think about it because thinking about why things happen the way they do around here can drive you crazy, dude. You wouldn't think you'd say that after you died, but that's the way it is. It's pretty bureaucratic," Ziggy explained, nodding his head for emphasis on the final word. "And don't ask what happened with me because it was different then. I was taken all the way to my new job, which is what I do now with you unless you return, which, I'm afraid to tell you, man, isn't looking that good."

John noticed they were now walking on a soft bed of green grass as he nodded in agreement. He also thought his fate had been decided. "What kind of experiences did you have along the way?"

"I didn't have many like you're having, man. But then, I don't think I did enough good or bad in my life to really make that much of a difference. I was just kind of there, you know?"

"Somebody must have been hurt when you died," John suggested.

"Oh, yeah, that was a bitch, dude. One thing I did have to do was attend my own funeral. My mom and dad were there and they were crushed, man. Lots of people were there, and I got a bird's-eye view of all of them. I could even see myself in the coffin, which, I'm not afraid to say, is really, really eerie. The whole experience was, like, epic, man. They're here now, too, but on a different level. They were pretty good people."

"Wow, do you get to see them?" John asked, his curiosity piquing on what the answer might be.

"No, but I can feel them sometimes. It's like we can sense and feel each other if we try hard enough. It's not words, but it does work, my man."

John stopped abruptly, almost tripping Ziggy, who was forced to perform a drunken ballet to stay upright. "Will I be able to do that with my family?" he asked urgently.

Ziggy began to reply, but another voice interrupted him.

"Hey, John," it said casually.

They whirled around, terrified that one of the body snatchers had followed them. When John did see who it was, he understood a new, possibly painful chapter was about to begin.

"Well, are you going to say hello?"

Standing before John, with the air of insincere superiority she always carried with her, was Olivia Williams. If it's true that everyone has a story about the one that got away - the true love that never was - then Olivia was John's story. They met each other while working for The Ubyssey, the University of British Columbia's newspaper. She was working towards a degree in political science to satisfy her ambition of running for office, but she also wanted to know what it was like being a reporter so she might be better able to answer their questions one day. His major was journalism, a young man with a burning fire in his belly to expose the fat-cat politicians for the thieves they were. They met, of all places, in a philosophy class they took for fun, and their attraction was immediate and white-hot. They would argue about everything that was right and wrong in the world and then make raw, hungry love through the night until they were both drenched in each other's sweat, their throats dry as sand. They needed each other like on the most primitive of levels, which, in the end, proved to be their downfall. They were unable to turn away from the other even if they had wanted to. Olivia possessed a tall, lithe body, mostly from the hours she put in at the gym, but also because she would've had it no other way. Imperfection was not her forte. Her cascading hair, the colour of a rich, dark red wine, caressed the long lashes of jade eyes that could turn from warm, inviting pools to ice without warning. High cheek bones, full lips, pristine, flawless skin and small, firm breasts gave her the air that she was no one to be trifled with. An expert chameleon, she would've looked equally at home on a Paris catwalk, playing pool in a bar, or taking care of business on Parliament Hill, Canada's equivalent to the White House. The fact that she naturally walked and talked with her head tilted slightly as if she was always thinking about something completed the look, and though she rarely felt superior to anyone, most people felt inferior to her. In her world, she was afraid, perhaps even slightly paranoid that life had it in for her, which is why she affected the air. It was to cover up her well hidden vulnerability and insecurities. But John had found her out, the only man ever to truly do so, and this had terrified her. To think that he had such knowledge of her inner workings was nearly paralyzing for the woman who habitually thrust her image onto others before they could thrust their own onto her. John knew her very core, her fears, her deepest secrets, and this kept her in turmoil many endless nights. She loved John as much as she was able, but in the end that fear forced her to break away leaving John a broken, bitter, and confused man. He begged and pleaded until tears stained his face, he cajoled and promised her anything, and when that didn't work he spat venomous, ugly anger out of hurt and frustration. Such acts only furthered Olivia's belief that she was doing the right thing by leaving him. If he truly loved her, she reasoned, he would've known enough to step back and allow her to return in her own time and under her own conditions. John did know this, but he needed her far too much to wait for that, not to mention that giving her such power was unthinkable. In the end, John saw the relationship as the perfect juxtaposition. She needed someone to intimately know how to handle her tumultuous highs and lows without ever overtly displaying such knowledge; a man who was able to see inside of her, while standing slightly in awe of her. There was too much devastation at risk, too much of her fragile self to lose with John. What Olivia Williams came to desire most out of college was her inner self back again. She knew she would never stop loving John, but she had lost far too much of herself to be truly happy. Olivia quit the school paper without notice and John never returned to the fateful philosophy class. They ended it all with less than their total selves, with less than they began with, but with more than they would ever feel again. This meeting, this explosive train wreck, would gratefully never be duplicated, but neither would ever be able to trust and give as much to anyone else again.

Lifetimes later, they accidentally found each other again while she was surfing the Internet. She had married the soft-spoken owner of a small rural hardware store chain, who ran for office in a federal election because his wife thought he could beat the other country bumpkins and because he sincerely wanted to do some good. She ran his campaign, wrote his speeches, chose his wardrobe, and tied his ties. When he did win, she happily moved to Ottawa to begin her role as the wife of a Canadian Member of Parliament with all of the social perks and behind-the-scenes power that went with the job. When he was a surprise choice as a cabinet minister, she blossomed into the position and held it to her heart tightly. Her husband, however, was another matter altogether. He treated her well, but was staid, stoic and boring - at least to his wife. However, losing the title and the respect it brought her was unacceptable and truly terrifying, and so she negotiated a pact with herself. She would love him as much as she was able, and in return she would travel in the right circles, meet exciting, intelligent people, and act the part of the genial hostess. Woven into the fabric of this performance was an incomprehensible need to keep in touch with her roots, as if to be sure they were still there when this dream somehow ended. She voraciously read the news from back home to see what everyone was up to, what was going on, and, most importantly, what was changing. She enjoyed the Vancouver Star for the big-city news and the West Island Chronicle for the smaller, more familiar community happenings. One day while scanning the Star, something caught her eye causing her mouth to open just far enough for her to hear herself gasp. The paper was introducing a new columnist, a guy named John O'Rourke, who would be writing about the city four days a week; every Monday, Wednesday, Friday, and Saturday. It said he had been working for a paper in Edmonton for a few years, but was happy to be coming home. There was a black-and-white picture of John looking into the camera very earnestly, so much so a giggle escaped Olivia's lips. Included was his new e-mail address, if you cared enough about something to write to him. That thought made her stomach rise to her throat as if on a roller coaster. She knew she shouldn't, but it was summer break in Ottawa, a time when politics sleeps and there are no dinners or affairs to attend or host. Without the socializing, Olivia was bored, so she convinced herself that a small note of congratulations from an old friend would be nice. If she had been honest, she would've known that although she had achieved a standing befitting her as a woman of substance, life had become dull. Even after the last time she and John had been together, the night they physically fought each other until both bled, she had continued to think of him. After all, he was always reliable when she masturbated with the Bronze Bullet, as she named her vibrator, and when she was sad enough he was there in her mind as the only true love she had known. Add to that the fact she was aging and afraid passion had left her forever, and the words began to slip out one after the other. "Just a small note of congratulations," she whispered, and that was really all she had sent, but in her head she felt a long dormant clock begin to tick again towards . . . what? He replied so quickly that she physically backed away from her computer when she saw his name on the screen. He had asked her a dozen questions, each one followed by a question mark and the exclamation point, he knew she had always despised. It took her two days and countless beginnings to reply.

"Hi again," the letter began, "sorry I didn't get back to you sooner, but I signed off right away and didn't see your e-mail until just now (she lied). You've asked a lot of questions and I'll try to answer as many as possible.

"Yes, I am married, and to someone you may have heard of. My husband is the Honourable Alex Wainwright, the Minister of Agriculture. We've been together for about seven years and all is well. (The second lie, she thought)

"I'm a consultant for a public relations firm here in Ottawa. I get paid well and don't have to work very long hours at all for it, so it's a nice deal. I guess my clients like the association with my husband. Much more of my time is devoted to working behind the scenes for Alex. There's a tremendous amount of work to be done, most of it pretty mundane and pointless, but someone has to do it. You know I liked politics, right? So here I am right on target.

"My health isn't all that it once was because of a traffic accident I was in a few years ago. My back got broken, so it hurts every once in a while, but I still go to the gym and work out as much as I can. Other than that, you know me (writing those words made her feel oddly uncomfortable), I have good days and bad days."

She thought about deleting that last part, afraid of letting him in too deeply again, but there was a mildly confusing compulsion that told her to leave as it was just to see how he might respond. Besides, he had known her, so he probably would've asked anyway.

"I have no kids because we've always been so busy. I truly don't see how I could stop everything to sit at home with babies for a few years. Maybe one day, but there's no serious thought to them right now. Well, I have no serious thoughts, but Alex has mentioned a few times that he would like to begin a family soon. God, can you imagine me as a mother?? I have zero maternal instinct. I even kill fish within a week of putting them in the aquarium! I've had five and they've all died within weeks of bringing them home. So that's the answer to that question.

"The rest of your answers will have to wait for another day because I'm getting grouchy and tired. It was nice to hear from you, John. Good luck with the new job."

John read the letter over and over before answering it.

"Hi Olivia," he typed, "I'm glad things are going so well for you. Of course I know who Alex Wainwright is. What the hell did you buy at the hardware store to make him fall for you? (ha ha) You didn't ask me any questions so I'm guessing that either you don't wish to communicate with me or you really were very tired. Regardless, I'll tell you anyway.

"I'm married as well to the lovely Wendy and we're thinking of starting a family. My career you read about in the introduction promo (damn stern looking picture, isn't it?), so I'll just add that my health is healthy so far as I know and other than the insanity of considering a baby, all is well.

"Thanks for telling me about yourself. I've often wondered how you were doing. I'll even admit that I've missed you; knowledge that I'm sure will have you running for the hills.

"I'd love to hear more about you, but will reluctantly understand if you choose to remain in stealth mode or seek entry into the witness protection system. I mean no harm and come in peace. It's up to you. This was nice."

John slept poorly that night, tossing and turning before surrendering and heading for the couch in the living room where he alternately watched TV and read until the sun finally came up. His emotions were a mixture of guilt and anticipation. He chided himself for writing her and opening the door to his life once again, but the possibility of a reply spiked his heart rate.

A full week had passed and John was sure she was never going to write again when her name surprised him for a second time in his inbox. He hesitated once, then twice, to open it, preferring to wonder only for a moment what it might say. He was sure she would either reply with a half-hearted maybe or - more likely - a terse no concerning writing to the other and he was nervous about which it might be. Surprisingly, he found himself afraid that this woman from his past would dismiss the notion as ludicrous. After all, they had been known among the few friends they kept as the bipolar couple; in love one moment, nearly coming to blows the next. Unable to resist opening it, he sat forward and began to read.

"Hi John,

I've thought about this carefully and believe we can write as long as it doesn't become too personal. I hope you understand what I mean. It's good that you're married. I don't think I would've continued if you had been single. We can try once a week to see how it goes. Is that okay with you? I'm going to open a new, private account because I've talked a lot about you with Alex and I don't want him to know you're back in my life, even from far away. And yes, I do see the irony of doing something wrong so that he doesn't think we're doing anything wrong, so you can keep that little pearl of wisdom to yourself.

"Remember, no drudging up the past. That's a hard rule or else I will go away. Talk to you soon. Keep well."

John exhaled loudly and sat back in his chair staring at the words on the monitor long after memorizing them. "Okay," he whispered to himself as a shiver ran up his spine, "she's back." And John O'Rourke knew beyond a shadow of a doubt that something had started the trains rolling towards each other once again, even while the romantic in him tried to believe that there would be no carnage somewhere down the line.

He took tentative baby steps in the beginning, careful not to write anything that might scare Olivia off. He took great pains to bandage old wounds as he reintroduced himself to her. As such, the letters were antiseptic small talk that left both empty and in need of more from the other. After three weeks, Olivia wrote the following e-mail:

"John: This isn't working very well for me. I hate how we have to be distant from each other, but I'm afraid of what might happen if we get too close. I admit to being just a little too screwed up to go through that again. I don't even know what the hell I want from this. You know too well how I worshipped you back then. It can't happen again, but it will if I'm not careful, okay? That's as honest as I can be. We can get a little closer, if you want. But you have to promise me, John, that it won't happen again. Promise me! If you don't, I'll close this account and never write to you again. I hope you see my point. I hope you follow instructions."

John knew Olivia well enough to keep his distance for the time being. He was also aware that the right words would, in the end, take her defenses down. He, too, was enjoying their thrusts and jabs as they used to be when he felt more alive than he ever had or ever would. He made sure every letter passed the most rigorous of inspections, rising in temperature only as hers did, and only after at least two such warm missives from Olivia. Even then, he made certain to ask her if what he was writing was okay. Of course, he would write, they could go back to talking about work and the weather all the time, but he knew that she would ask for more.

John told only Will that he was writing to Olivia. Will, for his part, tried to talk John out of it, predicting catastrophic disaster and heartbreak, but his old friend would have none of it. "We can be friends now," he argued.

Will replied in astonishment. "You can't really believe that, can you? I mean, you're not that stupid. You do know you have a wife, right? You remember this one's mentally fucked, right?"

"Shut up!" John shouted.

"Why, because we're having the exact same conversation we had a dozen times before she turfed you? The naked, brutal truth in Will's accusations stung John, but he refused to relent. "We're a lot older now, so you don't know what the hell you're talking about."

"You're the one hiding from the truth, asshole," Will countered. His anger over the thought of Olivia was surprising even him, and almost flooring John. "This is a woman you should not be in contact with because you're going to fuck her, yourself and your marriage up and you're going to kill her in the process." He was certain his words that made all the sense in the world to him had failed to breach John's closed ears.

"I wouldn't kill her," John said almost curiously. In the entire ridiculous conversation, it was the most ridiculous thing he said. "I might wound her a bit, but I wouldn't kill her."

"This is what I'm talking about, boy!" Will stormed. "You treat people's lives like they're your own private soap opera. You're never around to face the destruction because you're off seeking your next target to destroy, even with all your lame excuses about how badly they treated you. But let me tell you, John, there's always plenty of hurt and wounded to tend to after Hurricane O'Rourke has swept through."

John stood motionless, stunned at what he had heard. The truth was aching to seep through the cracks in his armor, while his default mechanism of pretending everything was better than it actually was fought it off. It was an epiphany,

John would say later, that sharpened the blurred images of past loves and used friends his mind had tried to camouflage with happy times and endless smiles. In one clean thrust into his belly, reality cut through him clean and true. He felt Olivia's flagrant desperation, the anger of friends let down and Judy's torment. Will's face was a movie screen for everything he thought. It was as if John had woken from that semi-sleep where one tosses and turns while fact and fiction blend into a single dream. More than anything, faced with this truth he felt humiliated and small. His previous boasts of barroom women captured and then released the next morning contorted his face in embarrassment and tightened his legs together. He'd never stayed there long enough to feel for his prey. There had been Annie, for example, who had always adored John from the time they were kids in their first year of high school. She had saved her virginity for him even as he dated other girls. Finally, as they were camping one weekend with a group of friends he had become drunk enough to sneak into her tent, where she said she would be waiting for him. Her friends had told her that she would never forget the first time. Years later, it would eat at her insides that they had been sadly correct. She was waiting in panties and a T-shirt, terrified that it would hurt and that she would be humiliated for her lack of experience as she pulled her sleeping bag up to her neck. John, on the other hand, was delighted with his patient prize as he quaffed a couple more beers down with his buddies before making his grand entrance into her tent. The act itself was at once awkward and devoid of any tenderness or love. Drunk, he fumbled with her small breasts pinching her nipples too hard in a juvenile attempt to see if she was kinky and would get off on him being rough. When she yelped and moved his hand away, John gently pushed the back of her head down to his cock hoping a good blowjob would harden what the alcohol had rendered useless. Although it was also the first time she had performed fellatio, she had become proficient thanks to Cosmo and bananas and it began to harden in her mouth as

John moaned softly in pleasure. But then he went back to business, pulling her up to sit on him even after she asked if he would be on top. As it was her first time, she believed it would hurt less that way, but John kept pulling her up until she was riding his rod like an old pro. It didn't hurt nearly as much as she had feared. In fact, what she had waited years for turned out to be pretty damn nice, except for John's rough play with her nipples, which he kept up through the entire, three-minute act. After they finished, three separate but equally crushing events conspired (the perfect storm, she would think years later) to radically change her from an innocent romantic in love with John to a world-weary realist. The first occurred immediately. After he came, John pulled her off of him, kissed her on the cheek and pulled her close so that her head rested lovingly on his shoulder. She hadn't experienced her first orgasm, but she knew John was the one and that she could wait a little longer. After all, she had just lost her virginity (she had!) and she was lying naked by his side. She closed her eyes and dreamily replayed the moment again in her mind knowing just what they would do differently the next time to make it better for her. As she was happily thinking of their future together, one of his pals threw in a can of whipped cream to the giggles of the other boys. While it mortified Annie, John laughed, pulled his pants up from his ankles and bolted out to join the fun. Alone inside, hoping he was coming right back, Annie heard their laughter. What was far worse, she heard John's laughter, too. Ashamed, she stayed in her tent the entire night sobbing quietly in her embarrassment. The second thing that happened turned out to make that abandonment more of a happy memory than not. The next night, as they all sat around the fire singing and joking as gangs that age do, she noticed John was taking a very long time in the camp ground's bathroom. In fact, as she glanced at her watch she calculated he had been gone almost half an hour. As her stomach churned, she saw him stumbling down the dirt road with someone she didn't know. It was a girl she didn't know!

PASSING THROUGH OBLIVION

The young lady who would forever be known as Frisby Nipples because of her large areolas, had that unmistakable freshly fucked look in her flushed face. As Annie's heart broke from betrayal and humiliation, the last piece of the puzzle was already underway as one of John's sperm managed to swim the distance. Almost five weeks later, Annie would discover she was pregnant. Six weeks after that, she had an abortion, which not only flushed the fetus but also her adolescence. John never knew a thing.

Meanwhile, he'd flit from one group of pals to the next being everyone's best friend and good-time guy. Someone or other might get a little bent out of shape over a girl, but by the time he made his way back to his other friends no one remembered what happened in the first place. There would always be a new guy or two in the group, who quickly idolized John as the hero of the adventures the others recounted and so he never lacked for reassurance.

That was the type of friend John would have most of his life, though. Guys that liked to have fun and blow off a little steam now and then. Pals you'd have a few laughs with while watching the game in a bar. And in the end, those were his friends at Matty's. John thought of how he spent his final night bitching about life with the doctor while inviting death into his body, two nostrils at a time. It wasn't unlike how he had spent most of his previous evenings and he cringed once again in embarrassment.

Back in his impossible reality, John found himself standing in an afterlife train station with Olivia Williams and a hippy crypt keeper.

"What happened to you?" he asked.

"Well, isn't that a nice hello?" she retorted.

"I don't think so," Ziggy agreed.

"Thank you," she said. Olivia was dressed in a white T-shirt and black jeans that clung to her athletic behind and firm legs. On her feet she wore long black leather boots with stiletto heels that added three extra inches to her five-foot-eight stature. Even in death, which John had guessed was the case, her emerald eyes shone brightly.

"You're welcome," Ziggy smiled.

"What I meant," John interrupted, "is what happened to you to put you here?"

"Oh," Olivia said, "You want to know how I died. What makes you think I died? That Judy woman saw you in a dream, so why should I have had to die to see you?"

"Olivia," John said.

"What?" she replied.

"Are you dead?"

"Yes, I'm afraid I am."

John blew out the air from his lungs in exasperation. "Was that so hard?" he asked condescendingly.

"I just don't think you have the right to simply expect that I'm dead." Her eyes were accusatory and full of both real and imagined hurt.

"You're kidding, right? I am in the process of dying myself, and while said process unfolds I'm being escorted from one weird scenario to the next by Casper the Friendly Ghost here," he said pointing at Ziggy, "and you're pissed off with me because of the way I said something?"

"Actually, he calls me Ziggy," said Ziggy. "I think it's kind of cool. It's much better than Casper, man."

"I think so, too," Olivia said warmly. "You look like a Ziggy."

"Thanks!" Ziggy smiled. "Did you have one of us?"

"Yeah, of course I did. He was a bit of a pain in the ass, to be honest with you."

"Why is that?" John asked, hoping Olivia would find something or someone else to bite into.

"Because it was like being led around by a scout leader," she answered as if John should have known already. "What kind of a person pisses me off, John?"

"Other than me?" he asked.

Olivia nodded and raised her eyebrows in that way that said if John had really cared about her he would remember what kind of a person pissed her off.

"Let's see," he began. "Someone who has very little or no personality; someone who obeys all the rules to the point of anal retentiveness. You hate people who don't have their own mind; who follow tradition simply because it's what people have done for years; someone who doesn't question the status quo; someone who doesn't answer phone calls and e-mails right away; who seems to take your friendship for granted; and who doesn't understand when you need to run and hide for a while when life gets a little too tough. Was that close?"

"I don't know why I'm here," Olivia huffed.

Chapter Eighteen

"Look!" Ziggy said to them all, pointing to what appeared to be a long dark gray train in the distance almost hidden in the mist.

"That can't be there because of coincidence," John remarked.

"Anything so that I can sit down somewhere," Olivia pouted.

As they cautiously approached it, they could see people through every window from the beginning to the end of the train that they all agreed had to be at least a hundred cars long and fifty years old. "It looks full," John said. "And I have no idea who's on that train. What if it's full of body snatchers? Where does it go and why is it here?"

"I don't know, man, but I have a feeling we're supposed to get on," Ziggy replied. "And I don't think those people are dangerous to us."

"Death is a cabaret, old chums," John said. "Death is a cabaret. Let's go see what destiny has selected for us now."

"Finally!" Olivia said. "I finally get to sit down."

Not surprisingly, every seat in every car they entered was taken except for three together in the last car just in front of the caboose. Olivia gasped and covered her mouth with her hand and John took an involuntary step backwards as they all saw each other suddenly wearing dark, gray suits and gray fedoras with black bands. The two newcomers looked to Ziggy - who somehow still looked like a Ziggy, even in his ill-fitting suit - for advice or explanations, but he, too, was flummoxed.

"Whatever!" said Olivia, as she tugged down on her hat.

Shrugging his shoulders in resignation, John led the way to the far end of the car and the open seats. As he neared them, the lone occupant in the fourth seat slowly turned in an exaggerated display of cool to see who was coming. In his own dark, gray suit, Olivia thought the man looked and acted the part of Jack Nicholson in China Town. He looked it enough in his usual college classroom attire of jeans and a shirt for some of his students, including John, to call him Jaaaaack behind his back, even though his name was Zachery Burnett. He stood a few inches short of six feet and he was balding like the actor, only Zach seemed to be doing it faster. He was known as a real prick of a professor because of his way of publicly embarrassing students in his classes who didn't apply themselves. In one incident, Zachary Burnett forced one hapless student to read his essay aloud to the class - a tradition that most often ends at high school. As he began to read, swaying from one leg to the other nervously, Mr. Burnett handed out copies of the composition - complete with his corrections and belittling commentary in the margins. He ordered the class to shout what he had written as the suddenly panicked author began to perspire. "Go ahead, young man, we're ready for you now," he purred sarcastically. Three words into his story about a movie he had found particularly cool, the class screamed at him. "MISSPELLING!" they bellowed as one, scaring the hell out of the hapless kid. He physically jumped back in terror and then stood open-mouthed in disbelief that this could be happening to him. "Go ahead, son, you just keep reading." The boy stood in rigid terror and said nothing. "Son, we're all waiting for you." Mr. Burnett's voice remained soft, but there was menace in his tone. He slowly sat back in his chair, crossed his legs, and moved the composition in front of his eyes, as did the rest of the class, none of whom wished to be singled out for even the tiniest of infractions. It should be noted that the student, Doug Norton, wasn't given a copy with Zach's scribble all over it. His was the original and it had not been touched. This gave Doug the added insults of not knowing when the next shrieking correction was coming and of being taught by his own peers.

When news of his heart attack and death reached the general population of students in the school, there was more a feeling of justice than one of sadness or shock. To most people, he was simply not a nice man.

"Well, well, well," Zach the Zach drawled. "Who do we have here?"

"Zach the Zach?" John asked, covering his mouth with his hands too late to stop the name coming out. "I mean Mr. Burnett. It's you, isn't it?"

"Mr. O'Rourke, if I recall. You almost spoke a complete sentence there. Death seems to become you."

John nervously smiled, but it was not being returned. "How long have you been here, Mr. Burnett?" John asked.

"Too fucking long, son, and call me Zachery, or Zach. After all, we're both men now and why adhere to such formality in a godless place like this?"

John nodded, taken aback by Zach's friendly greeting. He always believed that the evil English teacher went to the pound to kick puppies in his spare time. To be spoken to as a peer was almost as difficult to comprehend as anything he had experienced with Ziggy, but he did his best to appear nonplussed. "How long have you been here, Mr. - Zach?"

"Wait a minute!" Olivia interrupted. "Do you know this guy, too?" she asked Zach, who was already warming up to the idea of spending eternity with this woman.

"Yeah, I meant to say hi," he nodded, tipping his hat slightly with his left thumb and forefinger as his eyes dipped down to her ample chest.

"Eyes up! And I asked you a question. Do you know John?"

Zach's smile crept away from his lips slowly, as if it wasn't sure whether to remain or run. "I was his college English teacher, if I recall."

John nodded in agreement, but also to appease his teacher.

"Oh, this is great!" Olivia stormed. "So we're here because of you, is that it?" she accused John, who was about to answer when Ziggy interrupted.

"No, man, you're all here because it was your time, that I do know. They wouldn't do that to people, would they, John?"

"No, I'm pretty sure Ziggy here is right. I can't see them being that petty, first of all. And I don't even know if they have the power to do something like that. God, I hope they don't."

"Who are 'they?'" she asked? "What are you talking about?"

"You'll find out soon enough," John said. "Just be sure to be well dressed and know you'll be asked a lot of questions. Oh, and they won't feed you." Olivia cocked her head to the left and arched that eyebrow. "Whatever," she said in that dismissive tone of hers.

The old train began to shudder on its way, as the blue sky made way for darkness again. After a short silence, they told each other what they had seen and done along their own journeys. Olivia had been on the cruise ship, which surprised no one, but it turned out the entire crew, including the captain, as well as most of the passengers, were in various stages of decomposition, which Olivia did not like at all. Zach had walked as John and Ziggy had done, but unseen voices had screamed at him the entire way as he was forced to read the story the local paper had run of his retirement over and over. Zach said his guide had been abrupt and had forced him to read the story countless times as he walked. The community newspaper writer, who neglected to track down any former students for their thoughts, painted a glowing tribute of the old-school, kind-hearted teacher finally bowing out to rapturous applause from students and former students everywhere. "They screamed things like bully and phony, sentence fragment and sadist at me as I passed them," Zach admitted. "I must be crazy, but I could've sworn that I'd heard those voices before." He quickly looked ashen and much less like a movie star than a small man in a nice suit. The payback had obviously been a bitch, as some of his students promised one day it would be.

The foursome drifted back to silence as Zach concluded his story. No one had any magic words to cheer them up and no one had a clue about what was yet to come. It was when they were quiet with their thoughts that they noticed no one else on the train was speaking or making a noise of any kind. They were gray-suited drones with nowhere to go on a train that was getting there quickly. There was nothing to see out the windows and there was nothing to hear inside the train. Zach wondered if they were in purgatory or at least on their way there.

After a short while, the train slowed to a stop inside a dimly lit station that reminded John of something he might have seen in an old black-and-white western. Everywhere he looked he saw fading gray paint over old slats of wood as if they had traveled back in time. The clothes they were wearing began to make sense. After an initial flurry of conversation as they arrived, the group had been silent for what felt like an hour or so after the train had left the station again. Every once in a while one of them would attempt to engage the others, but because no one could answer any questions there seemed to be little reason to ask. Quietly, they all wondered what might come next and why this was happening to them. "It's not bad enough we have to die," Zach complained once as they sat lost in the rhythm of the train and the tracks, "but we also have to be someone's personal sitcom." Until then, none of them had thought that their journey might be a greater being's source of entertainment.

"I don't think that's the case, man," Ziggy countered earnestly.

"But how do you know for sure?" Zach asked. "How do you know? Who's to say? I thought at one time that the entire universe, the good, the bad, the ugly, your weak, your poor, your huddled masses were all part of the grand design of God. Okay, I didn't understand floods and earthquakes and children dying, but I figured God knew what he was doing in the grand scheme of things. I figured there were reasons that would become clear to me after I died. I admit I didn't attend church, I may have enjoyed myself a bit too much for immediate entry into heaven, but was I that bad of a person to be fucked around with like this? All I know now is that your death has fucked up my afterlife, Johnny boy."

John looked at Olivia whose green eyes had softened. "It's not his fault," she said firmly. "He's just a pawn in this as we all are. We all had meaningless deaths within days of each other, that's what pisses me off. It's like it was choreographed. But who knows what the reason is. Maybe John died to fulfill the destiny of one of us. Have you thought of that?"

"Give your head a shake," Zach retorted. "I think it's pretty obvious he's the central character here. We all went to him, he didn't come to us, see? And to top it off, missy, he's not even dead yet."

"So what? He will be soon enough," Olivia said before realizing it had left her mouth. "I'm really sorry," she whispered to John, who shrugged his shoulders in resignation.

"There's no reason to argue," he said. "There doesn't seem to be much we can do about our situation."

"Indeed," agreed a baritone conductor who had appeared out of nowhere to scare the wits out of everyone. "Last stop, everyone will have to get off the train." He motioned toward a door.

"Where are we?" John asked weakly as he tried to calm his heart back to its usual pace.

The conductor smiled and crooked his head slightly, as if tickled by such a naïve question. "Why, you're where you're supposed to be. This is the last stop. Now I have to ask you to disembark as quickly but as safely as possible. I have a very tight schedule to keep."

The group began shuffling to the door, unsure of what waited for them once they left the train. Zach, who was bringing up the rear, turned to ask a question, but the conductor answered before Zach had a chance to speak. "I've been here since 1934, sir," he said.

"You've been shuttling poor souls like us back and forth all this time, chief?" Zach asked.

The conductor nodded. "And I suspect I shall continue to do so for some time to come." He noticed Zach's puzzled expression. "It's entirely out of my hands, sir. This is what I was destined to do."

"Jesus," Zach mumbled under his breath as the others began to climb down the iron steps to the platform below. "Well, thanks for the ride, pal."

The conductor, on his way back to the front of the train, stopped halfway down the car and slowly turned. "That's very appreciated, sir," he said. "Very few people have ever thanked me for this."

Zach nodded just enough to be seen, then he went through the door and onto the platform to join the others.

"What were you talking about in there?" Olivia asked.

Zach shrugged his shoulders and dug his hands in his pants pockets. "Aw, nothing important. But maybe we ought to start thinking long-term here and what we can do to make it more pleasant." He gazed over the train station. It was damp and cool enough for them to see their breath. Olivia wrapped her arms around herself. Instinctively, John sidled over and draped an arm over her - except that when he did it there was nothing physical to feel. He leapt back in shock as they all stared at the other. He reached out to Zach, but his hand passed through Zach's body as though it was thin air. The two men locked eyes understanding the significance of what had just occurred.

"We can't touch each other," John said.

"No, dude, you can't touch anyone. Not yet, at least," Ziggy spoke.

Zach's eyes darted from Ziggy to John to Olivia, who held her hand out. "I have to know if I'll ever feel anything again," she said trying to mask the great sadness that was welling up within her. "Please try to touch my hand, Zach."

He slowly extended his arm to Olivia's waiting hand. John stood transfixed not knowing if he wanted them to touch or not. What if he was the only one who would never be able to feel anything again? The thought sickened him. Olivia gasped as Zach's hand passed through her own. "Oh, god," she cried.

Zach easily felt Olivia's hand blowing a sigh of relief from his lips as he rubbed his tired eyes with his free hand.

"Right, then," he said, "it seems you'll have to wait for your fate, my friend," he said to John. "I'm sure that once everything is decided - however that may be - you will be able touch us. As far as I can tell, we're here for good and we'll have to make the best of it. Other than those ghouls creeping here and there, we should be okay. And they're not the quietest of beings with their sniffing and such. We should be able to evade them, and even if not, as a band we should be strong enough to beat them - unless they have some sort of superpowers we don't know about yet," he finished, looking directly at Ziggy for confirmation.

"Uh, no, man, they work on stealth and look for strays, I think," he answered, happy to be part of the conversation again. But like I told John, this is pretty new to me. I didn't get any extra instructions for this, so we're all on our own. Man, I wish I was still on my boat. I wish I was still under my boat, or on the dock, or drunk. Man, I wish I was still drunk."

John listened, remembering how close the two of them had become and feeling for his friend's anxiety. "It'll be good, Ziggy. Whatever happens, we're here together and we'll find a nice place to live - or whatever the hell it is we're doing."

"It seems you are the one living, John," Zach interjected. "And while I believe our little band would be greatly enhanced by your everlasting presence, maybe it's time we forgot about our problems and started thinking about how we can save you."

Olivia shuddered and folded her arms tighter around herself. "I don't want to be dead," she cried. "I don't want to be dead. I don't feel any freer dead than I did alive. I'm still scared and I'm still cold and nothing is as it should be."

John reached out to her, but she recoiled violently. "What are you doing?" she shrieked. "You can't even touch me! Nothing has changed since we were alive. You still can't make me feel any better! Other than anger and frustration, you can't make me feel anything! Come on, can you touch me? Come on, big guy, try to touch me," she mocked.

"What is the matter with you?" John demanded.

"I'M FUCKING DEAD, YOU ASSHOLE!" Olivia screamed back. "And you're not," she whispered, holding her face in her hands as, she began to sob.

John stood impotently; there was no good response. Anything he did would be worth no more than a marionette involuntarily shaking as it tried to stand upright beneath its strings. He was mute.

"What I'm getting here is that you two have a past," Zach said with a forged smile. "Oh, goody for the rest of us."

Olivia uncovered her face. John began to focus.

"Well now, isn't that just a treat."

John and Olivia continued to stare blankly at each other, as if woken from a dream, their eyes wide and empty.

"Want to know why I think this is such happy fucking news?" he asked. "Or maybe, you don't even care. But allow me to refresh your memories, kids. You met, you fought, then you sparred, then you bickered, then you bitched, then you ignored. Shall I continue, or would you rather wait for the instant replay, which I think is what we'll all get throughout eternity unless we nip this in the bud right here and now."

"What, are you talking about?" John sneered.

"As I see it," Zach replied, "our actual lives might be nothing more than the blink of an eye. This," he orated as he opened his arms, "this is eternity. This is us and we are this. Why some idiot in charge of this cosmic mess wouldn't have taken our emotions away is anyone's guess, but I suppose we're nothing more now than dolphins jumping through hoops. Fuck this place!" he growled.

That jolted the others from infighting up on a train platform within a dilapidated station sometime in what appeared to be the 1930s, judging by the crowd of commuters bouncing from train to train and one end of the expansive station to the other. John marveled at the sheer movement of them, like a thousand ants all knowing what their job was and where they had to go. What he didn't know was whether they were dead or he was alive again.

"I'm leaving. Who's with me?" Zach challenged. He began to stride towards a door with a steel push rod to exit, but stopped short when he saw hundreds of others just like it all in a row from one end of the mammoth station to the other. He stopped in front of it standing rigid for minutes unsure of what to do next.

"Zach, are you all right?" Olivia squeaked. "Please, are you okay?"

He turned as if woken from a slumber taking a moment to focus his eyes on the gang before he spoke. When he felt suitably composed, he asked a question that, for him and the others, was the most crucial question they might ever ask.

"Which door do I choose?" he puzzled. "What if they're all different? What if each one is a different fucking destiny? Which door do I choose?"

"Ziggy?" John tried.

"Whoa, I don't know about this. I mean, this is really trippy, okay? I never even got the chance to choose, you know? You should be happy, dude. Maybe you'll get something really sweet."

"And maybe I won't," Zach said. "Goddamnit, this isn't right or fair," he mumbled. He moved forward for no reason other than to touch the door to see what it felt like, but he stopped after a single step, his hand no further than an inch away from the rod. He slowly retreated and sat down on a long wooden bench, to be joined shortly by the others. John felt an electricity shoot up his spine causing him to jerk violently. "What was that all about?" an annoyed Olivia asked.

John shook his head to clear the cobwebs. "Okay, that was weird," he panted. "It was like someone shocked me. It's gone now."

Scores of gray commuters were flitting here and there, off one train and on to another, yet never seeming to come in or go out of the station itself. He figured there must be 500 doors lining the walls with people coming in and going out of them all the time. "Want to know something weird?" he asked the others, all of whom waited to hear his response. "What's weird is that these doors never seem to take anyone anywhere. I've seen the same person go out one and within seconds enter again through an entirely different door." The gang began to swing their heads from side to side to find out for themselves that John was indeed correct. It was a difficult task with everyone wearing the same gray, but their faces were still unique, at least. "Go ahead, look all you want, but none of them seem to go anywhere. Everyone here simply caroms from one train to another, in one door and out another, without actually leaving this station."

"What's that supposed to mean?" Zach asked.

"I don't know," John replied honestly. "Maybe it doesn't mean anything. Maybe it means everything."

"Maybe we're supposed to get on another train," Olivia suggested. "Maybe -"

"Uh-uh, not me missy," interrupted Zach.

Olivia jerked backwards, startled by the force of Zach's response. "And why not?" she asked unsteadily.

"Maybe John's right, and maybe he's not," Zach said. "No offense, my friend," he smiled at John, "but we don't know what happens when they leave here. Maybe to them they're gone for a long time. And, I know now from watching closely that at least a few of them do not come back in the station."

This news startled the others, who until that time had been figuring it might be fun to see what was on the other side.

"You know that for sure?" Olivia asked as a chill darted across her skin causing goose bumps to rise on the back of her neck. "How do you know they didn't come in when there are so many doors? You can't see them all." Her tone suggested defiance because danger had not yet come into play inside the station. Boredom was already seeping in, but danger had not even been considered.

"Trust me girlie -"

"Don't call me that!"

Zach spread his arms wide in a welcoming motion. "I apologize unreservedly," he said with a smile. "It seems we're dead and we might be together for a very long time, so please cut me a little slack. I didn't mean any harm."

"Yeah, sure you didn't," answered John, as he tried to put an arm around Olivia, but again he watched it pass through her. "Shit," he spat.

"How chivalrous of you," mocked Zach. "Were you such a gentleman to your wife while you were alive?"

John lunged for him, grimacing with his teeth bared. "I'll fucking kill you, you son of a bitch!" Of course, he simply passed through Zach and ended up on the dirty floor, embarrassed and angry. Shit!" he screamed. "I . . . want . . . to . . . touch . . . SOMETHING!" Then he screamed again, but this time it was because of the pain. "What the hell is that?"

"Damned if I know," Zach answered. "Maybe you're being punished for past indiscretions."

"Leave him alone," snapped Olivia. "I suppose you never made any mistakes, right Mr. Perfect?"

Zach wagged a finger at her. "Hey, girlie, nobody's perfect, but maybe there's something to be said for karma, you know?"

"You bastard," she hissed.

"Aw, go to hell."

"Since I'm here with you, this is probably it," she spat before turning and walking a good ten feet away. For Olivia, that was as far as her comfort zone would allow.

Meanwhile, John untangled his legs and arms and was again standing, though he appeared to be a paler shade of his former self. Zach caught him out of the corner of his eye. "Wow, what's up with you? You look like Caspar's ugly brother."

John turned to him as if to lunge again, but remembered where that strategy had gotten him the previous time before he made the same mistake. "I don't know, but I feel pretty weird. Be sure of one thing, mate," he said to Zach. "If this is me morphing into one of you, be prepared to duck the second I can actually touch you."

"Oh, that's just what we need," Olivia sighed.

"I'm just trying to defend you," John pleaded.

"Who said I want or need you to defend me?" she countered. "The whole time we were together, you tried to baby me. Enough already!"

John's feelings had been hurt, but the frustration of being dead - or mostly dead - and bickering with his former lover was taking its toll. "Oh fuck, here she goes now. Let's find comfortable seats for the big show." Immediately, he wished he hadn't said it, but he had and it was too late to do anything about it. Almost every fight they had endured had come from him saying something she thought was stupid, mean or hurtful. Then she would unleash a white-hot flash of anger that wouldn't end until one or both of them was bruised, if not physically, then at least psychologically.

"Okay, you want it, you got it, buddy!"

"Well, this is getting interesting," smiled Zach. "I do believe I will find a seat."

Olivia ignored this taunt, so enraged was she with John. "How dare you? How fucking dare you say anything about me? I gave you everything and you treated me like something you'd wipe off the bottom of your shoe. Now I won't say anything about your wife like that jerk did," she said, motioning at Zach, "but you have a pretty bad history with women - and with maturity, too, I might add!"

John lurched forward in pain again. "Jesus . . ."

"He's not going to save you," Zach said.

"Go fuck yourself," John moaned.

Not far away, Ziggy, who had been largely forgotten in the melee, began to strum a guitar he had found leaning up against a pillar in the station. It was as if it had been left there on purpose.

"Stuck inside these four walls," he began to sing.

"Sent inside forever. . .

Never seeing no one . . ."

The sound quickly quieted the warring factions, for it was the first enjoyable sound any of them could remember hearing in what seemed like a very long time. They craned their necks to see Ziggy singing, the fight suddenly draining out of all of them.

" . . . nice again, like you, mama, you," he continued.

John smiled as he remembered which song Zig was singing. It was a favourite and one he liked to sing along to in the car. He walked over and joined in. "From the top?" he asked his old friend, the one who seemed to appear just when he was needed most.

Ziggy smiled and nodded. He didn't need to say anything. He only needed to sing. The others ambled towards him as well, seemingly oblivious to what had been happening only seconds before. The song had been a perfect choice because it said what everyone had been feeling. They all sang as Ziggy began again, from the top as John had requested.

"Stuck inside these four walls . . .

Sent inside forever . . .

Never seeing no one . . .

Nice again . . .

Like you, mama, you, mama, you . . ."

They all smiled, as Ziggy the hippy began to furiously strum the guitar. When he began the next stanza, they all screamed it out with heartfelt passion.

"If we ever get out of here
Gonna give it all away
To registered charity
All I need is a pint a day
If we ever get out here
If we ever get out of here"

Ziggy began to strum the familiar chords of the chorus to Band on the Run as every one of them smiled with innocent happiness, as if they suddenly knew that it wasn't going to be so bad after all.

In unison, they threw their arms in the air and screamed as loudly as they could, though Olivia remained more reserved for fear of ruining her carefully crafted image.

Band on the run!
Band on the run!
Band on the run!

And then one of them screamed something entirely different and they stopped at once. John fell to the station floor writhing in pain. Olivia rubbed her eyes because to her John was fading.

"ARGH!" John wailed. "Make it stop! Please, Ziggy, help me! ARGH SHIT!!"

It was true, he was becoming more transparent to them all.

"What do we do?" Olivia squealed.

"He's . . . disappearing," Zach whispered.

"We've got to help him!" Olivia pleaded. "Please do something," she asked of Ziggy, who slowly shook his head from side to side.

"There's nothing we can do," he smiled knowingly. "He's going back." And he began to sing again. "Band on the run
Band on the run . . ."

Chapter Nineteen

John clutched his chest again, his face a grotesque mask of pain. He closed his eyes and felt like he was on the rollercoaster from hell. When he opened them again, the face of a severely perspiring man was shouting at him in a thick French accent. "Wake up, you, wake up! Hey, I think we got him," he said in breathless French to his partner. "How long to the hospital?"

"Be there in less than five," the driver of the ambulance answered. "He gonna make it?"

"Can't tell yet. Just go as fast as you can, Jean-Marc."

The Urgance Sante ambulance crawled through the late-night traffic of Ste. Catherine Street, it's siren and flashing lights doing little to clear a path through the human wall of weekend revelers. Montreal on a Saturday night is much like most other large cities at rush hour. Most people don't even get dressed to go out until 10 p.m. or later. It has the distinction of being the only city in North America - and perhaps the world - with traffic jams at three in the morning after the bars close. This night was no exception. Jean-Marc Boudreau, the ambulance driver, had occasional nightmares of injured people dying in his rig because drunks wouldn't get out of the way. Sometimes those dreams came true, as he feared it would with that overdose in the back. "Come on! Come on! Out of the way," he shouted at the wave of people blocking his way. "Allons-y, let's go, tabarnac!" he swore. Only grudgingly did they part, but it was enough for the ambulance to make its way through. Block by block, the sea slowly parted as Boudreau's neck craned to view the traffic in front and the patient in the back. His partner, paramedic Phillipe Gingras, was monitoring the patient's blood pressure and breathing, both of which were weak at best. John O'Rourke's pupils were dilated and his heartbeat was too fast and irregular. Gingras knew his patient would die if his partner couldn't get them to the ER very soon. The defibrillator was close at hand, but Gingras had already used it to bring this man back from the dead. All he could do now was wait, watch and hope. If the man died, it would feel like a kick in the stomach, but he would get past it quickly, as he always did - as he always had to. Out of the back window, he could see the lights of the hospital's parking lot. They were there, and just in time. The back doors swung open as doctors and nurses reached for John's stretcher. Gingras pushed it towards them then took his end of it as it was pulled out. Boudreau sprinted around from the front of the truck and helped everyone expand the stretcher so it could be rolled into the emergency unit of the Montreal General Hospital.

The toxins John inhaled were doing exactly what they were supposed to do. By attacking his heart they were slowly killing him. Over the previous few months, John had graduated from a recreational user to a drug addict. He had increased both the frequency and the quantity, and now his body was doing the only thing it could do - it was shutting down. The truth of the matter is that his passing wouldn't have made a big difference in the entire scheme of things. He had never been a very good husband, before the plane crash he had been a reluctant father with too little time for his son, and his friends knew him as a fun guy but not someone who could be counted on when a big favour was needed. At parties and other social gatherings, he arrived late, left late, and drank too much while he was there. He played the field with reckless abandon when single, committed adultery when married, then played the hopeless drunk, begging for sympathy when it was all taken away. But there was something inside of him - I don't know if it could be called strength or faith or simply fear of what was on the other side - that made him fight to stay alive. There was something that wouldn't let him let go even when his body was begging to sleep because when John O'Rourke reasonably should have been dead, he did not die. As he was being wheeled into the ER, Dr. Michel Lemond read John's vital signs the paramedics had transmitted while en route. John had experienced acute myocardial infarction, a very common consequence of taking cocaine, which usually occurs in young, fit men with no history of heart disease.

Lemond knew that the potential of cocaine effect should be seriously considered in any younger patient with minimal risk factors for cardiac disease who arrive with acute MI, dilated cardiomyopathy, myocarditis or cardiac arrhythmias. Lemond immediately prescribed oxygen and nitroglycerine to make the arteries of the heart larger, then morphine for the pain. To his astonishment, the patient responded quickly to the treatment, so much so that John was alert enough to tell Lemond what he had done only 45 minutes earlier. He felt utterly ashamed with himself for the position he was in and all the people he felt he was letting down. He was used to thinking that he was John O'Rourke, Montreal's city columnist and immortal being. Sure, sometimes he looked in the mirror and questioned if he was doing too much, but that was always with the knowledge that he could stop at any time. Lying on a stretcher in an unfamiliar hospital, however, erased any notion that he was in control of anything. He asked for and received a mirror and looked at his own pasty, sweat-soaked face in the reflection. He saw the pale blue hospital gown he was wearing and was told his clothes would be thrown out because he had soiled them so badly. Every word was a knife to his belly, every look in the mirror an accusation of failure and lies. He had lied to himself, to his bar buddies and - during his rare calls to Will - his best friend. John spent an endless dark night thinking about what he had become. He also thought about the light he had seen, the one he would never tell anyone about, and Judy Hill and, strangely, Olivia, who had not returned an e-mail in two months. John would be told the next morning when he called Alex Wainwright's office that the MP's wife had recently been killed in an automobile accident while on the way to a dinner featuring the American diplomat. John wept as he realized he had missed her funeral, that he would never, ever see her again, and that he had kept himself too drunk and stoned to notice she was gone. In the midst of his great depression, he could almost hear her telling him to grow up and stop being so damn selfish. This time, he decided he would listen to that voice inside his head. He tried to feel his own embarrassment, his hurt and his helplessness. He wanted to hurt, to feel everything he had dulled with cocaine and vodka, even though he was terrified of what it would do to him. He begged Wendy for forgiveness, and as he sobbed on his pillow, he asked the same of Olivia. He cried harder, too humiliated to address his father who had been so excited about accompanying the family on vacation. John and his father had long been at odds with each other, but the rift had been closed in the months leading up to the trip. They had golf scheduled for the next afternoon after John's belated arrival. When he finally did sleep, it lasted only twenty minutes, but he dreamed of Wendy and Henry as they were before he began his affair. They were all laughing innocently playing on a beach, making sand castles and hugging Dad. He felt Wendy kiss him softly on his cheek, then Henry's sweet breath tickling his face. He saw Henry as a little man, shaking his dad's hand after another game of Memory. When John awoke in the darkness of his room, he solemnly promised them he would no longer desecrate their memory with drugs. He begged their forgiveness, pledging to become the man they had mistakenly believed he was already. By noon, John had already seen a psychologist the hospital had prescribed, a man who seemed to be most impressed with John's lucid thoughts and sincere remorse. Then John called Walt at the paper, told him what had happened and said he understood if enough was finally enough. "You're alive, son," Walt had said after listening to John's confession. "It was a hell of a tough lesson to learn, but I believe you're going to be okay. I'll be by tomorrow and we'll talk about when you might be able to come back to work and whatever help we at the paper can offer you." Walt said he would call the editors of the other English and French papers and ask if they would bury any story that their reporters might write. He said he was owed a few favours and that he would collect them now. John hung up quickly, but not before Walt heard John's voice quiver and break as he was being thanked. John's next order of business was his easiest. He called Matty's, where Tania answered the phone already sounding exhausted. He told her what had happened and said he wouldn't be going there anymore. He asked her to tell the doctor, who would tell everyone else. No flowers, no cards, no visits, John instructed. Tania had to hold on to the bar with her free hand to stop from falling down as her knees buckled upon hearing the news, but she reluctantly agreed to respect John's wishes and added that if he ever wanted to stop by he would be welcomed with open arms. As she hung up the phone, though, she believed they had all seen the last of John O'Rourke. That she was beginning to feel good about it surprised her. "Go get 'em, John," she whispered as she softly placed the phone back on the receiver. "Go get your life back."

Redemption

The pretty nurse with the long, blonde hair took John's pulse and smiled. "Strong and regular," she said. "I think you're going home tomorrow or the day after at the latest."

John returned her smile. "That would be nice," he replied. "Three days is enough, no offense." He knew his apartment looked as though a drug addict had been living there, which was the truth, but he had called his landlord, apologized for being late with the rent, and used email to transfer his saved coke money into the landlord's account. Walt had advanced him the rest to cover the overage. There would be a serious house cleaning, maybe some painting, but he was determined to make his pig sty a home once again.

"You're that newspaper writer, aren't you?" the nurse asked.

"Yeah, that would be me," John admitted.

The nurse smiled, her translucent blue eyes dancing in the sunlight that poured in through a far window. As she straightened his covers, John could see specks of dust float through the light like a miniature meteor shower. "I love your column," she said. "I hope you're back writing again soon."

John paused, soaking in her unexpected enthusiasm and the rush of inspiration it gave him even while his stomach still throbbed from the poison - and subsequent cleansing - it experienced. For such a long time, John had only been enthusiastic about going to the bar and snorting coke. Now there was this good-looking woman standing at the foot of his bed unknowingly instilling in him the ambition to write again. "I hope I go tomorrow," he said. "I'd like to get back to it, to be honest with you."

"I'll see what I can find out," she promised.

"Oh, excuse me, nurse, one more thing."

"Yes?" she asked.

"What's your name? I mean, we've spoken a couple of times now and I don't know your name."

"My name is Bonnie," she answered, as she pointed to her nametag pinned just above her left breast.

"Oh . . . yeah, I guess I could've looked, but . . . you know. Well, thank you, Bonnie. That's very nice of you."

She smiled again, a warm comforting smile made John involuntarily return one of his own. "I'll be back," she said.

"I'll be here."

Bonnie walked into the hallway on her way to see another patient leaving John alone with his thoughts. All the city's papers, including his own, had run surprisingly small briefs about his situation, as he liked to call it, but none had tried to capitalize on it. In Montreal, this was miraculous. He was indebted to Walt for smoothing things over for him like that. People now knew he was in the hospital, but why he was there was murky. Of course, Walt had told the other city editors - English and French - the semi-true story, but they were asked to refrain from sensationalism to give what Walt said was a good man time to recover in peace. "The man lost his family," he explained. "His wife and kids and his father. He's experiencing a long-delayed outpouring of grief. He's exhausted and his health is now paying for it." This worked because Walt had been around for three decades and had the respect of every important person in Montreal, so the pressure on those papers was immense to ignore what would usually have been a big scoop. The shit would surely hit the fan before too long, just as it had for Auf der Maur when he pissed in the ally beside Winnie's, but for now he had peace for the first time since the accident. Often over the past three days, John would remember that someone had told him that he would have to hit rock bottom before he could find redemption. He thought it might have been one of the doctors working on him when he arrived in the ER, but he couldn't get the confusing thought out of his head that it also had something to do with falling out of a boat. It'll come to me, he thought. Okay so the tough part is over, he figured, so the only way to go is up. He was still cringing inside with embarrassment, but when it became a little too confining he would remind himself that countless others - from the homeless to rock stars to business executives had fallen prey to depression and narcotics. In thinking about it, John decided the only way to get past it was to keep moving forward. "And I guess now is as good a time as any," he said to himself as he reached for a pad of paper and a pencil he had asked Bonnie to leave for him earlier. Walt had urged him to take all the time he needed before worrying about getting back to work, but writing had always been the one constant in John's life; the one exercise that until recently had never failed to calm his mind. He sat up in bed and stared at the paper for thirty minutes before he wrote a word. Then, when he started, he didn't stop until it was done. Writing his first column in a couple of weeks, and the first one with a clear head in months, was the therapy he needed to feel better about himself. John knew that as long as he could still write, he could live.

This is what he wrote:

Hello from hell,

By now most of you know that I'm in the hospital. I've been here for three days now, but the good doctors and nurses of the General say they'll be kicking me out in a day or two. This is good news for all concerned because I'm a lousy patient and worse when I'm bored.

What very few of you don't know is why I'm here. If you'll indulge me, I'd like to tell you, even though the very thought of it tears my guts apart. I am embarrassed, humiliated, and angry with myself for being here, but this is a story that I feel compelled to share with you because you're bound to find out on your own and - I hope - this is the type of relationship we've built with each other. Also, my ego is pretending that it may help someone else one day. Of course, my ego thought I was immortal, too, and that was almost proven to be untrue.

Almost a year ago, I lost my family in a plane crash. I didn't die with them because I wasn't on that plane. I told my wife and kids that I had some work that needed to be completed and that I'd fly down to see them the next day. The truth is that I was with another woman as my family fell to their deaths. I won't go into who or why or any other details about that. Other than being romantically interested in a married man, the other woman is a good person who values her privacy - especially at this time.

That's Secret #1, and I don't know whether to feel relieved or terrified for divulging it.

Since my family died, I have slowly fallen into a deep depression. On top of everything a man can feel after losing his wife, children and father, I had to deal with survivor's guilt and the awful reason of why I was a survivor. Please believe me when I say that if I could change the past so that I died and they didn't I would do it a thousand times over. The guilt became so crushing that for almost a year I have wanted to be dead. A few nights ago I came within a hair of getting my wish.

Again, details have to be left a little sketchy because other, somewhat innocent, people are involved, but I have been abusing alcohol and narcotics for quite some time. On the night this happened, I was filling in as a celebrity bartender for a breast cancer fundraiser - representing this paper - where I made a fool of myself. If you haven't seen footage of it, you either don't own a TV or you're blind. I've only seen it once myself, but it was the lowest I've ever been - until about three hours later, that is. I got very drunk - hammered, we used to say - at that event and I hurt some very courageous women with crass remarks and childish, boorish behaviour. Strike that; kids would have behaved better. Chimps would've behaved better than I did. I can only apologize truly and endlessly to those fine people. I pledge to do what I can to make it up to them if they'll allow me.

Because I was so drunk and humiliated, I stumbled my way back to a bar I used to frequent, but not before stopping to see an acquaintance for cocaine.

(John thought it wise to refrain from writing where the drugs really did come from)

Once I arrived at the bar, I drank heavily and did too much cocaine too quickly. In my delirium, I careened down the sidewalk in a mad attempt to get home, but I was disorientated and I went the wrong way. I fell through the heavy doors of a church where I had a heart attack brought on by the drugs.

That's why I'm here instead of my office or at home working.

In the nutshell of a column, that's what happened. Today, I feel better, inspired to turn my life around, to get and stay clean and to try to make a positive difference in the world. But I'm not naïve enough to believe I'll feel like this every day. I may not feel like this tomorrow or even tonight. It would make for a great movie if the flawed hero hit bottom and then made a triumphant recovery, but this is real life and the chance that I could relapse is a very real one. There are a number of programs available to me and others like me, but in this case I want to try to do this on my own. I do intend to begin counseling to finally talk about my grief, guilt and what kind of man I was and still hope to be some day.

For those who feel let down, if any, I'm sorry. For those who believe in me, who will give me the chance to work on this, thank you. And to those who battle an addiction of any kind, or who are dealing with guilt or fear or anything that's compromising your life and who you are, seek some kind of help. For we're now brothers-in-arms fighting every day to stay clean and stay alive. Write to me, if you like. You're not alone, and once this is printed and distributed, I won't be alone either. And, I'll write back to each of you.

Signing off - thankfully, not forever, but just for now. Good luck to us all.

John

He read and re-read his column, putting it aside only to pick it up again moments later, pen in hand darting from this word to that as if to stab them dead before anyone could read them. He felt the need for confession, but he hadn't yet convinced himself that printing it in a newspaper in front of a few hundred thousand strangers was the best way to do it. He rested the paper on his lap and gazed around his room again. It seemed he was hooked up to every machine medicine had ever invented, but Walt had somehow arranged a private room with a small TV and a laptop equipped with wireless Internet so he could surf the newspapers from across North America. It wasn't the worst of fates, all things considered. Still, the walls were a faded green, the bed was uncomfortable and it was almost as noisy at night as in the daytime with the near-dead shuffling here and there, in one door and out another up and down a gray, lifeless corridor. The food was awful, the room was too hot and stuffy, his bathroom door didn't close properly, and he had always hated the sick, antiseptic smell of hospitals, but he was alive and about to go home. The psychological withdrawal from the drug that his shrink feared would be so torturous had miraculously not occurred. The only one not surprised about this was John himself. He had been what people call a "social smoker" most of his life; someone who could take cigarettes or leave them depending upon his mood or location. He could smoke a full pack when drinking, but then could easily go smokeless for days without a care in the world. He knew the coke was more lifestyle or crutch than addiction, much as the smoking had been, and was used more as a method of forgetting reality than it was a physical need. There was no mistaking how tired he was, though, so he closed his eyes and drifted off into another fitful sleep with dreams of dead people walking the halls of the hospital. In his dream, which he would remember later, every patient in the hospital except for him was dead. The zombie patients never threatened John, nor did they really take much notice of him. All they would do is shuffle along the halls and enter and exit every room except the one he was occupying. They made no sound other than the sliding of their slippers on the floor. John awoke less than an hour later, sweaty and agitated, feeling as though there was some place he was supposed to be, but he couldn't nail it down in his mind. He turned on his TV and found Headline News. While a report about another suicide bomber in Iraq killing himself and five others ran, he changed his T-shirt and splashed cold water in his face. George W. Bush then filled the screen asking the American people to hold steadfast to their resolve, to be prepared to sacrifice for the good of the war on terrorism. John gave the screen a fleeting glimpse and a middle finger, then turned back to the sink and spit toothpaste into it. "What a wonderful world," he sang quietly. As more reports about other disasters flashed on the TV, John paced the room slowly. He already knew there were 68 tiles on the ceiling and another 24 in the bathroom, and that there were four outlets and eight different positions his bed could be moved into depending on if he wanted his head or his feet raised. As he paced, John looked for something else to count, but then an image appeared on the small screen that stopped him cold.

"And in entertainment news, David Bowie will visit Russia for a one-time concert to benefit the families of miners killed during a cave-in last month," the announcer said as images of the Thin White Duke flashed on the screen. "It's not the first time Bowie has loaned his talents to a good cause," the perky blond anchor continued, "but it will be the first time he performs in the former Soviet Union."

John stood transfixed as present-day Bowie sat behind a long table at a press conference smiling and waving. "Ziggy played guitar," he quietly sang, oblivious to the fact he had done so.

He spent the rest of the day doing crosswords and being examined by his cardiologist, who broke John's ennui by telling him that he seemed to be in pretty good shape "all things considered," and that he could go home the next day. John was both excited and nervous about the prospect of rejoining "the real world." He'd had brochures of rehab centres thrust at him, 12-step courses suggested, even some sort of a halfway house had been put forth, but John politely listened then smiled and shook his head each time. "Do you know what the chances are of you relapsing without some kind of program to help see you through?" Bonnie the nurse had asked. But John knew that if he were going to do coke again, all the rehab in the world wouldn't stop him. So at this stage of his life, when he didn't feel close to anyone nearby, there was only one person he could count on to help him through the difficult first days. Without the suffocating weight of guilt crushing the life out of him for more than a year, he would've still been living in Vancouver, still ... did it really matter? He picked up his cell phone and dialed a long-distance call.

"Hello?" the familiar voice answered.

"Hey, Will, how ya doing? It's me, John."

"John!" Will said with surprise.

"Yeah, I know it's been a while. I'm sorry for that."

There was a small pause. "John, it's been four months since anyone here has heard from you. I've left maybe twenty messages on your machine. I called the paper, but they wouldn't give me any information."

"Yeah, yeah, I know that, Will," John said quietly. "I think I owe you an explanation for that."

"I think you do," Will said dryly.

John sighed deeply and heavily before telling his friend the entire story. Will never once tried to interrupt with questions, allowing John to start at the beginning and finish at the end. By the time the story was over, Will had moved the phone from his right ear to his left and back again.

"It's almost impossible to believe, John," Will said. "I don't really know what to say. Are you going to be all right?"

"Yeah, it looks like I'm going to be fine."

"You know, it was like you lost your family and everyone here lost you. There are a lot of worried people, starting with Wendy's mom. She loves you, man, and she lost her family as well. Her daughter, her husband, grandchildren -"

"I know who died, Will," John interrupted.

"Okay, okay, tell me how you're doing right now," Will asked.

"Well, I'm embarrassed for starters, and I feel like shit on top of it. But the truth is that I also feel like I got a second chance and I want to do something good with it. I don't even want to ballpark how much money I spent on that crap the past six months, not to mention the cost of all that drinking.

My rent was behind, my apartment itself looks like, well, like a drug addict lives there, I've humiliated myself, and I came within a hair of actually dying." John pushed himself up into a seated position on his bed as he continued. "I have to come to grips with their deaths - and I have no idea how to do that - and I feel that everybody will be watching my every move once I get out of here tomorrow. I have no family here, my friends are the gang I hung with at the bar, so they're out of the picture, and I've just written a column that will tell the whole city what I did. You know what's funny, though?"

"What?" Will answered entirely unsure if any of the insanity could be amusing.

"I feel . . . pretty good, all things considered."

"Well, I'm glad to hear that, John, I really am. You know, I have a little vacation time coming to me and I haven't really made any plans. Do you think it would be all right if I went there and spent some time with you while you get your feet back on the ground?"

John sat silently for a moment, thankful his friend wanted to help, terrified of what Will might see or hear once he arrived. Since the time they were teenagers, Will had always joked that he was John's conscience. Now that conscience was coming to see the train wreck that John had made of his life. On the other hand, if John was going to tell the city what he had been up to in his free time in a column, what could Will find out that everybody didn't already know? John knew the answer to that question. Will would find out his friend was weak and needed a little help to get strong again. John had never been good at asking for anyone's help, but times had changed, hadn't they?

"I'd like that, Will. I'd like that very much. When do you think you could get here?"

"Okay, we're Thursday today. I'll have to work tomorrow, but I could leave Saturday."

"I can't believe that old bastard you work for actually lets you have some time for yourself," John laughed, realizing as he was doing it that he hadn't truly laughed for weeks. He allowed himself to enjoy its warm embrace, suddenly very happy that Will would soon be there.

"Ah, the rarified air of telecom sales is only for a chosen few, my friend, so say what you will, you dull normal. Soon, I'll be back at it telling some poor sap why my product is better than the other four hundred products out there that do the same thing. It is a sexy, sexy job, my friend!"

"Yeah, well, don't trip over your tongue on the way to the airport. And forgive me if I don't pick you up."

"Oh, and why can't you get me at the airport? You'll be sprung by then." That thought, for some reason, hadn't occurred to John. It quickly dawned on him that once he left the next day, real life would simply begin again. The daily dreary tasks of hauling himself out of his own bed; showering and getting dressed; bill payments; work; and what he knew would be a long, difficult night - on a Friday, of all things! - with no place to go. For a fleeting moment, John considered spending one last evening at Matty's, just to say goodbye to his friends, before Will snapped him back to reality, as if he knew what John was thinking. "Hello! John! You didn't crash your car, did you?"

"Uh, no, I can pick you up. I wasn't thinking. Call me tomorrow night once you have your flight plan."

"You'll be home tomorrow night, right, boss?"

John sighed again and slid back down until he was flat on his back. "This might not be as easy as I thought it would be."

"That's why I'm coming, John. The cavalry is coming."

John felt a shiver dart up his spine. Withdrawal from coke would be easy for him, but the drinking and the lifestyle would be more powerful and unpredictable foes. As they said their good-byes, John promised to hang on until his friend arrived.

Chapter Twenty

John paid the Lebanese cabbie and exited the car in front of his apartment building. The sense of foreboding was palpable as he left the antiseptic, safe environment of the hospital for his own lost world. Without really thinking about it, he looked left, then right in case anyone he knew was anywhere nearby before he ducked inside the building. He was wearing the green scrubs doctors and nurses wore in the operating room because his own clothes had been destroyed. Bonnie had been nice enough to "liberate" them for him while he was recovering because he had refused to ask anyone he knew to bring him clean clothes. He was touched that she would contravene hospital rules for him. In fact, the more John thought about Bonnie the more he realized how much he enjoyed her company. He briefly considered calling the hospital to see if she would like to have dinner with him, but when he opened his apartment door his heart jumped at the state he had left it in - and more to the point - the stench in which he had been living. Empty beer bottles littered the counter by the fridge, six dead vodka bottles stood in formation on the kitchen floor in the corner, which itself was littered with McDonald's bags, three full garbage bags and sundry other scum and stains. A sharp, foul odor constricted John's nostrils as the full scope of his personal destruction slapped him in the face, reminding him of who he had become. To think he was going to ask Bonnie the nurse out now seemed laughable. He quickly opened the balcony door to throw the putrid garbage bags outside, but he stopped short when he saw trash spread out over the balcony covered with flies, maggots and assorted other insects. The sight caused John to gag and recoil as if stumbling upon a dead body. "My God," he whispered as he closed the door. "I need a fucking shovel." Dazed, he shuffled into the living room, where a small mountain of newspapers was haphazardly stacked near the old, green couch. John carefully lifted the pile and kicked out the bottom section to look at its date, which said March 12 - more than five months ago. John's heart sank as the papers became top heavy and fell all over the floor as he tried to shift their weight. He saw them as the dated chronicles of the life he had wasted for so long now. March 12 had now become the official starting point of his descent. Although he had already begun drinking too much and had been introduced to cocaine, March 12 was the day he had given up trying. It was the day when he said "the hell with it" and his personal life became as unkempt as his apartment. He flopped down into his easy chair, stained here and there from bingeing after the coke would wear off and ravenous hunger would set in, and looked at the pigsty he had created. A thick coating of dust made everything look as though it was gray, giving John a strong sense of déjà vu, which strangely gave him the shivers. He looked around the room again falling into a deeper depression every time he spotted something new. Even though he had slept there less than a week earlier, it all looked unfamiliar to him, as if he hadn't been the one destroying the joint. His throat felt as dry as sandpaper, so he walked back into the kitchen to pour himself a glass of water. When he opened the cupboard, a large, black cockroach scurried into a far corner behind the only clean glass giving John a fright. "Cockroaches," he whispered again as the memory of his balcony flooded his head. He was thankful that he found only one other roach as he opened all the cupboards and the fridge, which also smelled. Arms hanging limply by his sides, he walked across the living room, over the newspapers, toward the bedroom door, which was closed. "God, I hope there's not a body in there," he thought sarcastically. The door opened, but not entirely, as another mound of newspapers blocked its way. The air hung heavy amidst an odor of dirty clothes too long left unattended. However, compared to the kitchen it was almost sweet. Instinctively, John scanned the room for bugs finding only a couple of silverfish in the closet, which he killed with a shoe. Clothes covered the floor and carpet and the bed sheets were a sickly shade of yellow, off the bed more than on. John opened a window but the stench of garbage from the balcony rushed in before he slammed it closed again. He turned around not knowing where to start, not wanting to know. At that moment, all John O'Rourke wanted was a drink followed by another and another. As he had requested, no one from Matty's had visited him, and he bore them no grudge for following instructions. He knew that bar friends - even the best of bar friends - rarely socialized outside their enclosed, dimly lit fabricated world. He also knew that no one of the coke blowers wanted to see one of their own lying in the hospital because of said coke. Only Matty himself had called, and John suspected that was to gauge how much information John had given the police or hospital personnel, who might then take such information to the police. A large vault in the rear of Matty's held a lot more cocaine that the old conquistador did, so Matty needed to know if he was going to be paid an official visit or not. John had assured him that no one knew a thing and that no one would know anything.

"You're sure?" Matty had asked for the third time.

"Positive, buddy, I enjoy going to your place. I sure as hell wouldn't do anything to change that."

"And you know it would change, eh? You know that would change a lot if you told anybody our secrets, Johnny."

"I'm aware of the consequences," John snapped back.

"Hey, what are we talkin' about this for, anyway, eh, Johnny? I just called to see how you're doin'."

In retrospect, John knew exactly why Matty had called, but he didn't blame him for it just as he didn't blame the others for not calling. As he liked to say from time to time: It is what it is. He was jolted back from his thoughts by a hard knocking on his door. Immediately, his stomach clenched, his recently repaired heart sped up and his mouth dried.

"Mr. John, are you in there?" shouted Muhammad, his landlord, who always smelled like curry and whose standard uniform - in the winter as well as summer - was a stained white undershirt and rumpled, baggy, blue dress pants. He sported one of the worst comb-overs John had ever seen and was by nature an annoying son of a bitch. In fact, the only person John knew in Montreal who was less attractive than Muhammad was the fat man's wife, a woman capable of putting a man off sex for years, if not a lifetime. John was not Muhammad's favourite tenant thanks to late rent cheques, the latest of which had bounced and sporadic noise late at night, usually the result of John bouncing from one room to the next while on a coke bender. The fact that it has always been difficult for a landlord to throw a tenant out in Quebec was one of the few reasons John still had the apartment, and it served as a scab that wouldn't heal for Muhammad, who didn't really give a damn that John had been in the hospital.

"Mr. John! I need to speak with you. I see you come in before. Please open the door so we can talk, Mr. John."

John stood frozen to one of the few spots on the floor that was not covered by newspaper. Under no circumstances did he want to see this man at this time, but Muhammad had spied him entering the building, so John knew his options were limited. Still, he would bar the door with his body if he tried to come in forcefully. Finally, he summoned the courage to say something. "I'm here, Muhammad, what can I do for you?"

"Mr. John, you must to open the door, please. I need to see you right away."

"I'm sorry, I'm just getting out of the shower," he lied. "You'll have to come back later."

"There are complaints, Mr. John. There are complaints about the smell of the garbage. You have to clean that up today, Mr. John! If not," he said as his voice rose, "I will have to cancel the lease. There are many bugs, Mr. John!"

"Okay," John answered.

"Okay? OKAY? It is always okay with you, Mr. John, but still I have to come begging for rent cheque, begging for mess. No more, Mr. John. That is clean today or you go!"

"It will be clean today, Mr. Muhammad," John called though the closed door.

"Six o'clock," Muhammad replied.

"No, come at nine o'clock," John retorted.

"This is too late, Mr. John. Why can I not come in now?"

"Nine o'clock, Muhammad. Take it or leave it."

There was an awkward moment of silence between the two men, as if the landlord was trying to come up with a more successful strategy, but then John heard him mumble something - a Middle Eastern curse, no doubt - before the man retreated with heavy footsteps echoing down the hallway. John had won a little time, but he understood that he needed to get to work quickly if he hoped to get much-needed peace from Muhammad. Even with the windows closed, the reek from the balcony was invasive. John felt a moment of keen embarrassment as he became aware of the fact that he was the reason so many people had been complaining to Muhammad. He even felt sorry for the big man, but just for a moment. "Okay," John heard himself speak to the empty room, "let's see what we can do about this." He walked to the kitchen and opened the cupboard doors beneath the sink to see if there was any cleanser or garbage bags. To his surprise, everything he needed was there, obviously from a trip to the grocery store he couldn't remember making. Deciding to get the worst out of the way first, he carried two large, green garbage bags and a dust pan to the balcony doors and stepped outside. His ambition lasted less than ten seconds before he escaped back inside away from the sickening odor. But the deed had been done, the foul air had come inside, and there was nowhere else to hide. John scoured the bathroom for cologne to dab beneath his nose, but he had never been one to wear that sort of thing and none could be found. Desperate for anything to mask the smell even a little bit, he came upon an idea he was sure only he could devise. He took all the empty vodka bottles and poured the last drops left over in them into a small glass that looked clean enough to just rinse out with water beforehand. Much to his happy surprise, John was able to accumulate almost enough for a shot. Without giving it much thought, he dabbed a little on his upper lip and shoved more up each nostril, a strategy he had developed with cologne while changing Henry's diapers. John then swallowed the rest, relishing the burning sensation down his throat and into his stomach. He sighed and smiled as it warmed him. "Where have you been?" he whispered. To the best of his recollection, John had never wanted or even needed anything more than the alcohol he craved at the very moment he tasted the leftover vodka. Even holding the bottle in his hand felt good, as if it was supposed to be there. The vodka smell, which had almost overcome that of the garbage, gave him a brief shiver of anticipation before it entered his mouth and coated his tongue with stinging pinpricks of forty-proof hootch. He gave a sideways look toward the maggot-filled mess outside and decided cleaning it up would be a lot easier if he attacked it with a good shovel, which he did not have, and a good buzz, which he desperately wanted. The only things that kept John in that apartment that day was the specter of running into that son-of-a-bitch on the way out, or, worse, on the way in with booze on his breath. Later in the day, after he had finally finished his job, was John greatly relieved he had not gone to Matty's, but the magnet that was pulling him there was far more powerful than he could've imagined. As he piled the last of the old newspapers into another box, he took another good look at the apartment and smiled wearily. It did look pretty good, except for the odd stain on the carpet, which would require a professional. The awful smell was still there, but the windows were now open and it seemed no more was coming in. The worst part had been the balcony, of course. John had darted in twice to throw up in the bathroom before he finally, weakly scooped up the last of the moist trash and maggots with the dustbin. His legs were burning from carting it all outside, something that took fourteen trips by John's estimation. What was worse was the dull ache he had in his chest, but time was not on his side. He liberally poured liquid cleanser all over the counter tops and bathroom, rubbing his hands raw with steel wool and elbow grease. To save time, he put on a pair of winter gloves and pulled the crusty, smelly plates, cutlery and glasses from the sink, which he then emptied and refilled with hot water and bleach. The dishes all were packed loosely for the garbage because it saved time and he never thought he would be able to stomach using them again, anyway. He could buy some cheap ones that would have better odds of survival than the shit he pulled from that sink. When he was done, he fell on the couch rubbing the sweat from his eyes, but his apartment looked more like a home again and he had an odd sensation of satisfaction. It was almost seven-thirty and he had been working for hours, but the job was done, and done well. Of course, his mind was urgently telling him he deserved a reward for all his hard work, while his overmatched common sense attempted to convince him otherwise. He could always go to a different bar, he reasoned, one where he was unlikely to know anybody or any way to get his hands on some cocaine. "But what if you get drunk?" the common sense asked. "The little willpower you have now will disappear entirely, you know that. You'll end up at Matty's slapping backs and celebrating your return." Quickly, John began to pace the apartment like a tiger behind bars, his breathing and movements becoming more static and rapid. "Okay," he said taking a different tactic against the small but determined common sense. "I'll get Muhammad up here and show him the place. I'll apologize adequately and all will be well. Then I'll decide what I want to do." The common sense knew that negotiation was futile, that his physical and emotional dependence on alcohol and the bar scene would win out in the end, as it always did. John sat down at the kitchen table and rested his head in his hands. He didn't want to go out, but staying inside amid the unnerving silence and solitude was impossible, especially knowing everyone was just around the corner. He placed his right hand over his heart feeling it beat beneath his shirt. "I don't want to do this," he thought. "Yes, you do," the familiar voice replied solidly. It was going to have its way. It always had its way. "I must be fucking crazy," he muttered into his hands. "Yep," said the voice, "but you know what you want."

John walked the long way up to Sherbrooke Street not realizing until he was halfway around the block that it was the same route he tried to take home less than a week earlier. There stood the church where he had been found and saved, and there he was off to become lost again. This time, though, the demons inside him were strangely subdued, only gently nudging him on his way to where they would be strong again. But the darkened church was reluctant to let him go so quickly. John slowly crept to the front of the big, oaken doors and gently reached a hand out to open them, but they were locked tight and wouldn't budge. John gave them a more forceful shove to no avail and wondered why they had opened the other night when it had been so much later in the night. He tried once more then backed away a foot at a time. "This is it, buddy," he said to himself. "Time to take a stand or give it up forever."

"One drink!" the voice implored. "We can go after one drink, maybe two at the most. We can watch a game, read a paper, stay out of trouble and go home before midnight to be fresh for Will tomorrow."

Will! John was astounded that in the mad rush to have a few drinks he had forgotten about his friend's arrival the next day. "Fuck," he muttered kicking a rock. He knew he could talk himself into a lot of things, but greeting Will with any kind of a hangover after what had just happened was impossible. He had to present a proper picture of contrition for the past and optimism for the future or risk his friend's wrath of lecturing and babying. In fact, the more he thought about it, the more embarrassed he felt. That he could even consider going to a bar so soon after he nearly died astounded even him, and he pivoted back in the direction from which he came. "You are one fucked up son of a bitch," he muttered. Still, there was one very vocal demon inside of him that was quickly persuading him into a triumphant return to Matty's - just for half an hour, of course. John tilted his head to the left and looked down the block, past the awnings and hand-painted signs of the small ethnic grocery stores, until he could see the blue and white beacon that had called to him too often. For a split second, John thought he saw Doc duck inside, but that might have been his imagination playing a trick on him just as easily. He rubbed his eyes and massaged his temples, then stood in the same spot for what felt like an eternity not sure of which road he wanted to take. The longer he thought about it, the louder and more persuasive that demon's voice grew until it seemed others joined in its arm-twisting. John took two steps back to see the entrance once more knowing that if he did see a familiar face enter he would likely not be far behind. But that night was not John's night to die again. Rather, he closed his eyes and pictured himself lying face down in a darkened church, alone and slowly dying in his own vomit as hundreds of people walked unknowingly past on a stifling Montreal evening. And he knew full well that he would never climb out again if he went back in. John O'Rourke spit on the sidewalk and shuffled his way home, shoulders hunched, clammy fists thrust grimly into his pockets.

Life Finds a Way

John's heart lifted as he turned the key in the lock of his apartment door. He didn't know why, he only knew that he felt . . good. The best part was that for a change he didn't feel good because of something he drank or smoked or snorted, he felt a marked lightness in his spirit because of something positive he had done. Or, as he smiled to himself, something he hadn't done. As he opened the door, John knew that inside the floor would be clean, the sink would be silver and empty and the balcony would be a place he could enjoy rather than a depository for rotting trash. There were no straws - cut in size or otherwise - anywhere, and his fridge didn't reek any longer, it shined and held good food that had been purchased that day, as opposed to sometime that year. His couch was unburdened of dirty clothes, ready and waiting for a night of watching TV, which was itself no longer a way station for beer bottles, newspapers and assorted chips and pretzels. And then, as will happen to people in John's turbulent situation, his mood took a nose dive for no more reason than it had taken flight, and he hated himself and his Martha Stewart apartment. He paced, perspired and fidgeted with whatever he came across. The remote turned the TV on, off, on again and then it took flight towards the couch. He opened the fridge door, looked inside, closed it and then opened it again as he desperately wished for that happy feeling to return. "Fuck," he muttered, as he threw himself on his bed, which did not smell of body odor any longer. He stared at the ceiling as he had done so often as a child when his mother and stepfather drunkenly fought, verbally and physically. It was a way to tune the horror out even if he could do nothing about the sound. It was also John's way of remaining inconspicuous, a way to hide quietly so as not to direct any attention at all toward himself. Too many times he had found himself cowering in a corner as his stepfather beat him because he had said something, anything, that gave the old drunk another reason to hit him. Too many times his mother had tried to intervene only to be beaten down harder than she had been before. Staring at the ceiling this time, while reminding John of those times when he was not allowed to be a child, served its purpose. He began to calm, and as he calmed the necessity to pace ebbed. He raised his sweat-matted head, and while he didn't find the euphoria of before, he felt at least a little more at peace and once again able to appreciate the fruits of his enormous cleaning labor. He began to think about Will's visit and what they would do and how he would explain what he had done to himself. But he hadn't done it just to himself, had he? A friend from thousands of miles away had been affected enough to drop everything to come out to see him. His boss was putting himself in harm's way, John believed, to protect him from the great majority who wanted him fired. A woman at work who he barely knew and who had her own barriers to overcome felt enough about him to touch his hand and to tell him people cared. He sighed deeply and decided that when Will arrived he would talk to him straight, as Will deserved, and he would not lie or try to minimize the events that had led to his heart attack and subsequent recovery. It was apparent the time for lying had passed and it had clearly not been a good strategy. He got up and walked to the fridge for a cold drink, then sat down on the couch and looked over the apartment again, and as he did so his mind wandered to high school, before Judy when he first met Will. John had liked him at first sight because they had so much in common, even while being such opposites in many other ways. John was hyperactive, always bouncing from one conversation or idea to the next while Will was a stoic leader both in stature and presence. Will had always been taller, thicker and more soft-spoken than John. He could've had most of the girls in school, but instead he stayed with the same one until she went to college and discovered that boys become men there. Even then, while acknowledging that he was hurting, Will said he could see her point. She was young and had been with the same guy for four years while every other girl seemed to be flitting from one to another like hummingbirds, staying just long enough for a taste before moving on to the next. John always felt that high school dating was incestuous and so when he met Judy he stayed with her like glue until that day he tasted something new himself. And that, as we know, was that. Left to his own devices, John chose to go after the entire smorgasbord, not just then but through most of his married life until the death of his family stopped him cold - at least for six months or so when his cock could pee but do little else.

Chapter Twenty-One

The day they met was like any other day. John knew someone who wanted to introduce him to this cool guy named Will. They said hello, sized each other up as young men will do and parted again as the bell rang for class. And so it was a mutual friend who called John to invite him to play poker at Will's place, an invitation John, who desperately wanted to be part of the pack, readily accepted. He told his mother that they would be watching the hockey game and that Will's mom would be watching over them. In a sense, John was telling the truth. The playoff game would be on the TV - it would be sacrilege to miss it - and Will's mother would be physically at home, but she enjoyed a sip of wine now and again, which, as it turned out, was really now . . . and then again. Hennie, as she would come to be called by almost every kid who came over, believed that it was as sure as death and taxes that teenagers were going to get into all sorts of trouble, so the best thing to do was to confine that trouble to her house, where she could keep an eye on them to make sure it didn't get out of hand. And while she enjoyed her wine, the company and the low roar of a full house pleased her that much more.

PASSING THROUGH OBLIVION

Her husband, Will's father, ran off when he was only five, leaving her to raise him and his infant sister, Belinda alone. Hennie worked as a seamstress, a waitress, a receptionist, and an office manager in that order as her kids grew. She always managed to pay the bills and a hot dinner was never missed. Will both loved her fiercely and was slightly embarrassed by how much she would drink most evenings, especially when he had friends over, but to those friends she was nothing less than perfect, everyone's favourite mom, who gave them hugs, reassurance, and sanctuary when they needed it. All she asked for in return was a little company and reasonable teenage moderation. John's parents fought wildly after drinking themselves, so to see an adult become more loving as she drank never failed to amaze and delight him, and as time passed he grew to love her almost as much as Will did.

That first night, though, when Stan invited him over for poker, John didn't know what to expect. It was two days before Mother's Day and he had ten bucks in his pocket with which to buy a present, but the opportunity to join the cool kids for a ripping game of poker was a siren he could not ignore. When Hennie answered the door with a glass in one hand and a cigarette in the other, he smiled unconsciously. The years of hard work and hard drinking had taken their toll on her, but she still had inviting, smiling eyes that helped settle John's nervous stomach. After all, this was his audition with the gang, so her warm welcome and gentle questions about his life put him at ease. There are few things worse than being a nervous teenager; Hennie knew it and lessened the trauma for them as much as she could. After the niceties, John went downstairs to the basement to find the gang already in full gambling mode with cans of beer in front of each of them. He was astounded. Will's mother was just upstairs. What if she came down? Before he could think any further, a can of Molson Canadian was tossed his way and a place made for him on the ratty couch he would one day sleep on after he finally beat the hell out of his stepfather after the drunk had hit John's mom. John tentatively accepted the beer and sat down to play some cards with his Mother's Day money. It never really occurred to him that he could lose that money rendering him unable to buy a present. It was just that kind of logic that followed him everywhere and almost forever. He said hello to Will, Max, Sean, and a couple of other guys he knew from seeing them at school, but whom he had never actually met previosly. He cracked his beer to raucous applause and bought ten dollars worth of chips. Three beers later he was a teenage drunk - and a broke one at that. None of that mattered, though, because by the time the evening ended, he had been initiated into Will's crowd and that meant a hell of a lot more to him than a present for his mother, which, by the way, was a character trait he would also exhibit throughout his life. He didn't much care, though, because he had become a charter member of the clique and a good friend of Will's - who would be in John's apartment in less than twenty-four hours. John took a quick look around and pronounced his apartment not only fit for Will, but for anyone, including the terrorist landlord of his. John would never forget that night when he played cards and won friends, and until the day he died he enjoyed telling the story of the night he lost his Mother's Day money.

Now Will was on his way and because of that John recognized how much life had changed for him. Hennie was long gone and so was John's innocence. Will was not flying across the country and taking time off work to shoot the breeze, drink some beer and play poker. No, his motive was far less playful that that. He was coming to save a friend.

John spent a restless night never fully falling asleep. The alcohol and drugs may have no longer been coursing through his veins, but in his head the need for both was like a hurricane crashing the coast reeking destruction and malevolence. In his spasmodic, choppy dreams, he was always lost in a place as dark as death where he could hear footsteps but not see who - or what - was making them. He could hear whispers but not words and though he could see nothing he tried to run through the darkness, but his legs were always too heavy as if they were stuck in mud. In one dream, he thought he could hear Wendy calling his name, but she was drowned out by what John believed to be a child's laughter and he bolted up as if electrocuted, drenched in sweat and shaking uncontrollably. That was the last dream he dared allow himself, so he unsteadily padded his way to the fridge to gulp down a bottled water as the clock radio flashed 3:15 a.m.

Exhausted, he fell to his couch and turned the TV on. Outside, he could hear the odd car but little else. The night was still and musty from the day's heat, it's scent heavy with the rancid odor of a large city suffering under the weight an endless heat wave. John mindlessly flipped from one channel to another not seeing what was on, but rather thinking of Will and what his visit would be like. John loved him, but he knew that Will could be judgmental and more than a little opinionated about some things - substance abuse being one of them. Will had experienced his mother's slow decline as she aged and he had come to hate alcohol because of it. John didn't even want to consider what his friend would have to say about cocaine. "Shit," he mumbled as he settled on the Weather Network after running the menu of channels four or five times. Pierre Elliott Trudeau Airport, the ticker tape scrolling beneath a map of Canada said. Temperature: 29 . . . Humidex: 35. "Too fucking hot," John said to himself as he gazed at the impotent open windows he had hoped would cool the place as he reconsidered, then decided against another attempt at sleep.

A raucous thunderstorm broke the eerie night silence just after four o'clock illuminating the city one moment, then shaking the hell out of it the next. A driving rain that bounced off the balcony pounded the dusty pavement below John's window, which he had been forced to close. Once, the lights flickered causing John to scamper for a candle, but for a change Hydro Quebec's delicate power grid withstood the storm until it passed as quickly as it had attacked. Afterwards, the foul odor John had noticed all too well earlier became more of a sickly sweet perfume, not unlike that of a fruit that has been left to rot on a kitchen counter. It didn't smell bad, it just didn't smell right. John spotted a large, black spider in the corner of his living room above one of the windows he had left open. Since childhood, spiders had terrified him, but he watched this one quickly crawl from the corner above the window on to the ceiling, where it stopped once again as if to get its bearings in this new world, then it was on the move again towards John, which did make him recoil slightly, yet for some reason he'd never be able to figure out, it scared him less the closer it got to him. "Hey, spider," he said softly. "You coming in to hide from the rain?" John surmised that the spider's web outside had been torn apart by the driving rain and wind. "Need a place to stay safe for a while?" The spider moved again, this time only for an inch or two, then it stopped about two feet from directly above John's head. Usually, he would've already jumped, but this night he stayed where he was. "That's okay, spider, you can be my guest tonight as long as you don't try to get to friendly with me, okay?" The spider did not move. "See? We can do this. We can do this for tonight only, buddy, but we can live together tonight. I'm not going back to sleep and you're not going to drop on me while I'm sleeping, so let's make a pact. You respect my privacy and I'll respect yours." The spider seemed to agree, as it stayed where it was, and while John felt uncomfortable with that black spot on his white ceiling, he intended to keep his end of the bargain. "I know what it's like to need a safe place to stay," he said. "I could use one, too, to be truthful about the whole thing, spider. If you're not gone by morning, we're going to have to reassess things then, but for tonight - cheers," he said raising the glass of cola he had poured earlier as if it were a real drink. "Cheers."

As the storm passed and darkness became dawn, John began to talk to his immobile spider, which hadn't moved an inch since he had been permitted to stay. "So what are we going to do, eh, my friend? Your home has been trashed almost as much as my life. What are we going to do?" The spider, a rather strong silent type, refused to answer, but stayed where he was, as good a listener as anyone could ever want. "Man. Have you ever fucked up? I mean, have you ever really fucked up a lot?" Silence. "Yeah, yeah, yeah, I've heard it all before," John smiled, as the sun rose bringing with it the heat of another stifling day, the kind Montreal gets often every summer. "But we made it, didn't we? And I'll tell you a secret; I'm not so bugged out by you anymore, pardon the pun. Don't get me wrong, I'd still like you to find another place to live - no offence - and I'm afraid that none of your family is allowed to move in with you, but we did alright, didn't we?" With that, John took a glass from a kitchen cupboard and tenderly nudged the spider into it, covering the opening with his bare hand. "Come on, little guy, time for us both to move on. Thanks for the company." John then opened the sliding door and gently placed the glass on the clean, wet surface of the balcony and removed his hand. "Run, Forest, run," he smiled. "But whatever you do, don't tell your pals about this. Last night was between you and me, okay? Be safe," he said, as the spider crawled not at all as quickly as John thought he would towards freedom. "Okay, Will," he whispered, "let's see what you have to say now."

John spent the rest of the day cursing the fact that he had been too busy getting stoned to buy an air conditioner and he began alternating T-shirts and underwear from the freezer to him and back to the freezer once the coolness wore off. Back and forth his clothes went; hot ones in, cold ones out. Will called at a little past two o'clock to say everything was on schedule and that he expected to land at about seven forty-five at Trudeau. John sounded appropriately enthusiastic, but the truth was he was afraid to see his old friend. It was when the acrid smell of curry began to waft into his apartment through the open windows that he decided to escape his self-appointed exile from the real world. "How in the fucking world can you cook that shit in this heat, for Christ's sake?" he spat to no one in particular. "Seriously, it's a hundred fucking degrees and you have to cook curry. Man, don't they eat anything else? I hope it's at least curry ice cream," he added as he closed the front door behind him. That was one thing about Matty's, he thought as he emerged to the sun-drenched street in front of his building, they do keep it cool in there. Like Pavlov's dog, he habitually turned in that direction before catching himself. A Metro station was about a block in the other direction, so John swiveled a hundred-and-eighty degrees in and walked quickly both to create some distance between himself and the bar and to burrow down away from the heat. Montreal has a unique underground city of stores, boutiques and restaurants that can take days to explore and it's connected by what John believed to be the greatest subway system in the world, though to be fair he had only actually experienced others in Toronto, which he found to be noisy, dirty and devoid of any character, and New York, which was far worse regardless of category. The only positive aspect of New York's subway was, well, New York itself. But Montreal's Metro was clean and quiet because it ran on rubber wheels, as opposed to the shrieking of steel on steel which Toronto and New York offered. The sky-blue cars were well lit and the riders were almost always courteous and kept to themselves.

He descended into the bowels of the Vendome station cooling off the deeper he went. After a wait of three minutes a train arrived, John boarded the mostly empty car and, to his great relief, sat down in a corner by himself. He transferred at the Lionel Groulx hub to the line that took him to the Champ des Mars station just on the perimeter of Old Montreal, where he debarked and took the two long escalators that climbed back up to the surface, where the heat was smothering. It was still early afternoon, too early for the inevitable thunderstorm that would wash away the dust for twenty minutes or so before the heat once again baked everything dry. During a heat and high humidity wave, late-afternoon thunderstorms were as regular as clockwork, as were the overnight boomers John and the spider survived together. They cooled things off only for a few liberating moments, but that was all the relief they could offer and if you didn't have air conditioning you went somewhere that did. For John, that meant an afternoon movie as much for the distraction as the cool of the theatre. The movie itself was a mindless shoot-'em-up with Bruce Willis saving humanity yet again while getting the girl and grunting his lines, but John managed to achieve blessed sleep for about twenty minutes. This brightened his outlook on life immeasurably to the point where he was almost looking forward to seeing Will. At the appointed time, he rode the Metro back to the Vendome station and home, where he splashed cold water in his face, brushed his hair, poured too much Visine into his eyes, and left for the airport. Once inside, he found domestic arrivals and scanned the banks of television monitors until he spotted Will's flight, which was on time. He then found a seat on a bench beside an older woman who was reading a Harlequin Romance novel to wait the fifteen minutes before the plane came in. "Excuse me," the woman said, "aren't you John O'Rourke, the newspaper writer?" John felt his stomach clench again at the recognition and his instinct screamed at him to get away, to find another place to sit, but there was a mob of people waiting for this flight and others and empty seats were at a premium. He smiled at the woman, nodded almost imperceptibly, and turned his back to her. By her appearance, John guessed she was someone's granny. She wore a shawl, even through the heat, and had glasses the size of small coffee tables balanced on her nose. Her hair was cut short for convenience and her face was an ashen colour with a slight moustache of fine hairs on her upper lip. "I'm sorry, I didn't mean to disturb you," she said curtly as she returned her gaze to one of the monitors.

"No, I'm sorry," John said too quickly, "I didn't mean to be rude. I'm . . . sorry." He felt his face flush and he unconsciously covered his left cheek - the one closest to the old woman - with a hand. He tried to smile, but felt his grin to be more a grimace than anything inviting.

"That's alright, young man," the woman replied with a genuine smile. "You're entitled to not be bothered by unsolicited questions from old women in airports."

This time, John smiled without trying to. It was an open, innocent smile that made him feel . . . safe? "My name is John," he said extending a hand. "How do you do?"

"I do fine, thank you," the woman said. "My name is Ruth. Such an old woman's name, isn't it? Ruth. I was old when I was young," she laughed.

John deduced she had used that joke hundreds of times, but her manner was friendly enough and her company was helping John feel less self-conscious among the throng of people who hadn't looked at him twice. "Are you waiting for someone?" he asked.

"Ha!" She yelped, loud enough to startle John. "Figured that out for yourself, eh? Oh, I'm sorry, that was rude," she laughed. "I forget myself sometimes." For such an aged woman her voice was rich and full of life.

It was John's turn to laugh, and he emptied it out of his stomach as if it had been years in the making. "No, no," he said, trying to control himself. "I deserved that. And, yes, it was that kind of grasp of the obvious that made me a good reporter."

"I read your column, Mr. O'Rourke. It's very, very good most of the time. I hope you return to it soon." John felt embarrassed again with the knowledge that she knew more about him than he wished she did. "Oh my, now look what I've done. I've gone and spoiled the spell. We were just beginning to enjoy ourselves."

John sighed deeply. "No, it's okay, really," he said. "I wrote about it, so I guess people know what an ass I've made of myself." He looked at his shoes, the right one softly kicking a dried piece of gum on the floor."

"Nonsense!" Ruth stated firmly. "Why, if I told you of all

the stupid things I've done in my life you'd have me put away in the loony bin." She shook her head slowly. "The difference between you and I, Mr. O'Rourke, is that I'm not a public person and so the only people who know about my indiscretions are my family and close friends, and not all of them know all of it. It's very much different for you, Mr. O'Rourke. Thousands of people wake up with you, if you don't mind the double-entendre. You've had your personal life splashed all over the place in this city. I don't know if I could've survived my life being so closely scrutinized. But there's one thing about Montrealers that you may not know yet, and that is that we employ a live-and-let-live philosophy. If you don't mind me saying, we've seen far worse than a writer with a drug problem. We've had politicians with drug problems and criminal records. We've elevated to almost saintly heights all sorts of colourful characters who would make you look like Rebecca of Sunnybrook Farm in comparison. No one who cares about you - and there are many of us who are fans - begrudges you your dirty laundry, but rather we just want you to feel better, to rise above it. In the end, we're all suckers for redemption. Are you in the process of redeeming yourself, Mr. O'Rourke?"

"Well, it hasn't been that long, but I'm trying," he admitted.

Ruth clapped her bony hands together. "Then that's all you can do, isn't it? Oh, I was a pretty fair sinner when I was young," she smiled as her eyes clouded over with memories of stories both true and false. "And look at me. I'm an old woman waiting for her adoring grandchildren and somewhat less adoring son and daughter-in-law." She laughed again, reminding John of how Goosey used to get after a couple of drinks, which is to say loving bordering on sappy. "If you don't mind me intruding, who are you waiting for, your dealer?" she asked, her eyes darting left and right in mock conspiracy.

"I wish!" John whispered, also very conspiratorially. Then he laughed and Ruth playfully slapped him in the shoulder. "No, I'm waiting for my best friend from home, who will no doubt straighten me up good and proper."

"Oh, Lord," Ruth groaned. "There's no hope for you, then, is there, if your friend is coming here to fix you up - how did you say it? - good and proper. Are you joking with me or are you dreading this visit from this friend who will shake the devil out of you?"

"A little of both," John answered. "He's a great guy, but he does see himself as my legal guardian sometimes, and I'm pretty sure this is going to be one of those times. And please call me John, Ruth."

"How do you feel about yourself, John? I mean, since you got out of the hospital, how do you feel about yourself? Do you still want to bottom feed with drugs and alcohol? I ask you only because drugs weren't such a problem when I was younger. I don't know what kind of pull they have on some people."

"I don't know how I feel," he confessed. "Last night I stood on the sidewalk about a block away from the bar I used to go to every night and I couldn't move for what seemed like forever wanting so damn badly to go back in. I went home, in the end, but I'm not sure of what I'll do the next time I feel like that." He hung his head to avoid her cloudy green eyes.

"So what? You say you didn't go inside, so what are you guilty about? My God, if I punished myself every time I've been tempted I'd be dead by now." She laughed again. "We didn't have drugs when I was younger, or at least if we did I didn't know about them, but we had all sorts of other things that society frowned upon and I found most of them. I liked the boys and I liked dancing and when I would come home past curfew, which was most of the time, my father would give me his belt on the palm of my hands. When I wouldn't behave in school, the principal would give me the strap across my palms. Between the two of them, I couldn't wash my hands for dinner without crying from the pain, but I was wild and I gave my poor parents fits. Girls just didn't do that sort of thing back then, you see."

While John was listening, he noticed the odd person glancing discreetly his way, peering over a newspaper or book, then ducking behind again as he caught their eyes. "So you liked to dance, eh?" he said. "I'm not sure that's really the same as what I've been going through."

"Only when my mother fell ill did I stop carousing. My father was a good man, but he didn't know how to take care of a house or a daughter, for that matter, by himself."

"What happened to your mother?" John asked.

"Cancer. She just grew sicker and sicker and shrunk smaller and smaller. I loved her so much because I knew my wildness came from her - as did my father. That's why I think he tried to beat it out of me so often," Ruth continued. "I know he loved me, but when he was beating the devil out of me he was beating it out of my mother, too, only he wouldn't dare touch her because she would've left him on the spot, even if that wasn't done then, too. Anyway, my mother died quickly, thank God, and she was never in too much pain. After that, I became the homemaker for my father. My two brothers, both of whom were older than me and both of whom have also since died were already out of the house, so it was just the two of us."

"How old were you then?" John asked.

"I was twenty years old."

"Did your father remarry?"

"No, he was a broken man. After my mother died, he didn't really care about much of anything. I cooked and I cleaned and I tried to engage him in conversation or games in the evening, but he was lost without her, and I think that maybe because I was so much like her it tortured him to see me every day because he saw what he had lost. In his eyes, she was so close, yet he couldn't touch her or talk to her. I finally met the man who would become my husband when I was twenty-six - which was quite old in those days to be single. I was verging on being called a spinster," she laughed. "My father died seven months after I left the house on the sixth anniversary of my mother's passing."

"The very day?" John asked.

"The very same," Ruth replied. "But enough of this maudlin talk, yes? You've experienced the pain of losing your family, but we're not so unlike each other, if you don't mind me saying, dear." John shook his head to say he didn't mind the comparison. He was enjoying her company so much so he had stopped noticing the curious stares from commuters and friends and family waiting for them. "The thing I learned, John," Ruth continued as she placed a hand on his shoulder, "is that the world keeps spinning whether you want it to or not, and remembering things can hurt even when you believe you're past it all. I'm an old lady now, sick more often than I'm not, but I lived my life and so I have no regrets other than the fact the good Lord hasn't called for me yet. Maybe peeing twelve times every night and hurting everywhere whenever the temperature falls below the seventy is His way of punishing me for my wicked ways when I was a girl," she smiled ruefully. "But if that's so, then I say I got the better of the deal. Oh! There she is, my beautiful granddaughter now!" Ruth exclaimed with a wave in the direction of a crowd entering the baggage area. "I have to go, John. I thoroughly enjoyed our chat and I hope we meet again one day. Until then, the world keeps spinning. It's up to you if you want to spin with it, but my opinion is that beats the alternative. Cheerio, my dear!"

And she was off in the direction of a pretty woman who hugged the old woman gingerly but with unmistakable warmth.

Chapter Twenty-Two

It was at that moment John saw Will coming into the baggage claim area with a big smile and a bigger wave. John knew at that second that he was happy Will was there, so he returned an enthusiastic wave and smiled broadly. As they neared each other, John extended his hand, but Will opened his arms wide for what turned out to be a breathtaking bear hug. "It's good to see you, man," John said truthfully.

"Look at you," Will smiled. "You don't look nearly the train wreck I was expecting to see."

John laughed at the familiarity between he and his friend. "Duct tape and Popsicle sticks, my man. That's all that's holding me together these days."

"Uh-huh," Will nodded, "we'll see."

As Will gathered his luggage and they turned to leave the concourse area, John caught Ruth's eye and mouthed "Thank you." The little old lady smiled and waved her hand at him. Then she pantomimed typing and pointed at him. "I will," he mouthed back, then waved once more and walked out into the heat of a July evening with his old pal, who he was very pleased to see.

"Is it always this . . ."

"Warm?" John asked.

"Warm isn't the exact word I would've used," Will said.

"No shit. It's been like this for about a week and a half now. Speaking of which, want to make a pit stop on the way home for something cool?"

Will turned sharply to stare down John. "Tell me you're kidding," he said sternly.

John smiled at his friend's alarm. "Don't worry, Mom, I'm talking about picking up an air conditioner."

"You don't have one?"

"Well, in my defense, I've been pretty wasted for a while and didn't notice the heat."

"Funny," Will volleyed back. "Very funny."

"Yeah, okay, there'll be time for all of that later. In the meantime, let's get cool."

"Copy that, amigo."

They found John's Miata, stuffed one bag into the miniscule trunk with Will putting the other on his lap. "I still can't believe you made it here in this," he said, as John pulled the soft-top back. "It must've been a hell of a drive."

"You don't know the half of it."

"You probably should've kept the minivan," Will said.

"No," John answered sharply. "That was Wendy's."

There was an awkward silence, then Will said, "Yeah, I guess you're right. Well, you made it, so it's a moot point, anyway."

"Yeah, I guess it is."

John wound the little car in a tight arc around the Dorval Circle and continued east down the 40 towards Montreal at 120 kilomotres an hour. Anyone who has spent time in Montreal knows that to drive slower would be to court disaster. Montreal is famous for a number of reasons, including the best smoked meat in the world, but it's the wild, almost reckless driving that absolutely startles visitors. Even at that speed, cars were whistling past John's car, sometimes on either side of him. Will silently stretched his right leg out as if to press an invisible brake. John noticed it and chuckled. "Sorry to tell you, but there's only one brake and it's on my side."

Oh, man," Will muttered. His face appeared to be turning a pasty green shade with every sudden lane change.

"Relax," John screamed over the wind, as he cut off a truck to enter the Decarie Expressway. "I can do this in my sleep."

"That's very reassuring," replied his friend, who was sitting with both feet jammed as far forward as possible, his bag on his lap and both his hands holding on to the dashboard. The Decarie was in its usual state of summer madness. Construction blocked the inside southbound lane and though it was evening, there was too much traffic for only two lanes causing them to creep along in second gear before the reached the Queen Mary exit, which seemed to suit Will just fine. "Traffic jam at this time?" he asked.

"All the time," John stated. "The Just for Laughs festival is ending and the jazz fest is beginning. It's summer and people want to be where the fun is. It won't take too long. Besides, it gives us a chance to catch up while we're waiting to get home. I have no beer or anything, of course, so let me know if you want to stop for something." John hoped Will would decline.

"No, I'll be fine, thanks. Glad to see you're off the booze."

John nodded his head. "Just for now. My willpower isn't strong at the best of times, so if I want to kick the drug thing it's best if I keep my head in the game. It's too easy to talk myself into going to the bar if I've had a few drinks. It was never a problem before and I doubt it will be when I start again, but I've been out of the hospital for just a couple of days and the orders are to lay low, eat healthy, take vitamins and all that shit."

Will laughed, happy John had brought the subject up. "It figures that it would take a near-death experience to make John O'Rourke stop drinking. I never thought you had a real problem with alcohol, either, but it has always been a part your life. A break will do you good."

John nudged the little car left into the passing lane, not because it was moving so much better but rather to get out from behind a white panel truck that was burning oil into their unprotected faces. Yeah, you're right about that. You know, with me it was never a case of needing alcohol, it was more of a way of life, if that makes any sense." Will nodded that it did. "I had this image of the great writer living the writer's life. That included hanging out at the press club and drinking with the boys. At home, I never had too much - or at least rarely had too much, to be accurate about it."

Will wiped beads of perspiration from his forehead and upper lip. His face had always flushed easily and the heat was no help in keeping the red blotches at bay. "I guess the question is how you're going to guarantee that you won't get into trouble again. There's telling me you won't do drugs again, there's even telling yourself you won't do them again, but the morgue is littered with people who had good intentions. I'm not having you die on my watch, which lasts long after I've gone back home, where you should be, too, by the way. This place isn't good for you," he said.

John waited almost thirty seconds before responding. They were nearing the Sherbrooke Street exit and he was busy maneuvering the Miata back into the appropriate lane to exit the expressway. When he did speak, his words were said quietly enough to force Will to lean left to hear them. "I don't think it's the city that's been bad to me, man. One thing I learned from all this is that wherever you go, you bring yourself and all the baggage that entails. You know, I moved here for a fresh start, but everything I was dealing with there came with me. I didn't stop thinking about Wendy and Henry and my dad just because I moved here. They came with me, too." John turned east on Sherbrooke Street, darted through a yellow light and stopped for a red at the next intersection. They were five blocks away from Claremont and John's apartment. "It's so much to deal with, you know? Not only did I lose my family, but I was committing a sin as they were dying. That's what's killing me."

"Committing a sin?" Will repeated. "I never thought I would've heard that come out of your mouth, you fucking atheist. Don't tell me you found religion." He cracked a sloppy grin and put his hand on John's right shoulder.

"No, I don't think so . . . no. It just seems so bad now considering what happened. I don't know if I could feel worse if I had shot them myself. His shoulders slumped and to Will he looked in that single moment beaten and tired.

"I don't know what to tell you, John. I wish I had the right words, but this goes way further than me telling you it was okay to cheat on Judy in high school."

"Judy," John quickly said.

"What?"

"I don't know. I think I dreamed about her recently, but I can't remember it." He felt a shiver run up his spine.

"Well, anyway," Will continued, "what you did, John, was cheat on your wife. Lots of people cheat on their wives. That doesn't make it right, it just means you did what thousands of other guys have done. Some got away with it, some got caught, and life went on." John found a parking space close to his building, took it and stopped the engine. "Hang on a second before we go in. I want to finish this," Will said. He had begun to sweat profusely, but he was determined to get his thoughts out before he forgot them. He turned in his seat to face John, looking him squarely in the eyes. "What you did is not unique. Women cheat on their husbands all the time, too. That perfect storm of being with her while your family died is all yours, though. I'd feel safe betting my house that you're on your own with that one. But you have to see it one part at a time, like a math equation or instructions from IKEA, okay?" He absent-mindedly wiped his brow with his right hand. "Fuck, it's hot."

"You want to go in?"

"No. I want to finish this because I'm nearly done. Okay, this comes in three stages. One, you met a woman and had sex with her; two, your family died in a tragic accident; three, you had to deal with all of it without asking for support because you had been cheating."

"Yeah, it's not like I could ask Wendy's dad for a heart-to-heart chat."

"Exactly. It was even too much to tell me for, what, almost a year. Back to my equation. You cheated on Wendy. Deal with that on its own. You're sorry it happened. I bet you would've been sorry it happened regardless of what came later. You're not a bad man, just a selfish one." John's face registered hurt. "I'm sorry," Will said, "but it's true. It's always been about you. Wendy knew it, your friends know it, and everyone is okay with it because you bring a lot more to the dance than just that selfishness. No one is perfect, John. Now, here come my words of such infinite wisdom that you'll forever be indebted to me. I am going to make you feel better, whether you want to or not. A plane crashed. It crashed because it was broken. Almost two hundred people on that plane died, not just Wendy, Henry and your dad. There are grieving people everywhere because they all lost loved ones that day. You did not make it crash. You had no idea it would crash. If you had been on it, you would've died with everyone else." John removed his sunglasses and dabbed a finger in the corner of his eyes. "Yes, you would've died and there is nothing in heaven or on earth that would've stopped it. You could not have saved them, nor - and this is important - nor could you have comforted them. They would've been terrified regardless of whether you had been there or not." Will lowered his voice as a young couple holding hands strolled past the car. "You survived, John. You may not like how you survived or why you survived, but you're alive and a lot of people are very fucking happy about that, even if you're not. So really it's a Greek tragedy in three acts. The Cheater; The Loss; The Guilt. But, and this is a big but, the first two acts are not related. Listen to me, the Cheater and the Loss are two distinctly different things. The plane did not crash because you were fucking some bimbo.

It was a horrific and sick coincidence, but a coincidence nonetheless. John, it wasn't your fault, man."

John had been crying quietly and as Will finished he wrapped a large hand around the back of his friend's neck. "You're a shit for committing adultery. That's it, John. That's all."

"I'm so sorry," John cried.

"I know," Will whispered. "So do they, John. They know it so much. Please don't disrespect their memory and the love they had for you by killing yourself just to escape your conscience."

"Oh, God, I'm so sorry, Wendy. Oh, God . . ."

"Come on," Will said gently, "let's go for a beer somewhere."

"A beer!" John yelped. "You gotta be kidding. After all this you want me to drink? I don't get it? Why would you ask me that after all this?"

Will left his hand on the back of John's neck. "Because you can," he said soothingly. "Because you're a man and you just learned something very important about yourself and you no longer need alcohol and drugs to dim your emotions. Here it is, John, all on the table finally. It's all been said and now you can start dealing with it. I want to have a beer with you because that's what we've always done and I've missed it. My best friend moved across the country and I miss him. I want to have a beer with you, John, because I know you're going to be okay. I know it I my heart. It's long past time to start healing."

John looked at Will through tear-soaked eyes. "I'd like to have a beer with you, Will. I really miss you, too, but I'm afraid of what might happen if I get drunk."

"You won't get drunk. You'll have a nice, cold beer and then you'll take me back to your apartment and then I might even let you buy me dinner for all this tremendous wisdom - which, to be truthful, was nothing more than plain, common sense - I've given you today. Can we walk somewhere close by?"

"I think I'd rather drive to somewhere further away, if that's alright with you."

Will shook his head. "Oh, yeah, good call on that one. Let's go and pretend we're friends, okay?"

John smiled warmly and patted Will's leg. "You're very attractive when you're trying to be serious, you know."

"I know, but keep your hands to yourself, cowboy."

The beer John did have was ice-cold and his first sip made him shiver. He thought about the one he had with that waitress in Kenora and realized how different this beer with Will tasted. It felt good and, more than that, normal. They shared a plate of potato skins and watched a few innings of baseball on the pub's TV before heading back to John's apartment without the air conditioner, which had been lost in their enjoyment of each other. It was the most normal John had felt since the accident. As they passed Matty's, John pointed to it. "That's where I used to go," he said.

Will took very little notice. "But not anymore."

John nodded. "But not anymore." And this time he believed he meant it. Will quickly fell asleep on the couch watching the same game that had been on in the pub, so John took advantage of the time to write his next column, which, on his new weekly schedule until he felt stronger, was due in three days.

"Hello again from Oblivion," it began. "I understand many of you have called and written the paper asking about how I've been doing since my last column. Thank you all for your concern. To have strangers care enough about me to take the time to do that is unimaginable. I've always been one to keep my personal life a good mile or two from that of being your faithful correspondent, but last time I felt it was time to share much more of myself with you. Your reaction to that still amazes me, but as the vaunted psychologist Dr. Will Traynor said to me today, it's long past time to start healing. I think the time has come to look to the future and let my family rest in peace. My wife, Wendy, would've been ashamed at how I've been acting. She would've expected so much more from me. She would've wanted to be proud of me. To havespent so long wallowing in self-pity would've disgusted her. I was my son, Henry's, hero. He looked up to me and he tried to walk like me and talk like me, as almost all sons do. Well, this has been a hell of an example I've been setting, hasn't it? Even if he's no longer here to see it, I owe him far more than this. I owe Henry and Wendy and my dad a better life than the one I've been living. They would've wanted to be proud of me, and so this is my goal now.

I owe my friend, Will, who arrived today on a mission of mercy, more than one phone call in four months. He's my best friend, counselor, conscience, and brother. He flew across the country on his own dime to make sure I would be okay. Will, your mission is and will be a success. I don't believe for a minute that I'm all-powerful and that I can do everything by myself. Before this newspaper lands on your doorstep, I will have called a professional to help me get through the next little while when temptation and fear will be my strongest enemies. I will, in short, learn to ask for help, which is something I've never been able to do before.

You know what I used to like doing before I dug and firmly entrenched myself in the Pit of Despair that is substance abuse? I loved watching baseball and going to the gym and I wanted to learn how to sail. I loved doing the crossword and reading the mammoth New York Times on Sundays. I wanted to get a motorcycle and I thought that I might start writing a book just to see if I had it in me. I was in a National Football League fantasy pool and I used Monty Python to make me feel better when I was down instead of booze and drugs. Cooking was a passion of mine, but the most elaborate dish I've made in months is macaroni and cheese. Wendy used to love it when I cooked for her and Henry. She adored mussels in a creamy white wine sauce. Henry's favourite was either tacos or chicken strips, but he was a good soldier and at least tried whatever concoction I whipped up before spitting it out.

I'd like to do these things again. I'd like to be happy again, but I'm not naïve enough to believe that all it'll take is a positive attitude and some elbow grease. There's a long road ahead of me, but with your continued support I hope to walk it all the way to the end. And this, my friends, is the last you'll hear of it and the last column with the word "I" in it so often. I'd (see?) like to write about you, and the Habs and all the other delightful and not so delightful aspects about living in this great city. Can I take your hand now as we begin this long journey forward to the undiscovered country?

See you next time, and, again, thank you all from the bottom of my heart. I'll work as hard as I can to live up to your support. And to make my family proud of me. I promise. John.

Chapter Twenty-Three

As John typed the final word, Will farted, smacked his lips, mumbled something unintelligible only those in his dreams would understand. "And with that," John smiled, "the deed is done." Before he sent it to Walt at the paper, though, he added one last sentence. Walt, I'd like to come back, if you'd like to have me.

He then dimmed the living room light, took a sheet from the freezer and let it warm closer to room temperature to avoid shock, then laid it over Will from his waist down, before padding into the bedroom in his shorts and T-shirt, both of which were also freshly frozen. That night, John slept like the dead, as he put it to Will the next morning. He didn't remember dreaming, or waking up. It was the flushing of the toilet that finally roused him and reminded him that he had to pee so badly his kidneys actually hurt.

'Morning, sunshine," Will cheerfully called as John scurried into the bathroom. "Have a good sleep?"

"Pee!" John answered.

"Well, aren't you the early riser? What's this I've been hearing about insomnia?"

"What do you mean?" John asked over the din of the waterfall.

"It's almost noon, man. I've been up watching TV for hours."

"Wha?"

"Except for when I went to the store."

"You what?"

"Went to the store," Will said. "Hey, you're going to overflow it, dude."

"Ahhh . . ." John replied as the stream finally began to ebb. He flushed the toilet and returned into view with his hair wildly splayed and crust still grimly hanging on to the corners of his eyes. "What are you on about?" he asked.

"Clock," Will replied, pointing at the clock, which read 11:52 a.m.

"Ha, ha," John laughed. "What time is it really?"

Will gathered the remote control for the TV and turned on The Weather Network, John's favorite station when conditions became too cold, hot or stormy. "You don't believe me?"

John looked on incredulously. "You have got to be kidding me," he whispered, at once embarrassed that he had slept so late and elated for the same reason. "I don't . . ."

"Okay, so there's surprise Number one, my friend. Now slowly turn your eyes straight down below the time to where that graphic of part of the sun being covered by some little, fluffy clouds is. See it?" John nodded, still busy clearing his eyes. "Okay, now look at that number just beside that happy, little graphic - and you better catch on soon because I haven't had enough sleep on that semi-ratty couch of yours to stay this cheerful for much longer."

John squinted his eyes, trying to focus on the number. When he did finally see it, he let out a whoop that even surprised Will, who had been waiting for a happy reaction. "Twenty-one degrees?" John whispered with awe, as if seeing a Mickey Mantle rookie card for the first time. "It's only twenty-one degrees? At noon? That's sixty-four Fahrenheit." Even though she had been gone for so long, John still translated Celsius into Fahrenheit for Wendy, who, of course, had been born and brought up in the U.S.

"Yeah, and get this, Kurt Cobain: it's supposed to get cooler before it gets warmer. Tonight, when you take me to some place that is not this apartment, we will bask in the glory that is eighteen degrees. Do you have a sweater or will your own natural fur keep you warm, Bigfoot?"

"Better find a sweater," John smiled. "Wax keeps the fur away these days."

"Not while you were busy being a rock star," Will said with disbelief. "You couldn't go to work or feed yourself, but you could go to a salon and sit quietly while someone poured burning hot wax on you before pulling out your body hair? Incredible."

"Yeah, I'm a real freak of nature," John said wistfully, suddenly aware of what his priorities used to be.

"Yeah, well, your long heat wave is over, pardner. Welcome to real life."

John's lips broke into a wide, sloppy grin as he looked his old friend in the eyes. "Thank you," he said quietly and as sincerely as any words he had ever spoken.

Now it was Will's turn to swallow a lump in his throat. "No charge, dude," he said just as quietly. "Are you sure you're going to be okay? I mean, this change has happened pretty quickly. You're not shitting me, are you?"

"No, I'm not shitting you, Will. Truthfully, I began feeling differently about everything the second I woke up with that paramedic pounding on me. I'm not kidding you. I don't really know how to explain it other than to say it was like an epiphany, and you know I'm not religious. I just needed you and your three-act play metaphor to help me understand things, but I knew from that moment in the ambulance that"

"Um, excuse me, but did you not tell me just last night that you stood down there on the corner - two nights ago, remember - fighting with all your strength to stay out of that fucking bar?"

"Yes, I did say that and it was true. But I know now that I wouldn't have gone in. Believe me, my willpower has never been that strong. If I had wanted to go back to that lifestyle, I would've gone back and that would've been that." He took a Diet Coke from the fridge as he continued. "And yes, your arrival helped me come home, too, but once I did decide to come back here that was it. I'm embarrassed that I did that shit for so long. I have nothing against the people I hung with, who I firmly believe like me and enjoyed my company. I enjoyed their company, too, especially the doctor, who I will miss a lot. But even he will slide down life's slippery slope if he's not careful. That entire bar is a train wreck waiting to happen and I hope they put the brakes on in time."

"Do you think they'll be able to stop in time?" Will asked. As much as he hated John's involvement with drugs and these people he spoke of, he did find it spellbinding. It was a culture he only ever saw in the movies, but it was his friend who lived it.

"I doubt it, sadly," John said. "But life goes on and you better be ready to spin because the world's going to no matter what. I wish them well, but I don't want to see any of them until they're as clean as I am, or at least will be."

Will slapped John's shoulder. "Feel like one of those smoked meats you told me about before I lost you?"

"I choose life," John said as his eyes drifted somewhere else. "and, yeah, let's get breakfast."

"Lunch."

"Right you are. Lunch."

A day later at the airport, John and Will hugged tightly as they said their good byes. Will felt confident, though not certain, that this would be his last mission of mercy, that the next time they saw each other it would be under less dire circumstances. He held John tightly and spoke quietly into his ear. "You listen to me, yes?" He felt John's head nod. "I love you. You're my best friend and you have been since you lost your Mother's Day money to me, even if I never told you that before. You're a good person, Johnny. You're flawed, but no more or less than the rest of us drones going to jobs we hate every day so we can pay the bills. And, in fact, you have a job you love, so go and do it and become the famous writer you've always wanted to be." He caught the flourish of a newspaper being opened out of the corner of his eye. As he looked closer, he saw a woman's face become very serious. As she read, it softened until she was finally smiling. Only then did he see the headline of the story she was reading. It read, "Hello from Oblivion." Will trembled as he held John closer, suddenly aware of his friend's near death and the compassion people in his adopted city felt for him.

"What the hell?" John laughed nervously. "I'm going to be okay, I promise."

"Yes, you will be," Will said as he loosened his grip. "I'm not so afraid of leaving you now because I know that there's a lot of people watching over your shoulder now. Look," he said pointing at the woman, who had sat down trying to wipe tears from her eyes as she shielded her face with the newspaper. "It's your column, man."

John stared long and hard at the woman, who had obviously been moved by what he had written. "Bonnie?" he asked gently pushing himself away from Will. "Bonnie?" he asked, this time hoping she would hear him.

"Uh, John?" Will stuttered. "She may not . . ."

"Bonnie?" John said loud enough for people far behind the woman to hear. This time, she peered cautiously over the newspaper at whoever it was calling her name as she did her best to compose herself. When she saw the man who had called her name, her mouth dropped open and silent words spilled out. "It's you," she gasped. "I just read your . . . I'm . . . it's you." She unconsciously got up to hug him, then realized what she was doing in public to this man she barely knew. "I . . . hello, John. You look . . . much better."

Will heard the final boarding call for his flight, and as he began to call a good bye he caught himself and instead smiled and nodded his head. "Well, I guess this place isn't all bad," he said to the ticket agent as he walked down the tunnel towards his plane without so much as a look behind. He knew John would call him that night, and he knew they would see each other again. "Waste of money coming here," he said to himself as he found his seat and settled in for the long flight home. "Thank God."

Chapter Twenty-Four

John O'Rourke and Bonnie Thomas found each other at one of life's crossroads for both, though her situation wasn't as dramatic or death-defying as John's experience. Still, as he got to know her he would sometimes shiver thinking about the bravery of this wisp of a woman, who he knew wouldn't hurt a fly if it landed on her. Bonnie had been shuffled from one relative to another after her parents died in an automobile accident when she was five years old. From an uncle and aunt who beat her for the sin of wearing a skirt that only hung down to her knees - in Grade three - to her father's parents, who blamed her for not dying with their perfect son, she still found some inner courage that you have to be born with to survive intact. As the months passed and John fell in love with her, he knew he could never do anything hurtful to her because, in the end, she had traveled a much longer and more terrifying road than he could've ever dreamed of surviving. He was her best friend and protector and she was his rudder and heart and together they looked to the future with each other, never doubting for a moment that they would reach it together.

Within weeks of Will's departure, John began writing his column regularly again and he would always try to impress

Walt, the quiet man who had owed him nothing, but who had given him so much at a time when he needed it the most. Walt never thought he had done anything special, but it's that type of solid person who does do that sort of thing. As far as John was concerned, he'd seen a lot worse over the years. There was the sports reporter who used to watch the hockey games on TV at his favourite watering hole while getting soused and writing his story as if had been at the game - complete with fictionalized interviews with the players. You could always tell how drunk he was when writing those stories by how outlandish the quotes were. His jig was finally up when he thought the team's best player had been benched and so he quoted the player ranting about the injustice of it all and that he had had enough of coach Scotty Bowman. "Trade me or I quit!" was the quote on everyone's astonished lips. The fact of the matter was his skates had been poorly sharpened before the game, so he went back to the locker room with the team's trainer to have them redone. By doing so, he missed a few shifts. The television announcers told everyone why he wasn't on the ice with his linemates, but this reporter couldn't hear it over the din in the bar. The next day, the offended player found the reporter nursing his hangover at the very same bar and beat the hell out of him. As for John, his column quickly grew in popularity to the point where even the breast cancer people invited him back to one of their fundraisers, but this time John did not drink too much. In fact, he did not touch alcohol at this one at all. What he did do was have his head shaved bald so that his hair could be made into a wig for women going through chemotherapy. When it was over, they all had a good laugh and hugged and shook hands. Finally, he had been forgiven. John doesn't talk about it very often, but I know that he carries that memory with him close to his heart.

John spent the rest of his life being true to Bonnie Thomas, who spent the rest of John's life making sure he would do just that. Their happiest memory together was a glorious burnt-orange sunset in Key West as they stood on the edge of a wooden pier with a dozen others who had walked out there for the same reason. Their hands held the other's tightly and Bonnie's head rested on John's shoulder as the sun slowly painted a burnt ornage and red masterpiece in the Florida sky as it slipped into the ocean. It was the perfect place to be together at the perfect time and the moment would live forever inside both of them. Bonnie eventually began to talk about kids, but this would often sadden John enough to push it off until another time. It wasn't that he didn't want children with her, but he felt that by having them he would be doing some sort of indignity to his own dead son. But it wasn't too long before John came around, though. He loved Bonnie, and he would've done anything for her. When she announced her pregnancy, he was the happiest man on earth. His heart sang for the first time in years and he loved her all the more because of it. He never told her, but John was terrified of anything happening to Bonnie and the baby, so when she needed something from the store at night, he went and got it for her. Although John's twenty-four hour care began to frustrate her own sense of independence, Bonnie said little to stop him. She understood his motives and so she allowed him to pamper her. "This won't happen with the next baby, John," she said one night after he had cleaned the house. "Next time I get to do something around here." He just smiled and nodded and gently rubbed her expanding stomach, blissful in his mothering. One night in her fourth month, she craved chocolate chip ice cream like a hungry lion craves an injured, fat zebra. The evening was a spring classic, as the soft breeze caressed her through an open window in the kitchen of their house fifteen blocks and lifetimes away from John's former apartment and bar. She wanted a reason to enjoy the night air, but knew that if she ventured out alone in the dark John would get cranky. Montreal is one of the safest cities in North America, but bad things do still happen, John warned. Sighing and shaking her head in contented resignation, she called John on his cell phone asking him to pick up the ice cream for her as he came home from playing hockey with some of the other guys from the paper. John was pleased she had called and asked him to get it. He knew he was being a mother hen, but it was just for a little while longer. Besides, he knew well enough that Bonnie didn't do anything that Bonnie didn't want to do. If he had fenced her in too tightly, she would've broken out already, but so far her worst reaction had been a mild pout that had endeared her to John so much at the moment that he picked her up and carried her into the bedroom, where they made love beside the cradle he had already built for the baby.

John walked with an easy, comfortable stride through the Metro station, up one crowded escalator, then around a corner to climb another, the perfumed scent of flowers blooming on a spring evening slowly replacing the staid forced air in the tunnel. He stopped himself from smiling for fear of looking like a goof in front of the other commuters, then allowed a wide, sloppy grin to crease his face. Upon reaching the top, he gazed upon the crystal lights of the city he had come to call home and felt the warm blanket of spring air tell him his long journey was finally over. He breathed it all in deeply and looked to the future he and his wife were planning for each other and their new baby. For the first time in forever, there would be a tomorrow, and a tomorrow after that if he was the least bit fortunate and he figured fortune was right by his side these days. But John O'Rourke was wrong about that. He turned a hard right into a convenience store for the ice cream just in time to accidentally provoke a simple robbery into something far worse.

Still smiling, he opened the door at the moment a young, terrified drug addict's finger was quivering on the trigger of the first gun he had ever held. Until then, the robbery had been playing itself out as most do. The bad guy with the gun was receiving the money, the victim was doing what he was told to do while fighting his panic enough to place the gunman's face to memory for when the police arrived. It all would've ended without incident except for the oblivious man who ambled in looking for some chocolate chip ice cream.

PASSING THROUGH OBLIVION

When the door opened, it struck a small tin bell placed just above it to alert the merchant that someone had entered. In this case, however, the bell served to spook the kid holding the gun, who had spent days planning this perfect crime in his drug-addled head. He had banked on a quick thirty-second holdup with no surprises and no casualties. Many years later, alone, homeless and in despair, he would recall the sound of that bell everyday as if it was the first time he had heard it. In his head, it was always the first time he had heard it and the sound never failed to make him tremble.

John stood frozen in the doorway, realized what was happening, and said "Shit," just as he was struck in the forehead with a bullet a young man was surprised he had fired. The shooter yelped at the sight and tore out of the store, the bell lightly clanging behind him as the owner tried to steady his finger enough to dial 9-1-1. Assured that help was coming, he raced to the man whose life was spilling onto the dirty tiled floor not more than a foot from the entrance.

"Mister, are you okay?" he asked.

John O'Rourke, who had weathered the storm that he had hoped would kill him many times over, tried to speak, but his mouth only trembled. Finally, he managed a word. "I"

"What?" the merchant asked. "Help is on the way. Hang on, mister, you're going to be all right. Just hang on." But he was very afraid the man on his floor near the entrance would not be fine at all.

John tried to get up, but blood loss and shock conspired against him and his head fell heavily back again. In the final seconds of his life, he had only a stranger to hold his head and stroke his blood-soaked hair.

"You're not alone," that stranger said. "You're not alone."

But as his eyes gradually closed, that wasn't the voice John heard as he was passing from one world to the next. Instead, he heard my voice asking him to get up. He felt my hand take his and it was my face that smiled at him. As he slipped away, the storekeeper heard him say a name that no one - not even Bonnie - would ever understand. "Ziggy?" was his last word on earth as John O'Rourke.

***

You could say I know John well, and although we don't spend as much time together as we used to, I can call him my best friend without a shadow of a doubt in my mind that he feels that way about me too. Bonnie nearly died herself that night when the police came to knock on her door. She almost lost her unborn baby, but the little girl she would name Jenn was born healthy and beautiful the following September. As soon as she left the hospital with Jenn, she drove to the cemetery where John had been buried five months before. She carefully took the blanket off of Jenn's little head of fine blond hair and held her out for unseeing eyes. "John, I'd like to introduce you to your daughter." She cried softly for what she had lost and for what she had gained. "She's beautiful, isn't she, honey? She has your eyes. Oh, John, she has your beautiful, blue eyes. I'm so grateful for that."

Chapter Twenty-Five

This story began with a loss, and it almost ended the same way. But the powers-that-be here - the ones John met in that restaurant so long ago - passed a unique amendment just for him. They sat him down when he was at his angriest and they apologized. I was there and I saw it myself, as hard to believe as it is. They said they would do their best to make it right again, and asked John to be patient, not that he had a choice, but after hearing them out he understood the magnitude of what they were about to do.

One day as Bonnie was at her lowest just about three months before Jenn was born, she woke up in the morning and didn't cry. When she felt she couldn't possibly go one more day beneath the crushing weight of her grief, something somewhere inside of her flicked back on. Years later, she would still never understand how it happened, but she suddenly acquired the strength to keep going. It would be three long years before she would be happy again, but she had found the bridge she so desperately needed to get there. I also heard that Jenn was given more than her share of strength, intelligence and many other fine qualities. They say she will have an extraordinary life. On the day she marries, she will toast her late father who she never had a chance to meet, as well as her mother and stepfather for their unconditional love through the years. Bonnie met her second husband three years after John's death. Reluctant to become involved again, there was something in this man that reminded her of John. It may have been the way he smiled or something about the way he spoke, but she could never isolate that one thing. On a sunny morning in May when Jenn was six she climbed into bed with her mom and dad and snuggled up with them. Bonnie was laughing about something silly when she stopped as quickly as she had begun. "Oh my God," she whispered.

"What's wrong, Mommy?" Jenn asked.

Bonnie looked quickly from Jenn's eyes to her husband's eyes and back again. It was at that exact moment that she found what had been eluding her. "Your eyes are so similar," she said quietly. "They're almost identical. You both have John's eyes." Hearing those words in her own ears stopped her short. "Oh, I'm sorry, honey, that was wrong for me to say."

But rather than be upset, which was not his nature to begin with, Michael Sweeney pulled his wife closer to him so that all three of them were as one. "Don't apologize," he said softly. "I'm not sure you could've said anything else that would make me love you more."

I still see John around here every once in a while, and when I do I smile. What makes me feel so good is that he does, too. He doesn't call me Ziggy anymore now that he knows my given name and I don't talk like Ziggy now that our journey together has ended and I look more like myself. Not too many of us get second chances. I've only ever heard of one person who was given a third. I'd like to think he deserved it.

Scott Taylor is an award-winning journalist now living and working in Ottawa, Canada with his wife, Ally, a cardiology researcher at the University of Ottawa Heart Institute. A native of Montreal, he grew up the son of a newspaper columnist at a time when newsmen still used the word "scoop" and kept a bottle of bourbon in their desk drawer. He has been nominated for Best News Story of the Year by the Quebec Community Newspaper Association twice, winning once, and has also been nominated for Best Investigative Series. Passing through Oblivion is his first novel.

Now Available from Amethyst House Book Publishers

But I Still Love Him…When love goes beyond sense or reason
Andreah   ISBN 978-0-9735663-3-7

Acceptance: A novel of the supernatural
Andreah   ISBN 978-0-9735663-4-5

Amethyst House Books for Kids

Book 1
Lincoln and the Lilac Lilies
Mary Stafford   ISBN 978-0-9735663-0-2

Book 2
Lincoln's Day of Discovery
Mary Stafford   ISBN 978-0-9735663-1-0

Book 3
Lincoln's Journey of Journey's
Mary Stafford   ISBN 978-0-9735663-2-9

Sofia's Pink Balloon
Zanita DiSalle   ISBN 978-0-973-5663-4-5

www.amethysthouse.com